Red August

H.L. BROOKS

Copyright 2015 H.L. Brooks

WEATHERHILL

www.hlbrooks.com

Book One of the Red August Series

Acknowledgements

This book would not have been possible if not for the love, support and hard work of William Hardy. He is a great editor, blurb-writer, snack-getter and life partner. He makes me want to do awesome things, just so he can see me do them. I also want to thank Brandi Brooks-Bemiss and Christina Collins for valuable input, proofreading and cheerleading when I needed it. Thanks to my daughters Amber and Jade for being such wonderful, loving and supportive spirits. Thanks to Natalie Gibbs for modeling for the cover and Leslie Gibbs for the zillion things she's always helping me with. Thanks to Amy S., Xochi, Sam, Meg, Mike, Amethyst, Dorian, Steve J., Erica J., Nina, Michael S., Angela, Mom Jan and all of my other friends who have helped me celebrate or gave me some encouragement when I needed it, had dinner with me when I finished the first draft, offered to throw me a party, and left me encouraging and thoughtful notes on social media. Special thanks to Barry and Scarborough Fair B&B for hosting a lovely reading and offering up his hospitality. To Erica Smith for being the first person to be the voice of August in the public readings and New Deal Café for being the first place that hosted a reading. To Erica Winter and Raven Heights Radio for my first interviews for this book. All of the support and encouragement has meant the world to me.

For Will

The love of my life.

Table of Contents

The wolf thought to himself, "What a tender young creature!
What a nice plump mouthful …"

~ The Brothers Grimm

~~Red Birthday~~

It's a clear night. A sky of indigo velvet is sprayed with stars that wink and peek beyond tangles of leafless branches. A hunter's moon, pinky-orange and bright, dapples the path in shards and pools of light.

She hears her heartbeat whoosh in her ears as she tries to outrun the beast. Her bare feet pound the peaty earth, a red cape billows out behind her, and dry leaves scatter in her wake. She hazards a glance over her shoulder as she runs, seeing nothing but inky blackness behind her. When she turns forward again he is there, standing in her path—six feet tall or more, lean and covered in fur, with a canine snout and glowing eyes. The mongrel is on hind legs, reaching out with paws like gnarled hands, flexing his shining claws. Even at a distance she can see his erect cock in the moonlight. Like the rest of him it is part wolf, sheathed in downy skin, and also manlike, with the pink of the working part standing tall and powerful above the sheath.

She pulls her cape around her to cover her nakedness, a thin veil offering no protection beyond modesty. She pants with fear, but there is also an ache, low in her belly, creeping down between her thighs.

The creature commands her in a seductive growl, "Take off your cape, girl."

A shiver runs through her body as she considers his menacing eyes. She tugs at the bow around the base of her throat, until the crimson silk slips free, clinging and caressing her body as it floats to the earth. She stands pale and naked in the moonlight, her breasts proud and her nipples erect, her flesh prickled and alert to every breeze. She trembles, and her breath comes in tiny gasps.

The creature drops onto all fours and leaps toward her—a snarling blur, covering the fifteen feet between them in one bound. He stands tall beside her, his breath hot in her ear. He reaches for her and she does not flinch. She wants him to touch her. She can't even remember why she was running to begin with. He lifts her in one motion, effortlessly. He cradles her for a moment, looks down at her face, and then lowers her onto a bed of silk, moss and leaves.

Now on all fours, he makes a canopy of fur and muscle over her. He is huge and powerful, and she wonders if she will be much of a meal for him.

Her breath catches, her flesh tingles with a longing both startling and overwhelming. The urge to rub against him lifts her hips upwards.

"My, what a morsel you are." His voice has a low vibration that travels the length of her bones.

"Your eyes, they're so big," she gasps.

"All the better to gaze upon your beauty," he says with unexpected tenderness. His fur settles and his expression softens. He leans down and inhales her deeply, his muzzle riding along her neck and down her torso. He lifts his head and savors the bouquet of her aromas.

She buries her fingers into the fur on his chest, and he gazes down upon her. She grabs fistfuls of fur and pulls him closer.

The great creature bows his head to her breasts, teasing each nipple with a long tongue, sending waves of pleasure through her spine. She quivers as the werewolf works his way down her ribs, tracing each peak and valley with wet tongue and soft, fur-shrouded lips, then explores the landscape of her belly. His tall ears flatten. She lays her hands between them, running her fingers through the soft grey and white fur at the top of his head. His ears flop and flick as she touches them.

"What big ears you have, my wolf."

"All the better ... to hear...the moans ... you will make," he says between luscious laps of her skin.

He sniffs and tentatively nuzzles as she parts her legs, while she cups and pinches her nipples, trying to ease the ache. She begins to writhe and press against his muzzle as he noses deeper into her.

"Your mouth, it's so big!"

"All the better to eat you with my dear!"

He guides her thighs to part, wide. "Let me look at you," he rasps, staring as though starving, then licking his chops.

She thinks she should be afraid, but cannot muster more than a whisper of panic inside, unheard beneath the cacophony of lust that is shouting over the fear.

He leans forward and slips the tip of his tongue along the center of her swollen cleft.

She wiggles and tries to press hard against him. He continues to tease her open with a deliberate rhythm of dips and swirls and plunges. He pushes his tongue into her until she feels like the ocean is cresting, and about to crash over her. She is so close when he slips away, and she moans with want for him.

"Now I'm going to put my cock in you, my beauty. Are you ready?"

She pulls him close and inhales. His fur smells of spices and wood smoke, iron and sex. The urgency to push herself against him becomes instinctual and she wiggles and writhes, pressing, pressing.

He puts the tip of his erection to the center of her and with one firm push he plunges into her. She cries out, her ecstasy overwhelming, and her passion reverberates throughout the dark forest. She begins to arch and push into him, grabbing handfuls of fur at his hips, moaning and pressing, wanting to swallow him whole inside of her—paws, tail, ears, teeth and all. She wraps her legs around him until they are moving as one. She feels his cock surge and pulse inside her, and he throws his head back and begins to howl into the night air. Gooseflesh covers her ... she is almost there ... almost ...

"A-hoo! A-hooooo!" He echoes into the forest.

"... a-hoo, werewolves of London ... A-hoo!" The clock radio rattled out Warren Zevon's nightclub voice. August thrashed awake, finding fistfuls of white and pink rosebud-printed cotton in her hands. She groaned and slapped the radio quiet, threw off the covers and realized she was sitting in a pool of blood. Her damned period had finally started, and with plenty of cramping—great, on top of everything else she had to deal with. As the sleepy haze cleared she felt a stab, remembering that her father was gone. Every morning now was like this—waking into a bad dream, instead of waking up from one—and nothing felt like it was ever going to be all right again. She was living in a world without her father's arms, without his sharp laugh and his glinting eyes, and without his voice. She was too numb to cry any more, but her right hand balled into a fist and she punched it hard into her thigh.

August rolled out of bed, trying not to make a mess everywhere. She eyed the battered *Blue Fairy Book* she had fallen asleep with, laying open to the illustrations of "Little Red Riding-Hood." She rolled her eyes. "No wonder," she said to nobody, then picked up the book and dropped it into a box marked "books."

She padded off to the bathroom to shower, and as she slipped out of her bloody underclothes she ruminated on her dream. It had left her feeling vaguely unfulfilled and a little pissed off, having come so close, but it also made her wonder if something wasn't wrong with her, being so turned on by a monster. *A drooling snarling beast? Really?* She felt like she was turned on all the time these days—angry and sad and lonely and turned on. Her mom kept saying her moodiness was hormones, but it seemed like it had to be more than that.

August swept up her long black curls and watched herself in the tall mirror as her body flexed and turned. She regarded the swells and valleys, the curves so often hidden under her shaggy dark mane, the body she still could hardly believe was hers since it stopped looking like a child's. She had always looked a few years older than everybody else her age, which left her trapped in a psychological space of never being able to get used to it. Starting in fifth grade, girls hated her for having developed early, and boys couldn't keep their hands and comments to themselves. The girls left her feeling betrayed and the boys made her feel ashamed. At least when she transferred to high school two years early she looked like she belonged there, but that first year hadn't exactly been anything to celebrate—it just brought on a whole new set of body issues.

Sometimes she wished her boobs were bigger, but she liked that she didn't always need to wear a bra. She liked how her waist nipped in and her hips flared out too—though maybe her bottom was a little too round, and her thighs a little too big, with some dimples here and there, judging from the nasty remarks she overheard from the girls in gym class. And even boys who said they liked her told her that her butt was too big or her tits were too small, or something else stupid—like she wasn't a whole person, just a collection of features that weren't put together right. Her mother Sylvia was petite, but had an ample pear-shape that men seemed to never tire of admiring—not that Sylvia needed them to. And even though she was bottom-heavy, she was graceful and could move through a crowd of people fluidly. Her father sometimes swatted her mother's backside and they would both laugh and then kiss. It was hard for August to imagine a time when she might have that sort of interaction with a boy without feeling a little used. She wondered if maybe just being together a long time meant there was sub-communication, tiny signals, boundaries and permissions that were formed over years of interaction—a sort of private contract that might be imperceptible to anybody else. She also wondered if her mother's bottom had always been as heavy as it is now, and then wondered if her own bottom would round out even more as she got older. In any case, she didn't think her body was something to complain about—and the way she had been feeling lately, if some boy had wanted to see it she would have been glad to show it to him. It had been a while since she'd been with anybody, but there wasn't anybody she was currently interested in, either.

August looked more critically at her plain pale face, and the bluish circles under her eyes that never seemed to go away. *Nothing for anybody to get too excited about*, she thought. Though she did have to admit she liked her emerald eyes, and she often got compliments on her full lips, which she didn't even realize were desirable until someone once told her so. She had always seen her mother's elfin features in her own, but now she caught something of her father in her expression, and she felt another pang. *They're both in me*, she thought, and at that moment she felt much more proud of the face looking back at her.

Still, as the warm water sprayed over her skin and washed away the red, she started thinking about magazine models and then about the cheerleaders at school—how those girls towered over her tiny frame, intimidating her with their long legs, ideal waist-to-hip ratios, golden tans, and large bouncing breasts. Girls who would not be caught "like, totally" dead without designer jeans—Gloria Vanderbilt, Jordache, Sergio Valenti, and Bonjour—would giggle en masse whenever August walked by, sneering and rolling their eyes, stewing in their cloud of Jean Naté and watermelon bubblegum, brandishing their candy-colored bags to match their candy-colored shoes, with Ray-Bans in different pastel hues for every day of the week. The whole idea of plastic smiles and matching status symbols just seemed so tedious—ridiculous, even. Then August realized that, even though she wasn't ready to move away, it was a relief that she'd never have to look at their smug faces again.

After her shower August slid on her oldest, softest Levis and a million-times-washed tee and tossed the rest of her laundry into the wash, prepared to spend her 16th birthday with her mother. As she rounded the corner into the living room she could see Sylvia was already up and busy, sashaying around the apartment, sorting and wrapping dishes, taping boxes and packing up the last of their essentials for the move the next day. Sylvia favored tight clothes in tropical colors, and today she was in a summer favorite, a clinging tangerine tank-dress, with her long brown curls bound up in chopsticks. Upon seeing her daughter, Sylvia put down the tape gun and gave August a tight hug.

"Happy birthday! Happy, happy, birthday!"

August pretended to be too sleepy and cool to meet her mother's cheerfulness, but she really did like it. Sylvia announced that they would have pizza delivered from Nino's one last time—thick crust, extra cheese with mushrooms and onions—which they could chase with the remaining Newcastle ales in the fridge.

The living room was stacked with cardboard boxes three rows deep, taped up and labeled with her mom's cryptic abbreviations. It was weird, seeing their crowded walls and shelves now so bare, and gave August the odd sensation that the apartment didn't belong to them anymore. She wondered how many of her father's things would just stay in those boxes marked "Evan," tucked away until

Mom could stand to open them again—if ever.

It was hours later, after mountains of packing and too much pizza, that August watched her mother curl up into the corner of the couch, almost like a painting. Sylvia's large round tangerine hip flowed into a curvy thigh, then calf, ending with her elegant bare feet that she flexed a little with each sip of wine. August figured if she herself became a bit heavier, she wouldn't mind it so much if she carried it like her mother did, without apology.

Once, when August was with her in line at a sandwich shop and Mom was ordering Dad a super-long double roast beef with extra cheese, a man next to them had the nerve to say that she might want to reconsider ordering that much food because she looked like she didn't need the calories. Other customers in line were stunned into silence and the entire room held its breath, all watching her. Sylvia turned to the man, raised an eyebrow and said, "I'm not sure I heard you. Did you say that I should avoid eating this sandwich because you think I need to lose weight?" The man seemed surprised that she acknowledged his comment, like a hunter who had shot a rabbit and the rabbit, instead of lying there suffering, asked him what the hell he thought he was doing. The man didn't speak, but he crossed his arms and put his chin up and gave a small nod. Sylvia laid a ten on the counter, then picked up the wrapped sandwich, opened it and said, "It's a good thing I don't give a fuck what you think of my weight, any more than you care what an asshole you are." She took a giant bite of the sandwich, chewed in his face, and slowly walked away, making sure to put plenty of hip in her step, while snickers and laughter rippled around the shop. August shot the man a look and a smirk too, put her nose up and walked out after her mother.

Sylvia finished off her wine with a flourish, and announced in a sing-song voice that it was now a birthday party. August picked up their grease-smudged pizza plates and took them into the kitchen. The birthday cake was on the counter, with "Happy Birthday August" written across the top in pink icing. Her mother hovered over the flowery masterpiece, her perfectly manicured coral nails wrapped around a cake server, poised for the task. She had ordered the cake from Sugarplum, three blocks down, and when it was delivered that morning Sylvia looked happier than August had seen her in the past two months. Almost like normal.

"Which piece do you want?" her mother asked, waving the server at her.

August considered a portion of smooth unblemished frosting. Who was she kidding? She pointed to the biggest pink sugar rose, next to the H in Happy.

"There. That one."

"You always choose the big rose."

"Then you shouldn't have to ask! You should already know what piece I want, woman."

Sylvia squinted at her and then smiled, high round cheeks tilting upwards. She carved out a perfect one-eighth slice of cake and tipped it expertly onto the little pink plate that was August's personal birthday cake plate. Then she pulled back the flap on a fresh brick of French vanilla ice cream.

"One scoop or two?"

"None, thanks. I want it straight up."

August set the plate down on the table and picked up the entire slice of cake, pressing her fingers into the icing. She loved the feel of it in her hands, the delicate crust on the surface layer, crumbling into the softer sugar and shortening underneath, and finally the yellow sponge, yielding. The thin tip of the wedge collapsed against her tongue as she bit it off, and her taste buds sent back tingles of sugary sweetness. But pleasure came with a tinge of guilt these days. Maybe she shouldn't be feeling so much pleasure, because her dad couldn't anymore. At least he couldn't feel pain, either.

"Happy birthday sweetheart," her mother said with a crooked smile, tipping her wine glass toward August in a nonchalant salute. Mom was hiding it well, but August could see the shadow of her pain just beneath the surface.

"Thanks, Mom." August swallowed all of the other things she wanted to say about how much she missed her dad, her stress over moving, and how she wished things could be different. It was easier to not talk about it right now. She knew she should try to enjoy the moment, so she smiled back and raised her glass of milk, toasting it against her mother's cabernet with a gentle clink.

"To us! And to me, since it's my birthday and all."

"To us. And, yes, to you, sweetheart."

August sipped the milk and watched her mother walk away and almost lose her balance as she left the room. Turning her attention back to the cake, August scooped up the rose with her finger and put it onto her tongue, pressing the sweet lump to the roof of her mouth. She licked her finger, leaving the flesh stained pink, and rubbed the sticky residue onto her jeans. Everything had become so sensual to her lately, it seemed all of her senses were clamoring for attention.

"Why don't you start on this pile of gifts?" her mother called from the living room. "We've got to pack the damned things as soon as you unwrap them."

August mustered a laugh for their sad little party, but she was amazed by the stack of presents awaiting her. "It's a good thing I don't have many friends or we'd have to put a trailer on the car. Look at this pile."

"You know how excited I get about birthdays," explained Sylvia. "I can't help but spoil you." August caught an edge of sentiment creeping into her mother's voice—a side effect of several glasses of wine, no doubt—and saw her blue eyes were swimming. "Even if you weren't my daughter I would want to be your friend," Sylvia went on. "It's a true privilege to be your mother."

August sniffed as she teared up a bit at her mother's sincerity and tenderness. Mush. Pure mush. But she didn't hate it. All of this change and loss reminded her how easy it was to lose someone you thought would always be there.

"Way to make me all emotional on my birthday, Mom," she teased. "I love you too."

August gratefully endured one of her mother's deceptively strong hugs and buried her face in the waterfall of hair that had been liberated from the chopsticks some time after Sylvia's third glass. August breathed in her smells of wine, Herbal Essence shampoo, garlic dressing and lavender soap, and hung onto that moment, tucking it into her memory, and when she stepped back she noticed, for the first time, that as tiny as she herself was, her mother was no taller. August really did love her, and she wanted to better appreciate her. Now, more than ever, the clarity of how temporary everything could be clung to her.

The gift pile was a bounty of books, music tapes, concert tees and stonewash jeans. There were also a number of handcrafted silver hair ornaments, each beautifully tied up in its own tiny parcel. Sylvia was famous for wrapping gifts into as many lovely little packages as possible, prolonging the process, and presumably the joy, of opening surprises. The most exciting present was a short stack of albums that had belonged to her father. There was a note on top from her mother.

Sweetie,

Though these weren't necessarily your dad's favorite albums, they were important to him for various reasons. I thought it might be nice for you to have them for your own since you shared his love of quirky music.

Love, Mom

The stack included *Mermaid Avenue Vol. II*, a compilation of Billy Bragg, Woody Guthrie and Wilco that was definitely in the quirky category. *Back to Basics* was another Billy Bragg record, and August saw it had one of her dad's favorites on it, "Milkman of Human Kindness." She felt a catch in her throat as she recalled her father leaning back in his chair with the sincere call of Bragg's plaintive pleadings echoing in his study. August didn't recognize *The Tourists* at all, but the jacket featured a dramatic-looking female vocalist named Annie Lennox. Finally there was *King of Skiffle* by

Lonnie Donegan, which had "Does Your Chewing Gum Lose its Flavor (On the Bedpost Overnight?)"; it was a very silly song she and her dad would sing together.

After reading over every song title and every artist associated with the albums, August was feeling very satisfied with her birthday haul. Then she noticed there was a large flat box next to the couch, different from the others. Instead of pastel-colored paper with "Sixteen" printed all over it and long curls of ribbon, this package was wrapped in deep red paper with flocked black scroll designs, tied up with a giant red velvet bow. It was almost too grand and opulent to belong in the same room with the others.

"Is that for me too?" August looked at her mother, who was smiling to herself.

"Yes, sweetie, your father wanted you to have it. He actually wrapped it himself not long before.... He was always teasing me about how overdone my wrapping was—look at that package! It looks like it's straight out of a vampire bordello." Her smile this time was wistful, and August could see some happy memory of Fletcher Evan Archer in her eyes.

August approached the mysterious package and fingered the flocked decoration. She felt a lump in her throat and her face flushed—she wanted to know what was under that paper, but she didn't want to open the very last gift she would ever receive from her father. She could feel the sting of tears welling up in her eyes, but she knew her curiosity would win in the end. Attempting to preserve as much of the wrapping as possible, she gently pulled at the velvet bow until it came loose, and then felt along the ends of the package looking for tape to pop free. Instead, she found dollops of red sealing wax. Each was stamped with an arrow encircled by Celtic-style knotwork.

"What is this stuff?"

"It's a wax seal, with your father's family crest," Sylvia said, as if it were perfectly obvious. "It's the symbol of his people," she explained in answer to August's blinking stare, "from his ancestors, sweetheart. That's an arrow, for Archer. Your dad came from a long line of Archers who were skilled hunters and leaders in their lands."

"Our name is literal? As in, we actually had archers in our family?"

"Lots of names are literal, but over the centuries, the crafts gave way to modern careers." She raised an eyebrow and sipped her wine.

August found she was more annoyed than impressed with this new revelation. *Why hadn't anybody ever mentioned this before?* She cracked the wax seals finally and eased the lid off of the box.

Inside was a garnet-hued robe of some kind, fitting with the red theme of the packaging. August's jaw dropped open. She couldn't speak. She grabbed the sides of the thing and lifted it out of the box, and the heavy garment fell open, scattering dust into the fading sunbeams. It was a hooded cloak, nearly two yards long and made of what looked to be felted wool. The inside was lined with silk and edged with a velvet that was softer than any she'd ever touched before, not at all like the stretchy synthetic varieties she was used to. This was no costume piece—this cloak was special, from some other time. Some other place.

"It was his. It's been in his family a long time," her mother said.

August shook her head. "Why would dad have something like this?"

"You should talk to your Gran Sorcha about it."

"You don't know?" August felt her curiosity beginning to burn. Each question her mother answered just raised more questions, and it was making her irritated again. She didn't like this hydra game.

"I do know—I just think you should talk to your Gran. She's the one who should explain these things to you." She tipped back her goblet and finished off the last swallow.

August challenged her mother with a look, but it fell flat. Sylvia wasn't budging. *Why all the mystery?*

August stared at the cloak, then hugged it to her chest and inhaled the faint scent of her father rising up—that mix of old books, pipe smoke, dark spices and some other scents she could never quite figure out. These mysterious smells that had been comforting for so many years were now tinged with sadness, and something like anger, but softer.

Sylvia stood and embraced her daughter, the cloak sandwiched between them. "It's been a long day. Tomorrow will be longer. Why don't you go get some rest? I'm going to do the same."

They said goodnight and August went to her room and laid her gifts out on her bed to admire. She didn't bother to wash the pink off of her stained fingers or even to brush her teeth. She curled up on her father's cloak to rest a moment and fell into a deep dreamless sleep.

She awoke to the sun in her eyes, coming through bare windows, and the sounds of movers tromping through the apartment, stacking boxes and hollering to each other. A flash of anxiety washed over her—she wasn't ready to leave her home—and a moment later, the memory of her father stabbed and made her heart skip. It felt like she had a hole torn in her that could never be mended.

She looked down and saw pink icing stains on her shirt, and there was a bloody spot on her jeans because she passed out before taking care of anything. Thankfully the cloak was saved by sliding onto the floor in the night. She locked her bedroom door, ran to the tub to rinse out her clothes and clean herself up, then dug out her new David Bowie shirt from the gift pile. David was all in red, but the shirt was white and a little tighter across the chest than she had expected. It clung to her slightly damp body, and her bra was so thin that even together they didn't hide much. August decided she didn't care. She liked how the tee showed off her form, and how you could practically see her nipples. It made her feel sexy. Maybe a new start in a new town wasn't so bad—she could try to leave some of her insecurities behind. And if somebody didn't like her big butt, they could kiss it. *Hah!—they should be so fucking lucky*, she thought. "Life is too short," she said aloud. *And you never know when it will be over.*

She threw the last of her laundry into a grocery bag, stuffed her new clothes into a duffel, and then reached under the bed and pulled out a finely crafted wooden box. Here she kept her treasures, and she wanted to take one more quick look at them and put her journal away inside before packing the box into her suitcase. She traced her fingers over the wolf burned and carved into the lid, and the border designs of knots and arrows, which meant so much more to her now that she knew they stood for something. She grasped the chain around her neck, pulled out the old-fashioned key that hung from it, and turned it in the lock.

Inside, on top of the pile—the most recent addition to her treasures—was a bracelet of braided rainbow cords from a girl named Beth, who had wandered into and then promptly out of August's life just after her father died. Beth was an exceptionally beautiful girl, with thick golden hair in fat bouncing waves. She was sturdy but petite, with a classic face of delicate arched lines that made you want to paint her portrait. The relationship was awkward, but a defining one for August. Or at least she thought it was. It had been such a relief for her to have some distraction from her grief, to have someone new and different to be close to. But it was hard for Beth to be honest about her own feelings, and then one day she just stopped coming by. August wondered what she might be up to at that very moment, and if a phone call would be welcome. She supposed it didn't matter now, since she was on her way out of town for good. She took the bracelet out of the box and studied it for a moment, then hung it on the end of a naked curtain rod and said goodbye to Beth. She didn't feel any sadness, and wondered if she had ever actually liked Beth in the first place. Or maybe no one could have really reached her while she was grieving for her father.

August sat back down and picked through the more familiar items: A folding antique knife that her father gave her when she was 12, and farther down were three agate marbles and a silver arrowhead that had also been his. A dry Zippo lighter from when she was dating Luke, and a flattened, flaking cigarette, which she removed and tucked into a trash bag. Luke, the quintessential bad boy in leather—that was a short-term romance brought to mind whenever she smelled leather steeped in stale beer and cigarette smoke. There were also two notes and an I.D. bracelet from Jackson, her sixth-grade crush and her first real lover, along with a small, hopeful box of condoms that August ruefully imagined she would never get to use. Underneath all of these was a packet with a few antique family photographs and some snapshots from the 1950s, as well as a sketch of her father done by her mother on a Nino's placemat, and also a four-leaf clover—her mother was famous for finding them with ease—that had been pressed between waxed paper.

The box held another secret as well, a false bottom with a small compartment underneath. Inside the hollow was a beautiful antique key made of silver and copper, larger than the one that opened her box, tied on a length of red satin ribbon. Her father had promised he would explain the meaning of the key on her eighteenth birthday. Her whole body flashed with anger to remember that he was gone before he ever got to tell her. And now there were so many other questions—things she guessed she would never know. Instead of hiding the key away again, August removed it from the ribbon and slipped it onto the silver chain to let it hang with the other one around her neck. Then she braided her hair and tied the end with the ribbon. She wondered for a moment about Gran Sorcha and if she'd remember anything about archers and Archers and keys and heavy red cloaks.

She pulled her journal from her nightstand drawer and tossed it inside the box, then locked it up and stashed in her suitcase. August took one last look around her childhood bedroom, brushing her fingers over the chipped lavender walls. There was a pang as she stepped over the threshold one last time, and glimpsed her height measurements on the door frame. She didn't want to give in to the clichéd nature of all of that, and so tucked the pain away, letting it coil into a lump in the pit of her belly, where it remained all the way from New York to Maryland.

The ride out of the city was slow and smelly, especially at the bridges—*Looks like we're not the only ones trying to get the hell out of New York*, August smirked to herself—so they kept the windows up and the AC on. There were only four working 8-tracks in the Bonneville's glove box, so after the third go-round of the Carpenters' hit singles (Mom's choice) August was more than a little relieved to get on the highway and roll the window down. The wind roaring in her ears felt like freedom, but the turnpike didn't smell any better than the city and it wasn't any less crowded, just a lot faster. After maybe a half-dozen episodes where somebody cut them off to pass ("Asshole," her mother christened them each time), August was glad when they got off the beaten track to take the old roads south, and even more so when Mom took a side trip to a rail crossing with the cutest little nickel-plated diner August had ever seen. "Before you were born, your father used to insist we stop here whenever we visited your Gran," she explained. There was only one waitress, and when she brought August her pancakes and eggs, she winked and called her Hon.

August was still licking syrup from the corners of her mouth as they wound their way around rolling farmland and little towns that hadn't changed much since the railroad came through. Occasionally they would crest a rise to be greeted with a spectacular overlook view, or catch a smattering of summer rain. Sylvia once started to say something about Evan, but then trailed off mid-sentence. August pushed in a Moody Blues tape just to fill the silence.

The only other time they stopped was well into Maryland, at a small café with a gift shop and bookstore next door. August discovered there was a whole room dedicated to a local author there, and she realized the woman probably owned the store, and the café too. *That must be a sweet deal,* she thought—*write a book and then put it right out on the shelf.* She was just leafing through a paperback about Maryland legends and lore when her mother came up to her with a surprise. The gift shop was loaded with handmade ornaments and jewelry, and Sylvia had bought them both bracelets of woven red thread, peppered with beads. August squeezed her hand into the loop and ran her finger over the rows of bumpy beads. The tag on the bracelet declared the artist's name was Hyacinth Dovewalker.

"Mom, this says it's for warding off werewolves," August chuckled, flipping over the tag.

Her mother shot her a look warning her not to laugh. "Anyone could know anyone in a small town," she'd told August just last week.

"Gosh, it's really just so beautiful. What fine craftsmanship," August enthused, earning another dirty look for over-acting. She stopped talking.

Back in the car Sylvia said, "Fun fact: I have some family members who are deathly allergic to mistletoe. Your great-grandpa

Ada, for instance, and his siblings."

"Well, okay," August replied, a bit mystified over the direction of the conversation.

"I'm hardly allergic at all, though," her mother noted as she pulled on her new bracelet, which was a slightly different shade of hand-dyed red. "And how nice is it that there's such a lovely way to wear mistletoe beads? We used to just ... well, it's just a very pretty bracelet. Don't you think?"

"Yeah, sure. Thanks, mom." August chuckled to herself. Her mom was always a fount of surprises, as her dad used to say. She didn't offer any reasons about what compelled her to buy them, but she insisted that August wear one, and so she did. It actually did itch a bit, but nothing too bad, so she didn't mention it.

After another half-hour on the road, August saw signs for Mahigan Falls, the town where Gran lived. The hills and the abundant trees reminded her of parts of Upstate New York, but the sleepy town that greeted her was like nothing she recognized. She shivered a moment, despite the heat. This place was so unlike the city blocks she knew.

Get a grip, August told herself. *It's not going to be a disaster. Dad lived here through his whole childhood. I'll find friends and maybe even a job. If I'm really lucky I'll find some hot guy to touch my boobs, and maybe even use those condoms.* August didn't take that thought to its fruition since she was still in the car with Mom, but she planned on thinking about it more later.

Gran's house was on the outskirts of town, and August was astounded by the huge old Victorian standing there, a deep royal blue with gingerbread trim painted canary yellow, coral, powder blue and white. Flower beds and bushes skirted the house and fence, echoing the trim colors in bright yellows and pinks, with muted clouds of foliage. The best part was a turret rising up like a rocket ship from the porch, peaking above the main roof, and all August could think was how much she wanted to get inside that tower. The movers were already there, manhandling their furniture up onto the porch and into the front door. At the white picket gate there was a wooden sign with raised letters reading "The Blue Rook." There was a ceramic tile next to the lettering with a relief of a raven sitting on a castle tower. A house with a name—this really was a different world.

"Jesus, Mom, this thing is three stories tall!" August marveled.

"It's four, counting the cellar and the attic," her mother corrected her matter-of-factly. "Grab some of the stuff from the trunk and go choose a room. The big one with the bathroom is mine. You can have any of the others you like."

"Seriously, Mom, this house is huge."

"Yes. Which means it's going to be a pain in the ass to clean."

"What does 'The Blue Rook' mean?"

"It's just the name of the house," Sylvia said distractedly as she bent over collecting paper cups and snack wrappers out of the car, her bottom bouncing this way and that in her stretchy green sundress. August could tell Sylvia was in her own world.

"Don't you like it, Mom? It's a beautiful house."

Sylvia stood and faced her, tendrils of hair clinging to the sweat on the sides of her face, and her cheeks were bright red. August put a hand on her mother's shoulder.

"Are you okay, Mom? You know, we don't have to move here. We could move anywhere we want to."

"We need to be here, sweetheart. It's okay—I'm okay. I just miss your father."

"Me too. This is the house he grew up in?"

"It is."

"I like it. There's something special about this place. I can feel it."

Sylvia just gave her the hint of a smile and kissed her on the forehead with her overheated lips.

August started unloading the trunk onto the gravel, stacking boxes by the fender until she could reach her own luggage. The late summer heat was oppressive and before long August's clothes were sticking to her; what little she'd had covering her was now more like something in a wet tee-shirt contest. She shouldered her two big bags, grabbed the suitcase with her treasure box, and hiked down to the porch.

As soon as August stepped into the house, however, she found fans and air conditioners going full blast, and it immediately made her nipples bump out. She knew there were men all around and she felt herself flush, but she realized this was one of those moments when she could just try to relax and go with it. So instead of putting everything down and covering up, she strutted right by two movers—one gray and wiry, the other young and muscled—who were trying to carry her mom's overstuffed purple sofa around a narrow corner. She wondered if they would even notice her, but as soon as she was past them she heard the sofa thud to the floor, and some cursing, and she had her answer. She laughed to herself imagining which one had dropped his end.

On the second floor she found a wide hall with several rooms, including the one her mother had already claimed. She surveyed the master suite—nice, but her mom could have it. August headed for the opposite end of the landing and nudged the door, and sunlight came flooding into the hall. Still blinking, she realized that this was the room with the turret on this floor, and she dropped her bags on the dark pine boards. No question, this was the room she was going to have. It was huge, and standing in the windowed alcove she could see more than half of the property, from the treeline to a sloping ridge, where a stream trailed off into the distance. There was a window seat running all the way around the alcove, and she curled up on it and watched the trees starting to gently sway, and saw ominous-looking clouds rolling in over the ridge. The air was changing. August realized she was feeling somewhat detached from everything, as though there were a veil between her and the rest of the world—it felt like she was looking at a photo, rather than out of her new window. Despite that, she had a sense that she had come home, even though she had not been to this house or this town since she was an infant.

There was only one other house in sight, up the hill to the north, with the stream tumbling down past it in a small cascade. It didn't look anything like their Victorian grande dame with its boastful colors and wrap-around porches; instead it was long and modern, made of beige brick and steel, with clean straight lines, big windows and overhanging balconies. There was a man pacing on the balcony, and his shadowy silhouette was somewhat hunched and lean. Then he looked over at their house, like he wasn't sure what to make of having new neighbors, and went inside. *What's eating him?* August wondered.

She leaned back in her alcove and listened to the movers shoving things around downstairs. *What if that young muscly one came up here with her mattress? What if he came into her room and said, "Where do you want this, miss?" And saw her sitting there in her thin white shirt with her nipples bumping out, and then he put down the bedding and walked over to her slowly? What if he looked in her eyes and she nodded, and he reached over and filled his hand with her breast? And then slipped it down her neckline and into her bra? What if she ran her hands over his arms and down his back and into the back of his jeans? And what if she led him over to her mattress on the floor?*

August's eyes flicked open and she realized she had been making sounds and wiggling in her seat. She shot a look to the door, but no one was there. *Too far,* she thought. No way would she really let some sweaty stranger paw her up like that. Maybe a little. If he was cute. Then she thought, *Shit, who cares? I can imagine whatever I damn well please until the Thought Police are a real thing.*

She sighed and grabbed the seat edge as she rolled off of it, and it moved. She looked closer, tried lifting the seat up, and found a hollow beneath it. The whole thing was like a big trunk, and the hinged part of the seat was the lid. It was stiff and it stuck, probably due to moisture and about fifteen layers of paint, but eventually August managed to pry it open. The only thing she found inside was an old, stale-smelling quilt, which she pulled out and set aside to be laundered. She grabbed her treasure box and tucked it into the window seat, and then, inspired, she ran down to the car and came back up with her father's cloak. She folded it carefully and slipped it into the window seat as well. She gazed at her treasures for a moment with a sense of satisfaction, but as she lowered the lid she noticed the underside of it had faded crayon marks—the names Fletcher, Tom and Tav in youthful handwriting, as well as drawings of trees, people and dogs. This must have been her father's room, too. She smiled as she closed the lid—this was the best hiding place she'd ever found, and it made her happy to know that her father had lived in this room too.

By early evening August's new room was populated with all of her own furniture and several items left behind by her gran. Sorcha had lived in the house for a long time, and it was still hers even after she had been moved to a small nursing home across town when August was a baby. As the family story went, Sorcha had started to forget things—important things—soon after her husband Bryan died. When she once left the gas on in the kitchen, her son, Fletcher Evan, felt he had no choice but to move her to the facility for her own safety, and Sorcha was so angry she stopped speaking to him. She still wasn't speaking to her son when he died, after which her regret ran deep, despite her memory loss.

Sorcha gave the house to her daughter-in-law and granddaughter and begged them to move into it, close to her. August suspected the story was missing some things, but she wasn't going to push for more answers.

It hadn't taken Sylvia long to decide she didn't much want to stay in New York. She had made a few good friends there, but she really only moved to the city because of Evan's work at NYU, she had told August. And although she'd loved nursing for the first few years there, her job had become more and more administrative. And after *that night*, when her husband came into her ER so mauled and torn, and died there in front of her, Sylvia hadn't been able to even walk back into the hospital. So here they were in Mahigan Falls, a town more like Sylvia's childhood home, and August decided she would start getting used to it.

After two weeks of exploring the grounds, dipping her toes into the stream, helping her mother hang pictures on the walls and put books on the shelves, and poking into whatever cubbies she could find in the dozen or so rooms of the Blue Rook—including a brief look into the attic, which was another whole floor and even had windows, but no AC—August finally turned her thoughts to the coming school year. She had been resisting the idea, not looking forward to walking polished linoleum halls or smelling freshly re-painted cinderblock—things she associated with anxious feelings and embarrassment. She didn't want to suit up for gym class, or catch guys complaining about her ass. She didn't want to deal with gangs of bitchy cheerleaders, or feel the burn of frustration as small minds yawned over literature that was brilliant to her. Most of all she didn't want to be the New Girl. She spent most of Labor Day trying to work out an outfit and accessories that wouldn't call too much attention to herself, but wouldn't make her invisible either. She wanted to "be herself," but honestly, she wasn't sure exactly who that was yet—not in this new place, anyway. *Does the place determine who you are?* she wondered. How do you try, but not look like you're trying too hard? How can you be cool, but not indifferent? And how exactly are you supposed to be yourself with all of that spinning around inside of you? "It's fucking distracting," August muttered, surveying the clothes she'd thrown around her room.

Tuesday morning finally came, and August woke to the braying of morning deejays. She groaned and rolled out of bed. All she could think of was how much she wanted to sit down with a plateful of her dad's homemade waffles and smell the strong coffee he always made. She missed how he would start talking about politics and current events while he read the paper. She used to watch how his dark, sleek hair bobbed above the newspaper, his head nodding or shaking. In that moment she didn't think she could feel any sadder in her life, and then a moment later, she was ready to jump out of bed after all and say *carpe diem*. The roller coaster of emotions was wearing her out, and she wondered if the hole in her heart would ever begin to heal. Or maybe it wouldn't heal, exactly. Maybe she'd fill it with other things.

Taking the bus, the school would have been 20 minutes away, and she could have easily walked down to the end of their road to catch it, but August had already figured out a shortcut. By crossing the stream at the stepping stones, walking through a couple hundred yards of woods, and then cutting along the edge of an old farm field, she got there in less than 15 minutes.

From the back, the school itself looked like a brick bunker, and she shivered a little. But the front of the building seemed, if not friendlier, a little more inviting, and the students were running around, laughing and hitting each other. Some of them noticed her new face, and when she smiled, most of them smiled back. It seemed like everything was fine, so August decided that it was fine, and she tried not to let her body language show how nervous she really was.

The first thing she saw inside was a mile of shining tiles, cream and pale green, stretching out ahead of her. She found the main office and stood behind two other kids waiting for late registration. August thought about her father telling her that if you acted confident, people would respond as if you were, and in time you'd actually become confident. Standing there in that strange place though, she didn't feel she was much good at it, and she wished she could go home and cuddle up to her dad on the couch and have him tell her all about confidence and how to emulate it. Another half-learned lesson that she would have to complete by herself, August thought, and felt her throat tightening and tears trying to well up. She quickly swallowed them down before they could gain momentum.

She tried sauntering through the day. She made a point to make eye contact, introduced herself to classmates who approached her. She paid attention to their conversations and tried to sound like a confident senior. It was exhausting. Many of the juniors were already older than her, and she wondered if the seniors could tell. Probably not—she'd always been able to pass for older, ever since she grew hips at 10. Some of her fellow seniors looked like they were 18 already, particularly this one boy she couldn't help noticing, Tanner. He was big, muscled, and wore a varsity jacket despite the heat. He looked like a quarterback, and August had seen him in three of her classes by the end of the day. He was confident, bordering on cocky, and he always seemed to have a thick knot of friends around him. She wondered if she and Tanner would ever be friends and couldn't help but notice how attractive he was. Though, after a while she began to pick up the scent of something unsettling about him.

By her last class August was congratulating herself for having made it through the day without too much trouble, and she had started to let down her guard a bit. The teacher was in the hall talking to another teacher and the class was getting a little louder, when August heard a boy call out, "Hey you! Hey! New girl!"

She turned and looked in his direction, half smiling. It was Tanner, and he was looking right at her. She thought he was going to say hi or introduce himself or ask where she was from. Instead he showed his white teeth and said, "August? That's your name right?"

August smiled her best, "Hello, yes that's me," smile and gave a little nod and wave.

He just grinned, not a friendly grin, and said, "Well, August, I can smell your pussy from here! Oh, and nice camel toe!"

Most of the class burst out into laughter. August's smile fell. She tugged at her jeans and took her seat. She felt her face get hot and her stomach turn sour. She was a city girl and she was used to catcalls and crass comments—she even had a few good comebacks—but this was a sucker punch that threw her off balance, and Tanner had landed it perfectly. He just sat there grinning while the girl next to him laughed her ass off and whispered in his ear and glared at August.

The teacher came into the room and everybody shut up and turned to the front for the rest of the period. It was the longest 40 minutes August had ever endured. She heard snickers ripple occasionally around the room as she sat thin-lipped and seething, staring at the board the entire time.

All the way home she kept thinking of witty retorts, and she tormented herself for the rest of the night for not saying something smart and condescending. She had, essentially, let him get away with it.

September 7, 1982

Well that sucked. In the history of first days of school, this will go down as the worst. Started out just fine. I noticed this jock named Tanner early in the day and, idiot me, thought he was cute. Gag! He yelled that he could "smell my pussy" and see my "camel toe" in front of the whole fucking class! Where does that shit even come from?!?! I couldn't even believe it, and I didn't get to say ANYTHING because the teacher came in and everybody shut up.

I wish my dad was here. I wish he could tell me why boys are so stupid. Oh my god he would have reamed that smug bastard a new one! Mom would probably march straight down there and tell off the principal, but that would make things worse. Plus, she's having such

When August woke the next morning she thought of her father first and then her humiliation, and her anger burned like a hot coal in her belly. She suited herself up in her downtown New York City don't-fuck-with-me gear: spiked wristbands, black Doc Martens, ripped jeans, dark eyeliner, and two layers of her dad's old punk tees—the Stranglers on top.

At school, people parted like the Red Sea around her. She spent the day with a wall of anger up, giving no smiles and waiting for anyone to be shitty to her. She pretended Tanner didn't exist—but if he got in her face, she promised herself, he'd find out how hard those spikes really were.

It seemed to work. The rest of that week and all of the next she stayed puffed up like a cat, and at lunch she sat in a corner of the courtyard and read books. She noticed that people were leaving a zone of clear air around her, and even some of the teachers looked a little nervous when she stalked to the back of their classrooms. But she could still hear Tanner and his gang, whispering and snickering. And she could only keep up the angry girl bit for so long. She was worn out by the end of the second week. Beyond that, she really did want to make friends, and now nobody would come near her.

Almost nobody. There was one girl August noticed who didn't keep her distance. In fact, just when August thought she wouldn't make friends with anybody, this girl had her own book out at lunch, on the next bench over. August noticed she was reading Kurt Vonnegut, and tended to favor Star Wars T-shirts, flowered skirts, pigtails and a beat-up pair of combat boots. If August was going to make any friends at all, this seemed like a good place to start. She put down *The Stand* and looked at the girl, until she finally noticed and put down her own book.

The girl looked at August, open and unguarded. "I'm Lainy," she said, with a hint of a half-smile. She only hesitated a moment before launching into a stream of information. "These boots used to be my mom's. She was in the Marines. Now she stays at home with my little sister. I liked that book too, but I liked *The Shining* better. This is my second time reading *Slaughterhouse-Five*. Did you see *The Empire Strikes Back*? Yoda's my favorite. I like everything Frank Oz does. Did you know he's Miss Piggy too? Tanner is the biggest buttwipe in the whole school. Everybody hates him but none of them has the guts to stand up to him." At this point Lainy stopped for breath, and August guessed it was her turn.

"I'm August. I just moved here. I love *Star Wars*, too. Oh, and I love Grover. Is that ... Frank Oz, too?"

"Yes! Alright!" beamed Lainy, and held up her hand for a high-five, even though August was eight feet away. She turned it into a wave instead. "August? That's cool. Is that your real name?"

She was going to answer, but as soon as she opened her mouth the bell rang for class, and the two girls hopped off of their respective benches. "Listen," said Lainy, "don't pay any attention to Tanner. He thinks he can do anything he feels like 'cause he's captain of the wrestling team, but he'll get bored and find somebody else to annoy."

"Thanks, Lainy. I'll see you in sixth, I guess." August watched Lainy skip off into the hallway and felt her spirit lift a little. *I've got one friend, anyway*, she thought.

Unfortunately, Lainy was wrong about Tanner. He seemed to have decided that he was going to step up his campaign against August, and with some less defensible tactics. Twice he came from behind her in the hall and banged her shoulder as he passed; the second time he slapped her ass at the same time, but August was so distracted by the notebooks and papers he'd knocked out of her hand that she didn't have time to respond before he was far down the hall, laughing and looking over his shoulder. The hairs rose on the back of her neck. There was something in his expression—something predatory, August perceived. She said so, in a note she passed to Lainy later, but her new friend just shrugged. Clearly she had never been the object of Tanner's relentless attention.

September 22, 1982

I met a girl named Lainy last week. She seems smart and real and knows about a million bits of trivia. I'm glad to have somebody to talk to at least. At last. The hardass bit really worked—I didn't think anybody was going to talk to me ever.

She's into Star Wars and Muppets, but I don't know about her music yet. I'm looking forward to having a friend—tho I don't want to get my hopes up. She told me to ignore Tanner, but he's not letting me. Knocking me over, putting his damn hands on me—and always with no teachers around. He's totally creepy, but she doesn't think I should be worried. I hope she's right.

Except for Lainy, school stinks. Even the subjects I should like are miserable because I'm just waiting for somebody to say something gross or push me around. I still haven't told Mom about it, but if it keeps up I may have to. It seems like people in school must know about this guy but they just don't do anything about it.

Maybe I should just get my G.E.D. I'm already two grades ahead—what if I just start college early? At least those people would be adults.

This town has been such a roller coaster for me. It's beautiful, but it's so little—and quiet. And I haven't gotten to see Gran yet. Mom said we should get all settled in first, and also set up her room for long visits. I have so many questions to ask her.

I do really like the woods tho—more than I thought I would.

Fingers crossed that tomorrow is better.

It was a week later, just before seventh period, when August felt someone behind her in the hall again, and spun around. But it wasn't Tanner, it was his girlfriend Crystal, just inches away. She was half a head taller than August, but thin as a rail—except for her boobs, which she always dressed to reveal. August had never seen her up close before. She wore purple sparkle eye shadow, and her mascara was so thick it had flaked onto her cheekbones. Crystal always seemed to have her lips parted, as though she was forever on the verge of asking an insipid question. But at this range August could see that she wasn't really pretty, just very done up.

"What is your problem, you ugly little bitch?" sneered Crystal. "You're in my way."

She was trying for intimidating, but August saw nothing there to be afraid of. Instead she shrugged. "Go fuck yourself, Crystal." It was an automatic response, but it seemed to shock the girl. Her expression froze, and she drifted backwards a step or two, but then charged up in August's face again.

"You just stay away from Tanner, you freaky little cunt! You hear me?" she hissed. "And don't say my name! Got it? I don't want my name coming out of your fugly mouth!" She stalked around August and into the classroom.

Fugly. August rolled her eyes. "Sure, no problem, *Crystal*!" She couldn't resist. But if Crystal heard her, she pretended not to, chatting with her friends, facing away from August and tugging casually at an earring.

August just shook her head. She couldn't believe Crystal really thought she wanted anything to do with Tanner. In fact, August would have been thrilled if he just dropped off the face of the earth any time in the next five minutes. How could anybody be that clueless about what was going on? Would it even do any good to try to tell her otherwise? August couldn't decide whether she felt sorry enough for Crystal to try to reassure her, or just wanted to punch her in her ever-parted mouth.

The bell rang, but instead of walking into class, August turned back down the hall and headed for the nurse's office. She decided she had a migraine and would need to sit this class out on a cot in a darkened room.

Things went along pretty much the same into October. August looked forward to her lunches with Lainy, who could actually sit quietly and listen when she wanted to. But most of the time August had her guard up, watching for her varsity nemesis. One day, walking into class, she caught a whiff of danger just before she felt someone else's leg step between hers. She jumped and then went down hard, her knees and elbows cracking onto the cold linoleum. She looked up to see Tanner standing over her, grinning and offering a chivalrous hand. She wanted to kick his leg out from under him, but Mr. Poul was standing right there, looking at her like she'd forgotten how gravity worked. After that, August took to walking along the walls between classes, her head half-turned to watch behind her, using her peripheral vision to look ahead. She was increasingly aware of how ridiculous all of this had become, to the point she was seriously considering that G.E.D.

~~Red Woods~~

August had joined the yearbook committee at Lainy's
suggestion—"You'll totally meet like a ton of people who know
everybody but aren't all stuck-up"—so now she was staying past
5:30 on Wednesdays for the after-school meetings, talking with new
friends and helping Ms. Kinney file their photos and notes away in
the school office. By the end of October however, she realized the
trouble with staying so late at this time of year was running out of
daylight. The walk home through the woods that night would be
gloomy, but there was no way she was going to ride around on the
activity bus for 45 minutes with the wrestling jocks headed
home—particularly Tanner. She could hear the coach's whistle in the
gym. *Maybe if Dad hadn't died, I'd have gotten my driver's license
by now*, she thought, and then cringed at how selfish that sounded.

August took a peek outside of the auditorium doors. The sun
was already below the trees, and the woods were looking murky. She
sniffed the cooling breeze and listened, but all she could hear was
the chattering of birds. She shivered, and then realized she didn't
have a jacket either. She didn't want to call her mom, but it looked
like she was out of options. Once she got to the office however,
August noticed the box of lost-and-found items behind the counter,
and most of them were jackets. What could it hurt to borrow one, she
thought—she would just bring it back tomorrow, and she wouldn't
have to bug her mom for a ride. At the bottom of the box was a beat-

up hooded sweatshirt in Mahigan Marauders red with the school's wolf mascot on the front. August zipped it up and pulled the hood over her head before slipping through the auditorium doors and into the cloudless twilight. The schoolyard was creepy quiet. She imagined being the last teenager on Earth, and wondered how long it would take before she broke into a supermarket and ate all of the Breyers mint chocolate chip.

A few leaves came raining down with each breeze and August watched them as they fluttered towards the ground and waltzed a moment on the sidewalk, silhouetted by the light of a waxing gibbous moon. At the edge of the school property, where the trees became thick, there were a few straggling workmen repairing the fence where a tree had fallen. One of the men was preparing to cut the wood with a chainsaw and nodded a greeting as August walked by. She nodded back, but made sure to check over her shoulder a few times until she was deep into the woods. When she was far enough away that she could barely hear the buzz of his saw she turned her attention back to the darkening path ahead of her.

The wind chilled her face and she pulled off the hood and let it blow back her hair. She felt so alive, vibrant and crackling with energy. She kicked and crunched through the leaves on the path, and picked up the faint scent of chimney smoke blending with the musty smell of ground cover and pine. August caught herself smiling. She mused over conversations with her new friends and thought about holiday shopping with Lainy to buy presents for all of them, and something special for Mom and Gran. She was actually happy; the veil between her and the rest of the world was falling away and she was beginning to feel connected again.

Then she heard something, a rustling between the breezes. A twig snapped, deeper in the woods, but she couldn't see anything but trees and underbrush. *Must have been a squirrel.* She continued on, treading silently on the mossy bottom land and listened as though she could hear the song of the wind itself. When she heard another rustle it was much closer, and she stopped. The breeze settled for a moment, nothing was making a sound, and then the wind shifted and she smelled him. The hairs on the back of her neck stood up, and her heart started pounding hard and fast. She turned and saw Tanner standing a few feet away. Along with the musk and mildew of soured sweat, August could almost taste the stench of anger on him, and when he sprinted toward her she knew he was going to hurt her. Before she could get two steps away he grabbed her by the hood and hair. He spun her around and shoved her against a huge gnarled oak tree, pinning her there with a forearm across her chest and clamping his hand over her mouth. He was pressing with such force August could feel the bark digging into her through two layers of clothing. Time slowed and her mind raced, noticing everything. His eyes were two mouths, hungry and dark. There was a small sharp pain and something warm and wet ran down the side of her neck. He was crushing her and she understood the silent panic of a rabbit in the jaws of a dog. A scream gurgled in her throat and he cut it off with a shake of his meaty hand against her mouth.

"Shut up," he barked, and then leaned in to hiss in her ear. "You shut the fuck up or I'm going to crush your goddam head like a melon against this tree. Got it?"

August couldn't even nod. She tried to relax some of the tension in her body to indicate she would obey. She could feel her heart pounding in every part of her body but she couldn't get a breath with him crushed against her. She panicked at the thought of passing out, and instead tried to focus on slowing her breathing and forcing her muscles to relax. August's forced calm rewarded her immediately, as Tanner eased his pressure and she remembered that she had a knife in her right front pocket.

The hulking animal regarded her with a smug and possessive gaze. "Oh look, you have a little blood on your neck." He leaned his head into her, licking and sucking the blood from her skin and pressing his hips against her. August tried to cheat her left hip out so he wouldn't feel the knife in her pocket. How was she going to get it out? Her heart started racing again and her body tensed. Tanner pressed her harder against the trunk.

"Don't fucking fight me you little cunt!" he spat. Now, I'm gonna take my hand off of your mouth if you promise to be a good girl and be quiet. You got me?"

She nodded.

"I fucking mean it. No noise. I'm not going to hurt you if you stay quiet. But if you make a fucking sound I will rip you inside out and leave you for the fucking wolves."

She stayed as still and quiet as she was able, her body trembling hard against her will. His weight still pressed her, but he pulled his hand from her mouth. Her lips were stinging and her whole face felt oddly numb and prickly at the same time.

He pushed his foul mouth against hers and clumsily shoved his tongue into her. She didn't fight or even resist, but devoted her attention to trying to sneak her hand into her right pocket. Her body convulsed in small gags as his milk-sour tongue pushed between her teeth. She had the impulse to bite hard, but she didn't think she would have enough time to get away. She was trying not to vomit. Her fingertips found the end of the bone-handled knife.

Tanner leaned back and started pushing up her shirt. His hands on her belly were like cold slabs of beef, but she pushed the chill far away. Maybe an inch more and she could grasp the knife well enough to retrieve it, she thought, but if she wasn't careful he could catch her and use the blade against her. Then Tanner shoved her tee and sweatshirt up together, grabbed the front of her bra, and tore it open at the clasp. Her stomach recoiled and a wave of nausea rushed over her. She swallowed hard. This is really happening, she thought. This pig is going to rape me and then do God knows what else to me.

"Tell me you want it," Tanner prodded her. "Tell me you want it you stuck-up cunt!"

The knife was almost in her grasp. If he moved just a little to the left she would have it.

Then Tanner grabbed her waistband at the button and ripped open her jeans. The button went flying, the zipper jammed, and he yanked her pants down past her hips, past her knees. The knife was gone from her reach. Something inside of August switched off and any hope she'd had of escape drained out of her. He was twice her weight, and a wrestler. She understood finally that she was not getting out of this, and her mind abandoned her body. Tanner pushed his fat hand down the front of her and squeezed her hard. August twitched involuntarily. He pushed his sweatpants down to his knees, and the smell of rancid sweat and musk engulfed her and she gagged again. She didn't look down. She looked into the night and tried to maintain numbness.

"You want this, don't you? Walkin' around teasing me. Watching me like you want it. Asking for it. Now you're gonna get it. And you're gonna like it."

He pushed against her thighs, hard.

August looked up at the moon, more than half full. She guessed it should be full by Saturday. She sent her mother an apology into the ether, for not trying harder. For not being bigger. For not being stronger. She wondered if she would see her father, wherever it was she was about to go. Tears streamed down her cheeks.

Tanner's groping and pressing seemed to go on for an eternity, though it must have been only seconds when a low growl came out of the darkness. He froze and shrank away, finally leaving air between them. There was a rustling, and a snap, and the growl came again, louder and closer, but August couldn't see anything in the shadows. It sounded like a large dog. Tanner's breathing went shallow.

"Fuck. Fuck!" Tanner spat.

He slowly edged backwards, straining to see into the gloom. The growl deepened to a vicious snarl and Tanner tried to run off, tripping over his pants and scrambling away into the darkness. August watched him from someplace above, seeing her own body standing against the tree, wondering without concern whether she would see the creature that frightened him. The growl moved around behind her at some distance, and went silent. She heard something run, with a sudden burst of speed, into the dark woods where Tanner had gone.

Then August realized she had not been breathing, and gulped a lungful of air—sharp and strangely scented. A wave of heat flashed through her and she was back in her own skin. She pulled her clothing into place, plunged her hand into her pocket and pulled out the knife, extending the blade and pointing it into the darkness. It shook in her grasp. Her breath began to heave and she sobbed. *Keep it together!* she snapped at herself. Whatever was out there, it was going after Tanner right now, and it was her time to get out and go home. Long step. Shaky legs. *Don't fall!* Next step. Next step. She was moving. She could see every tree, every bramble in her path. She didn't even break stride when she heard the scream in the woods far behind her.

Then August was at the mudroom behind the Rook. Her grandmother's house. Home. Her next thought was that she didn't want her mother to know what had just happened. She was ashamed for her carelessness, for not being on guard, but more than that she was feeling fiercely protective of Sylvia. She was still so fragile. That ape may have put his foul hands on her, August glowered, but no fucking way she was going to let him touch her mother. Her hand tightened on the knife.

Easy! Don't lose it. Just breathe. After taking a moment to calm down she folded the knife and slipped it back in her pocket. She balled up what was left of her bra and shoved it in the sweatshirt pocket. She smoothed down her shirt, combed her fingers through her hair, pulled her jeans closed and tied the sweatshirt around her waist to hold them. She steadied her breathing and stepped in through the back door. Fortunately, her mother barely looked up from her book. She had a glass of wine and two bottles next to her, along with an oatmeal dinner that looked untouched. August sailed through the kitchen, sounding as casual as possible.

"Hey Mom. I'm gonna go get a shower and go to bed. I love you! Goodnight!"

"Wait, August, it's awfully early for bed. What's that smell?" Sylvia shouted after her, her words a little slurred.

"I know, I need a shower," August called back. "It's been a long day. I'm just going to do my homework and go to sleep."

"Okay, goodnight sweetie," Sylvia gave up. "Let's spend some time together tomorrow, okay? I love you! I love you so much!"

"Sure Mom! Goodnight! I love you, too!"

August dashed for the bathroom, barely getting the door shut before starting the shower. Then she lurched toward the toilet and began to dry heave, trying to keep it quiet and praying that the solid walls and the sound of the water were enough to cover it. She peeled off her clothes, pulled a plastic trash bag from under the sink, and tied them up into the bag. For safe keeping. In the mirror she discovered a crusted line of blood down the side of her neck, under her right ear. She was surprised she wasn't aching or sore, but she guessed that may come later, and made a mental note to slip back downstairs and take some painkillers before bed. She wondered if she should tell her mother after all, and go to an emergency room. But she was afraid if anyone except Mom touched her now she might punch them. Even the thought of having to do one more thing filled her with the overwhelming sense that she was going to disappear, or explode. All she knew was that all she could do now was take care of that one minute, and the next minute.

She stepped into the spray and lathered every part of her body, but she couldn't wash away the layer of filth she could feel beneath her skin. She turned down the flow to make the hot water last longer and sat in the tub, letting the shower pour over her head, which had finally started to throb. The sobbing came on again, and this time it took hold and didn't stop until the water had gone cold.

August wrapped herself up in her fluffiest robe and crept down toward the kitchen. It was empty. She heard the floor above the kitchen creaking and knew that her mother had gone to bed, and the relief of not having to perform another act for her washed over August. She toasted some bread and made a cup of tea, grabbed some aspirin and headed up to her room, where she wrapped up in Gran's freshly laundered quilt to calm down the shivers, and curled up in the window seat. She wasn't sure she would be able to eat, but the buttered toast was just what she needed, and the tea made her finally feel warm again.

She watched the moon and thought about her father and wondered if he saw what happened to her tonight. She decided he couldn't have or he would have done something to prevent it. Then again, that creep was chased off before he finished whatever he came there to do. She pictured Tanner stumbling over his pants, scared by a stray dog, and felt glad. *Fucking deserves whatever he got!* And what was that strange smell? She remembered it now. Whatever that scent was, there was something so familiar about it, but she knew she'd never smelled it before. *I really have to report this*, she thought, just moments before she fell asleep, right there in the window seat.

The next morning August crawled into bed and complained of menstrual cramps, and parlayed her feigned discomfort into Friday as well. She managed to largely steer clear of her mother, which was made easier because Sylvia had a new job at a doctor's office in town. But by Saturday August was not only sick of lying in bed, she also realized that she missed her mother's presence very much, and hovered around her for most of the day, staying bundled up in Gran's quilt and feeling like a pint-sized sasquatch. Sylvia clucked her tongue and felt August's head for fever, but eventually was satisfied that her daughter was having a blue day. She reminded August that it was "Hallowe'en-e'en," her dad's name for the night before Halloween, normally a very excited night at the Archer household, though August couldn't muster much more than a weak smile.

"We might get ghosts and witches and maybe a few E.T.s at the door. This town is very into Halloween. It was a big to-do back when your dad was a kid. And even in her saddest days, your Gran gave out caramel apples and big candy bars. And I hear her friends have kept up the tradition. Kids know to come by here. We shouldn't disappoint them. Next year when you're feeling more up to it, you'll want them to know they should come back."

"I guess."

"I got a bag of fun size candy bars and Jolly Ranchers, too—but don't give those to the littler ones, they'll choke," her mom cautioned.

"I'll think about it."

Then Sylvia told her about her day at work, including the tale of "a boy from the high school" who had been attacked in the past week by a wild animal—maybe a bear, maybe even wolves. The doctor she worked for had to treat him at the emergency clinic before he was transferred to Johns Hopkins in Baltimore. Sylvia whispered gravely, "He almost bled to death. His injuries were severe and he'll need special types of physical therapy for a year or more. He's never going to have kids, at the very least."

August knew it had to be Tanner, and though not proud of it, she couldn't help but gloat a bit that justice had been served so quickly. Besides, now she could let go of some of the guilt she'd been carrying about not reporting Tanner's attempted rape. He wasn't going to be trying that again with any other girls.

"Oh," August managed, hoping her mother hadn't read her first reaction. She felt her entire body relax, and then realized she was starving.

"Boys should be careful walking through the woods by themselves," Sylvia said, then patted August on the head and went off to another room.

That night, August went upstairs, opened her nightstand drawer and took out the letter she had written for the sheriff. It detailed Tanner's assault on her, a physical description, the arrival of the dog that she never saw, and her own state of mind after he was chased off and she went home. She re-read it and folded it over and over into a tiny square and tucked it in the bottom-most corner of the window seat. She thought of Sylvia, sitting in the living room with her wedding album while quietly finishing off a bottle of cabernet. God, or karma, or whatever avenging spirit had punished Tanner for his crime. Maybe there was some order to the universe after all.

August spent most of Halloween Sunday writing in her diary, working through her guilt and anger. She wrote a memory in her journal of her mother, cleaning a slice on her leg when she was nine. Sylvia told her that the butterfly bandage would keep the wound shut and if she took good care of it, washing it and re-bandaging it, that it would heal neatly, in time. But if she kept taking the bandage off, looking at the wound and poking at it and picking the scab, it could become infected and fester and even get as serious as poisoning her system, and if it did finally heal it would leave a nasty scar. *Maybe emotional wounds are like that too,* August wrote. *If you keep picking at them, maybe they don't heal, or they leave nasty scars. Maybe they can even poison you.*

She often worked things out in her journal. Maybe that was the bandage she needed for her soul right now. Would any good come of writing down, over and over again, what Tanner did and how angry and violated she felt? Wouldn't that be like taking off the bandage, picking the scab and poking at the wounds? If you hold every horrible moment close, would that nurse the hate into a monster? Tanner attacked her. It happened. It's done. Now it was behind her. You can't fix things that have already happened. Her father's death had taught her that.

She listed off things she felt she could do to expedite recovery, and "Be stronger" was at the top of that list. Maybe she could take karate or something; she would figure it out soon. By the end of twelve pages she was feeling much better and looked forward to Halloween night.

That evening the sun set quickly, the temperature dropped into the forties, and the moon came up full and round, a perfect night for Halloween. August happily volunteered to handle giving out the candy, since Sylvia had hoped to start studying the state's nursing registration guidelines. She suspected that it had more to do with Mom not being up to having a Halloween without Dad, so August resolved to get into the spirit of things herself, like her father would have wanted.

She dumped all of the candy into a giant bowl and dug her father's cloak out of the window seat for an instant Red Riding Hood costume. The cloak floated around her as she rushed down the stairs to prepare for the trick-or-treaters. She was determined to envelope herself in positive memories of her father for the next few hours. A spark of joy lit her up from inside.

All night the nostalgic smells of candy from the bowl and her father's cloak were with her. The wool was heavy and made her feel safe and protected inside of it. August even found a small pocket on the inside where she could tuck her knife. She did pause a moment to imagine her father in such an ostentatious piece of clothing—he a man of brown tweed suits and understated tartan ties—and August couldn't wait to talk to Sorcha about all of these things. Her father did go all-out for Halloween though, so maybe the cloak was part of an old costume. For a moment she entertained a fantasy of her father in a billowing ruffled blouse and tall boots, sword-fighting with some evil pirate, the cape blowing in the wind behind him. She smiled to herself and snuggled the cape tighter.

The cadence of the trick-or-treaters who ventured up their road in packs stirred up memories for August. She remembered her father from Halloweens past, dressed up like a ghoul and popping out into the hall to surprise the little ones. The apartment would be filled with fake tombstones and spider silk and flashing strobe lights, accompanied by cheesy screams on tape and sometimes fog, which oozed out into the hallway. Everyone in their building knew to come by at Halloween, just like here. She imagined carrying on the tradition, and maybe even turning the Blue Rook into a haunted house next year. Her father would have loved that.

Eventually August had to shed the too-warm cloak, though it didn't matter so much once the stream of Halloween hordes had slowed to a trickle. What did matter was that they were still coming when she ran out of candy, so she taped a note to the door, slunk shamefully into the darkened house and turned off the porch light. She wouldn't let that happen again next year.

August noticed that moon beams lit up the glass around the door and made a pattern on the floor. She hadn't looked at the designs in the stained-glass transom before. It was an outdoor scene, a forest of some sort and a round yellow moon.

She took the bowl back to the kitchen and discovered her mother had conked out on the table in a sugar coma, with a half-dozen candy wrappers scattered around next to her wine glass and her nursing book. August nudged her gently and admonished her to go find her bed. Sylvia hugged her daughter and lumbered off up the stairs, and August once again thanked her stars and angels that Tanner had not taken her away from her mother.

August knew she wasn't going to school tomorrow, if ever. She felt restless and ready to be past all of it. She wanted to go out and shop or see a movie or something—now, this minute—but it was Sunday night in a dinky little town, and everything was closed. She thought about calling Lainy, but instead she picked up what was left in Sylvia's glass and went into the living room to watch some cable. The family programming was done for the night and most of what she found was sex comedies or straight-up soft-core erotic fare. She settled on the couch and let herself be taken in by the flash of skin and the sounds of kissing. She felt herself becoming aroused, which at that moment she found extremely comforting. It was all very cheesy, soft-focus stuff, but seeing people who wanted to be touched, who happily caressed each other's tender places, made her feel like sex could be normal. This scene had a cowboy, tongue-tied and cute, and a barmaid who was kissing him and reassuring him. He kept putting his hands on her and she kept smiling and being playful. It was sweet and romantic, and August couldn't help but feel turned on. She noticed that the barmaid's breasts, now naked in his hands, were shaped very much like her own. *Maybe mine aren't so bad after all*, August thought. The lovers' kisses and heavy breathing, punctuated by gasps and quiet moans, had her gently rocking in her chair.

As August watched these eager strangers nuzzle and caress each other in soft focus, she began to pet her own thighs, inching her skirt up, and then bent her legs open. She slipped her hand into her panties, brushing the soft patch of fur with her fingertips and feeling delicious tingles. She slid her fingers towards the cleft between her thighs and started stroking herself. As the excitement of the lovers on screen crested, August rubbed faster and pressed harder, and her fingers became slick. The tingling climbed up the center of her body to her breasts, and they grew warm and achy. She slipped her left hand up her tee, and began brushing and pinching her nipple with her fingertips. Her eyes closed and her lips parted in a silent moan, and behind her eyelids she watched the lovers as she imagined them, hungry tongues and restless hands, cupping and stroking and squeezing, set to the music of their passionate sounds. Soon she was rocking her hips rhythmically, filled up and overflowing with her own lust and want. She began quaking with ecstasy, pushed over the edge by the lovers' cries, and her body shuddered in waves. August's orgasm melted into quiet spasms, leaving behind a spent euphoria, and she pulled the nearby cloak around her. She rode the tranquil streams trailing after her peak and allowed herself a moment to hang there in complete pleasure and relaxation, momentarily swept clean of worries, and fears, and loss. She slipped into a gentle doze, and there were no monsters in her dreams.

She awoke with the clock creeping up on midnight and the full moon staring down at her through the window. She tried to stretch and relax, tried to re-cover herself with the cloak and settle back into sleep, but nothing doing. She was wide awake and restless. Nothing on TV but static and people trying to sell stuff—and judging by their volume, the louder you yell the more you sell. She couldn't sit still.

August dug through the hall closet, slipped on boots, and

grabbed her pocket knife and tucked it into the inner cloak pocket. She surprised herself, not feeling afraid to go out into the night. In fact, with her knife in a handy pocket and her father's cloak wrapped around her, she was feeling almost invincible.

The chill of the first November night was hanging in the air, but the moon was kissing every tree and hill, every roof and fence. August felt so much a part of it all, she would have hugged this night to her bosom if she could. She set a path towards the tree line, following the stream and a light in the distance. She stood for a moment at the edge of the woods and thought, *Gotta get back on the horse*. She stepped into the trees and began walking. The night was big and filled with a thousand tiny sounds, each in their own key and timbre. Clicks, whistles, tiny clucks and whirs were all around her, suspended inside middle-of-the-night stillness.

Soon she could see a lantern in the yard of their neighbor's house, looking like a sculpture in the moonlight. In fact the side of the house facing the woods was dotted with a circle of lanterns and torches. As she made her way closer, August could just make out a figure moving around. She pulled the cloak tight around her and put the hood up over her head, as though it would somehow make her invisible, a part of the night mists. She fingered the knife's shape through the pocket, confirming its existence.

August crept around to the side, staying close to the bushes. She could see him better now, her neighbor. All he was wearing was some kind of wrap. No, a kilt, over a furry Halloween costume. She almost giggled, but bit her lip instead. The firelight of the torches alternately threw shadows and amber light over him. He was saying something, a low sound like humming or chanting. August could almost make it out—a ritual perhaps, or a rite of some kind?—and she was mesmerized. She edged in as close as she dared, and she could see he was holding some kind of small ceramic bowl up to the sky.

He was bringing it to his lips, about to drink from it, when August shifted her weight. She momentarily lost her balance and grabbed the bush for support, and the rustling seemed to reverberate through the night. She gulped and held her breath, and at that moment felt an urgent need to pee. Her neighbor stopped and threw a searching glare in her direction, and she froze. She could see his mask now—it was so realistic it was spooky. A chill shot down her spine. He looked like a real hound. Maybe it was a movie costume. Why would he have a movie costume? Even his eyes seemed to have an icy blue glow. He tipped back his head and waved his snout around, like he was sniffing the air, looking even more wolf-like in the process, and August thought her heart would stop. Then he went back to his ritual, drinking whatever was in the bowl and chanting some more. His movements and chants left August feeling a deep sense of numinous beauty, a feeling of oneness with the trees and the moon, as though she were witnessing something ancient and secret. The man extinguished the torches and lanterns, picked up his bowl, and walked into the house. She watched as lights turned on and off as he moved through the rooms. After a few more minutes August guessed nothing else was going to happen, so she rose up out of her crouch and turned to go home. She was so startled to find someone standing there behind her that she yipped and then just stared at him.

"Hello neighbor," he said with a hint of Scottish brogue.

"Uh ... I ... um. Hi. I'm really sorry. I didn't mean to ..." She was feeling for the knife inside of her cloak, just in case he was not as friendly as he seemed.

"You won't need that," he said calmly, and her fear inexplicably melted.

She reminded herself not to let her guard down too quickly, but there was something about his manner that was soothing and familiar. She also felt like she could smell that he was safe, the same way she could smell that Tanner was dangerous. She had no words or context for these things and didn't quite trust them fully, so she slipped the knife out of her pocket and opened it beneath the cloak and looked for a clear path to run, if necessary.

"I didn't mean to spy," August went on, anxious to make herself understood—to explain her trespass. "I was just restless, and bored. I went for a walk and headed toward the light in your yard. I didn't even realize it was your yard until I got here. I've never walked this way before."

The man crossed his arms, cocked his head slightly to the side and studied her coolly. Despite the patchy moonlight, August could see him pretty clearly. He seemed lean and strong. Maybe in his forties, with slicked-back dark hair and pale blue eyes.

"There wasn't anything on TV," she faltered, not sure what else to say. She felt herself flush when she recalled what she had been watching. She hoped he wouldn't notice.

"It's alright," he said after another moment. "I just didn't know anyone was watching. My rites are rather private. This is a small town; people sometimes get upset about things they don't understand."

"Oh, you don't have to worry about me saying anything," August returned, relieved to be on conversational ground and eager to engage this intriguing man. "I actually found it kind of interesting. Well, maybe the costume was a bit spooky, but it's Halloween, right? You managed to get out of it quickly enough," she added as an afterthought. She noticed he was still wearing a kilt, but had on a loose, thin white shirt, almost a blouse, really. He rolled up a sleeve while she watched. Something about his body language was attractive to her. So relaxed and calm, but confident.

He regarded her with a slight smile, devilishly crooked at one corner. August tried to study his face. He was handsome in an academic sort of way, yet somehow he also had a rugged quality. She thought of Indiana Jones. Not that he looked like Harrison Ford exactly, but that he could have easily played the part himself.

"I would invite you in, but if I did you should say no," he admonished. "You don't know me and it's late and I'm guessing nobody really knows where you are."

She gripped the knife a little tighter and eyed her escape route. It was stupid not to tell her mother she was going out.

"Absolutely," she said. "You're absolutely right. Maybe some other time."

"I'm not so sure that's a good idea, mon petit chaperon rouge."

"Little Red Riding Hood," she translated automatically. "Charles Perrault." She gave a stunned half-smile.

He smiled back, a relaxed, yet glorious smile. "Quite right."

Little Red Riding Hood. She couldn't tell if he was trying to endear himself or not. By all reason, she should be scared shitless right now, but she wasn't. In fact, she had to keep pushing aside the thought that she would have to stand on her tiptoes to kiss him.

"And why would it be a bad idea? " She responded, tilting her head.

"Because, I'm a stranger." He said it like it was the most obvious thing in the world.

Her empty hand emerged from the cloak. "Hi, I'm August. You can call me Red if you want to, though. What's your name?"

He did not meet her gesture.

"Look, Red, I think you may have the wrong idea. We can't be friends, okay? Trust me, it's nothing personal. I told you—this town. It's small."

Feeling stupid with her hand hanging there in mid-air, she went for being adorably assertive, and thrust her hand out further. "I said, what's your name? If you introduce yourself, we won't be strangers."

"I think you'd better go now," he said finally, and turned and went back toward the house. She was stung, even a little choked up, by this flat rejection. She realized her sense of disappointment was far in excess of what it should have been, considering she'd only just met the man, but she couldn't help it.

She didn't mean to sound bitter when she yelled after him, "Guess I'll have to call you Wolf!"

All the way home she couldn't stop thinking about how embarrassed she was. She also thought about what he might look like in the daylight and what it might be like to kiss him. She then wished she could stop thinking about kissing altogether. It brought nothing but confusion and complication.

Even when she was back in her bed, her night was restless and full of unresolved longings. When she awoke in the sunlight he was the first thing on her mind and her stomach was queasy and she doubted she could eat anything for a month. Exhausted, she groaned and burrowed deeper into her covers, cupping her breasts, rubbing and rocking for comfort and release until she finally fell back to sleep. She dreamed peacefully of wolves and fairies and sexy older men.

It was bright daylight when the phone woke August again.

"Hello?"

"August?"

"Lainy?"

"Yeah. Why weren't you at school today? You've been absent forever! There are a lot of rumors going around. I really think you need to come in and clear things up."

"I don't care. What time is it?"

"It's like 2:30. I'm coming over, I've got to talk to you."

"Oh, Lainy, I don't feel like—"

"Too bad. I'll be there in 20 minutes." Lainy hung up. August was only slightly annoyed at having to deal with this intrusion of reality, but she also had to admit that she really did need to get some of this off her chest, and she couldn't think of anyone she'd rather tell than Lainy.

August did a quick tidy of her wrecked bedroom, tucking the cloak into the window seat and gathering up scattered books to pack them into the already overstuffed bookcase. Then she caught sight of herself in the mirror looking thoroughly disheveled, wearing only underwear and a threadbare tee. She tied back her hair, threw a cardigan over the tee, slipped jeans on over her hips, and socks onto her chilly toes. She headed for the kitchen—all her late-night wanderings and sleeping-in past lunch had left her famished. She felt her breasts bouncing as she trotted down the stairs, and she watched how they moved. She thought how she wouldn't mind if her neighbor was here to see her like that, then wondered if he would even be interested in her small tits. "He might actually like them," she said aloud, and then rolled her eyes. She figured it didn't matter anyway—it wasn't like she was ever going to find out.

Lainy arrived in a flurry of agitation and concern, her pigtails bouncing. She was talking so fast that August couldn't get in a word, so she munched on buttered toast and let Lainy unload. She explained how Tanner had told the police a story about being attacked by a pack of wolves in the woods. He'd been in the hospital ever since that night and had to get a series of rabies shots. They'd even sent him to Baltimore for more treatment.

The story going around school, at least according to Tanner's gang, was that August had come on to him after his practice Wednesday night and that he turned her down. But because he was worried about her feelings and he was such a great guy, he offered to walk her home through the woods. Then these wolves or dogs or whatever came out of nowhere, so he sacrificed himself by drawing them away, letting August run to safety. So now, as Lainy reported, Tanner's this big hero and Crystal's been going around with weepy eyes collecting sympathy all day and everybody is mad at August for abandoning the wrestling legend of Mahigan Falls High School and not even bothering to call for help.

By the end of the story August's simmering rage had turned into raw, jagged anger.

"So ..." Lainy finally prodded her.

"So what?" August replied casually, but felt her face flush.

"Oh my god? So, is all that true?"

"What do you think?" August set her jaw and fixed Lainy with a look. She'd been hoping she could count on Lainy not to be suckered into such a ridiculous tale.

After a beat Lainy asked, "Well, what did happen then?"

"Tanner tried to rape me," she said icily. She saw Lainy react, physically.

"Then some animal, a dog or something, came and chased him off and I fucking went home."

"What?!" Lainy sort of shouted, utterly disgusted and probably louder than she meant to, and August loved her for it. "What do you mean he tried to *rape* you?"

"He pinned me against a fucking tree, and tried to stick his terrifying dick inside of me. Some big dog came along and growled at him and he ran off into the woods. I walked home and threw up and took a two-hour shower. And now you know the rest of the story."

"Holy shit! We have a wolf problem around here. Did you know? No one can ever find them, either."

"No. But I'm glad. And I doubt that asshole actually told the police about me, or they would have come and asked me some questions, don't you think?"

"Well, did you call the police about ... you know ... about what he did?"

"No! And don't you, either! I didn't want to upset my mom. She's shaky enough these days. And I don't think anybody will believe me anyway. The hero jock wrestler, most handsome guy in school, with a girlfriend that looks like Crystal, and he wants to rape scrawny, little me? Yeah. Nobody's going to buy it."

"Rape isn't about that. It's about assholes like Tanner thinking they can take what they want. What you look like, what you were wearing, none of that shit matters. You can't just let him get away with it! What if he tries to rape somebody else?"

August looked up sharply.

"Sorry, I didn't mean to make it sound like you don't care ... that you didn't consider that."

"I get what you're saying, Lainy. But, he didn't get away with it. My mom works with one of the doctors who treated him after the attack. Sounded like he got his thing torn up. She said he wouldn't be having kids."

"Oh shit!" Lainy's eyes went wide and she seemed to have broken out in a sweat.

"My father always said that things have a way of working themselves out."

"I mean, it does sound like he got what was coming to him. I don't think the police could have done worse to him."

"Yeah, well that's kind of what I'm thinking, too."

"Shouldn't you talk to a counselor or something? Did he hurt you?"

"You mean besides the emotional terrorism? My ear bled when he shoved me against the tree. He pushed up my top and ripped my bra open ... I don't want to recount all of the details, it makes me nauseated. It was terrifying. I thought he was going to kill me."

"Oh my god, I am so sorry! I didn't know. I didn't know he was capable of that. I just thought he was a jerk. I'm sorry I didn't listen to you when you said he was creeping you out. I'm so sorry. I'm glad you're okay. Let me know if I can do anything. I mean it, anything to help. Okay?" Lainy put her hands on August's and looked full into her face. Her eyes were welling up with empathy and August began to understand the true comfort of friends.

"I'm not going back to school, Lainy. I tried, I really did, but I've felt wrong there since day one. I'm just going to take my G.E.D. and go to college next fall."

Lainy gave her a sympathetic nod. "I keep forgetting you're such a genius."

"Well thanks a lot," August retorted with a smirk.

"You want a hug?"

"Yeah."

So Lainy hugged her and stroked her hair, and it helped.

August was a little surprised that her mother didn't fight her too hard on the G.E.D. idea. She began applying to Maryland colleges, not wanting to be far from home. But the more she thought about starting school again, the more she found herself wanting to take a break. Sylvia decreed that, since August had finished high school almost two years early, that meant she could take two years to get herself together for college. August suspected that it might have been more about her mother wanting her to stay home for a bit longer, and that actually suited her just fine.

August tried to convince herself that she was all better, but she began to have flashbacks about Tanner attacking her. It seemed to be more troubling now than in the week after. Like a delayed shock or something. Sometimes just a stray chill breeze reminded her of having her clothes torn off and she would spend the next hour shivering. Or even just hearing his name mentioned in town would set her stomach into turmoil and her heart to pounding hard. She tried whatever she could think of to not let the memory make her feel helpless or vulnerable. She visualized over and over the look on Tanner's face when he panicked and stumbled into the darkness. But always in the background somewhere was that crippling feeling under his weight, and sometimes it crept into her mind without warning.

Sometimes, in dreams, he squeezed her so hard her head came off and she woke up gasping and shaking; other times she had a sword, and it sang with a metallic ring as she pulled it from its scabbard and started hacking off pieces of his mountainous body. Sometimes she had a bow, and let an arrow loose—right into his black heart. There was one dream, when Tanner ran away with his pants down, where the dog that chased him off was a wolf. After Tanner was long gone the wolf came back to find August. He bowed low at his approach and called her "My Lady," and then laid down on his back, supine and vulnerable before her. She pulled away the rest of her clothes and climbed on top of him, petting his chest fur, looking into his half-man half-wolf face and rubbing herself against his shaft until she woke up climaxing and thrashing in damp sheets.

Unable to get the therapy she badly needed, August took to other coping mechanisms, like running around the property and building up her physical strength. Or watching movies on cable with kick-ass heroines like Pam Grier, or reading sappy sweet romances. It didn't hurt to put on the occasional Runaways or Heart album, either.

Sometimes she just sat on the window seat and cracked the sash open, letting in a nippy breeze. She was glad it was chilly outside now, since she had taken to wearing her dad's cloak whenever she was outside of the house. It made her feel safe somehow—held and enshrouded and warm—and she liked having her knife handy in the inner pocket. She wondered where she could learn how to properly handle it.

The first week of November, Sylvia and August went to the nursing home to talk to the staff about off-site holiday visits, and so August could finally meet her Gran Sorcha. It already felt like too much time had passed since they arrived in town, with no visit to the home. Any more time and it would have just been rude. For her part, August was very excited to finally meet the family matriarch.

Out front they were greeted with large dark blue and yellow lettering, Sunnyvale Nursing Home. The facility was a cheerful building of brick with white trim. Tall pillars out front suggested a Georgian style mansion, but the automated doors and large industrial windows gave the building away as medical. Indeed, it was an old mansion with medical building tacked on all around it. The place was gleaming and smelled of a mixture of cleaning products and antiseptic solutions—a smell August's mother was probably used to, but always set August a bit on edge because it reminded her of the unpleasantness of a visit to the doctor's office.

Sorcha's room was near the rear of the building—a corner space with windows on two walls. August imagined this was one of the more desirable rooms in the facility. For that she was glad, but it also made her sad for the residents who couldn't afford the corner rooms, and it made her wonder for a moment just what the worst rooms looked like. But the facility seemed nice enough that even the worst rooms couldn't be too bad.

Sorcha was sitting in a wheelchair near a window facing Sunnyvale's manicured green lawns. Sylvia approached the wheelchair while August hovered near the doorway.

"Sorcha? Hello, Sorcha?" She was saying it in that cheerful sing-song way that she had. "It's Sylvia. I'm going to turn you around, okay?" Sorcha didn't respond and Sylvia turned her chair around slowly.

Sorcha's hair—wavy, long and silver, with one band of black running along the left side of her face—tumbled down to her shoulders and onto her big quilted robe, decorated with tiny pink and blue rosebuds. Her skin was pale and smoother than August expected for an elderly lady. She did have some deep furrows on each side of her mouth, where her cheeks and chin drooped a little, and some minor crow's feet and two forehead creases between her brows, but overall she looked more sickly than old.

Her limbs were a bit longer than August expected—lanky, like Fletcher Evan's. But the rest of her was covered in the tent-like robe, so August couldn't get much of a feel for how she was shaped.

August inched forward towards her, but Sorcha seemed tuned-out.

"Hi, Gran." She paused and got no response. "Hello."

August looked at her mother—*what should I do*? Sylvia gave an encouraging nod. August inched closer and squatted down. "Hi. I'm August. I'm so glad to meet you." A blink here, but no real recognition in her eyes. Then August clasped the old woman's soft, warm hands in her own and it seemed Gran tensed a little, and then relaxed. Perhaps just an involuntary response, but August thought she saw a flicker behind her eyes. "Gran, I'm August and I've been waiting a long time to meet you. I'm going to come visit you as much as I can. I have so many things I want to tell you." The woman didn't budge and August's legs were starting to go numb, so she stood up and let Sorcha's hands slide out of her own.

"I'll come back tomorrow and I'll bring a book and read it to you. What kind of books do you like?" Sorcha remained a statue, though her breathing seemed to get deeper and August thought she recognized another flicker. August studied her for the tiniest of clues, then looked again to her mother, who only gave her a crooked mouth and a shrug. "Okay, well, I'll bring one of my favorites. I'll see you then, Gran."

August turned Sorcha back towards the window and they left the room, both she and Sylvia saying goodbye as they exited.

The car ride was quiet. Once home, Sylvia started to make lunch.

"She's in there," she told August. "She's hiding. If you keep at it, she'll come out."

August was confused. It was a medical condition, wasn't it? But she was too tired, and frankly a bit too down about it all, to question it further today.

"Okay," she acknowledged. "I will."

The following week August returned to Sunnyvale four more times, and each time she read a sliver of *Tuck Everlasting* and brought snacks that she thought Sorcha would like. Most of the snacks were a failure, probably because they were snacks a teenager would prefer, candy bars and chips. But on the way to see her on

Friday, August passed the Wynda's Bakery just as they were putting fresh scones in the window, and at Sunnyvale fifteen minutes later she presented Sorcha with one blueberry and one cinnamon, and let her choose which one she wanted. That was the day that she finally seemed to surface a bit and looked at August. She didn't speak, but she did give a small smile and a happy blink and slowly ate her scone while August finished off the book. Sorcha was actually smiling by the end of the visit and even quietly managed, "Goodbye."

The rest of the next week August ended up coming later in the day and Sorcha seemed more awake. At one point they even ate together in the dining hall and played a game of checkers, and August was delighted when Sorcha became a little moody and stubborn. It was her first real flash of personality, and August couldn't help but love her spirit.

Sylvia had decided that Thanksgiving would be the perfect time to gather the whole family and a couple of Sorcha's friends around the table, and since August was now home all day, she was the ideal candidate for getting the preparations together. August rolled her eyes and groaned when this was announced, but she didn't really mind. In truth, having something to do all week helped her keep her mental monsters at bay, and on Tuesday she donned her cloak, grabbed the little red wagon her father once played in, and went into town for the groceries they would need.

This drew an unexpected, though gentle, protest after the fact from Abel Jefferson, the gardener and handyman her grandmother kept on duty—though August suspected he was more than that to

Sorcha. He had been away for most of the past couple of months, taking care of some family business in Alabama, which was the only reason he and August hadn't already become better acquainted. It seemed to Abel that Thanksgiving cooking was his job to do, thanks to a long-standing tradition at the Rook, and the household was big on maintaining traditions, in part to give Sorcha something to look forward to through the seasons. Not that Abel minded sharing the kitchen, but there were going to be dishes on that table that August hadn't even heard of, and he had been planning his shopping for weeks.

A lean, wiry man in his seventies, Abel had dark skin and a handsome white afro, close-cropped, and he never seemed to tire. He had lively, laughing eyes, and always found ways to keep himself busy, yet he had an easy air, as though nothing had ever ruffled him in his life. August had realized one day that, even though the trees were bare and the garden cut back, the lawn was immaculate, as though no dry leaf dared drop itself on Abel's grass. Not that there weren't clover and dandelion and other so-called weeds on the rolling greens, but even they seemed to understand where Abel wanted them and where he didn't, and they dutifully obeyed.

August and Abel came to an understanding over the Thanksgiving meal: she could cook a turkey and make gravy, since that was what her family did on the holiday; but Abel, being vegetarian, would cook the rest of the dinner—with August's assistance, of course, since it couldn't hurt for a young lady like herself to learn how to cook a few things. "Everybody should learn how to cook properly," Abel advised. "It's just part of growin' up."

There would be a ton of food for the five of them—August, Sylvia, Gran, Abel, and a woman named Brigid that August hadn't met—but as Abel explained in his lyrical southern accent, "Thanksgiving's not just for eatin' yourself into a stupor. It's also about preparing for the coming winter, and you'd best have some leftovers canned up for the long nights." He then launched into a soliloquy about canning foods, like spiced peaches, pickled peaches and peaches stewed in brandy. August laughed at how much the man loved peaches. That topic then morphed into boasts about his mother's legendary cobbler recipes and ended with a lament about losing his favorite pecan pie recipe, which he knew by heart but had been written in his mother's hand.

August was looking forward to seeing Gran Sorcha at the table. The matriarch had had a fearsome reputation in the family, but August could already feel that Gran had a special spot for her in her heart. And for Abel too, it seemed. At the nursing home just last week—the first time August had ever met Abel—she was astounded when Gran started complaining loudly about somebody on the staff. Abel simply laid his hand on her arm and said her name, and she quieted right down. "That man," her mother had marveled, "is the only person in the world who can take the worst your grandmother can dish out, and still worry about *her* feelings." August got the distinct impression there was some important history there.

She watched Gran closely during the feast, worrying a bit about how she was faring away from the home, but also because there was something in Sorcha, buried deep down, that August wanted very much to reach. "Ask your Gran," her mother had said about her father's red cloak, but whenever August managed to get her to talk about family things at all, it was only ever for a moment, and then Gran's face would cloud over and she would be quiet for the rest of the visit. There was a mystery at the heart of this family, and sooner or later something had to come out. So August decided to be patient, and wait for any opportunity to steer the conversation in that direction.

She was intrigued with the new person at the table, Brigid, who was good friends with Abel and kept an eye on Gran almost as closely as August did. Sylvia knew her, too. Brigid seemed to August to be what her dad would have called a wise woman—a healer who understood herbal remedies and ancient ways of medicine. Brigid had a shop in town that sold unusual teas and dried herbs, some of which she had brought with her for the dinner. She looked to be about sixty, August guessed—definitely older than Mom, anyway—with long pewter hair that gleamed in the candlelight. She was draped in colorful silks and wore elegantly handcrafted silver and crystal jewelry around her neck, in her hair, and on most of her fingers. Along with what August thought was a light Irish lilt, Brigid had an easy laugh and a confident nature that seemed to radiate calm, as though nothing could ever go too far wrong, and soon August felt completely at ease with her.

But something had nagged at August through the evening, and not until after Brigid and Abel had rounded up Sorcha's bags, packed her into Brigid's van, and driven off toward the nursing home, could August put her finger on it. She had gotten the sense that everyone at the table knew something about her, about the family, and she was the only one who didn't know. And the more she thought about it the more certain she became.

The plan was that Sorcha would return to the Rook in a few weeks for Christmas and Hogmanay celebrations, and stay in the suite behind the kitchen they had prepared for her. And during those weeks, whenever August visited Sunnyvale, she found Abel there too—the receptionist told her he usually only left after Sorcha was in bed for the night. Finally, on the Tuesday before Christmas, Brigid brought Abel and Sorcha to the Rook. She hung up what she called Winter Solstice charms, made of wood with mysterious symbols burned onto them and strings for hanging on the Christmas tree. She cackled as she put them up and said, "Two worlds collide again!" She stayed for dinner and the Bûche de Noël, complete with meringue mushrooms, that Abel had picked up from the bakery. Sylvia cut cross-sections of the log-shaped cake and feigned difficulty, as if she was sawing a real log, and everybody laughed. August hadn't had Bûche de Noël since she was a small child and it made her feel very cozy and nostalgic.

Brigid came again to the Blue Rook on Hogmanay to be the first-footer of the Scottish New Year holiday, bringing a huge basket loaded down with shortbread, black buns and whiskey. August was starting to enjoy the warmth of having Abel and Brigid around. It gave her a new sense of family bonding, and plenty of conversations and stories to look forward to.

January 4, 1983

The holidays turned out to be interesting. Abel made some

delicious food, like cooked greens and sweet potato pie. I think my favorite was his macaroni and cheese, though—I'm going to have to learn to make that so I can eat it for three months straight. It was amazing. He insisted I call him Abel, instead of Mr. Jefferson, so I am trying it out. He did the sweetest thing. He made me recipe cards and gave me a recipe box with little fruit and vegetable graphics all over it to put them in. I got to make the turkey, which Abel won't eat. He's a vegetarian, which means he doesn't eat meat. For a minute I thought it was weird, then when I really thought about it I could understand why somebody would do that. I'm just so used to meat, I never thought about it before. Plus, I just feel like I have to have red meat sometimes. Anyway, for Christmas he brought us one of those Yule log cakes with the meringue mushrooms and for some reason it made me so happy. There is something regal about him. Like a quiet and brave knight. In any case, I'm glad Gran has his friendship, even if she isn't fully aware of it much of the time. I think he may be sweet on her, actually. I tried to get some stories out of him about my family history, but he's pretty tight-lipped. I've tried to pry things out of him in clever ways, but he sees right through me. I think he is what they call "discreet." One thing is for sure, everybody around here knows something they aren't telling me. I thought any minute trumpets were gonna sound and somebody was gonna stand up and say, "August Archer, you are the long lost Princess of Perthshire," and Mom would come over and put a crown on my head and the cloak around my shoulders. I'm probably just imagining things.

Celebrations are weird without dad. I feel unfinished, unsettled ... something is missing. I may never be able to shake it and, really,

I'm not sure I want to. His ghost was at the table and hanging around the Christmas decorations. And I think he would have really enjoyed Hogmanay. I wish we'd been celebrating that all along, even if the name is kind of weird. I'm not sure why we haven't, but with Brigid there was no question, we were going to have a celebration over it and that's all there was to it. Dad loved holidays. He loved life, so I guess he made me love it, too. So many things made him happy, it made everybody want to be around him.

There are some things I've realized about myself and Dad. I've had a lot of time to think about this stuff. I think I wanted to be good so he could see me be good. You know, I was all "Dad look at me! Daddy, watch this!" I'd pick up the biggest book I thought I could read, just to impress him. And I remember wanting to be able to kind of hold up my end of the conversation with him. We'd sit in his study, him on his big leather chair with the overstuffed arms and his pipe smoldering in the ashtray. He'd cross his legs and ask me pointed questions about what I'd just read and I'd thrill inside whenever I had an answer that seemed to please him. When he asked something I didn't know how to answer, his eyes would narrow ever so slightly and I would feel a ridiculous amount of disappointment prick my heart. Now I would give anything to feel that hurt. Now, there are lights inside of me that won't flick on. But sometimes happy memories crowd out the pain a bit and I feel a smile creep across my face. I hope that keeps happening until all that's left is happy memories.

I guess the other thing I want to write about is the attack. Ugh. I want to just not think about it anymore, but I'm still working on getting better. For one thing, all of my running and exercise makes me feel stronger and more capable. My muscles hum and I sweat until my mind is clear. My agility surprises me, jumping from rock to rock across the creek, climbing trees and swinging around like a monkey. There is nothing better than feeling the rubber of my shoes bite into bark as I make my way from branch to branch. The blisters on my hands have given way to callouses, which I'm kind of proud of. From the tops of trees I've been memorizing and falling in love with Mahigan Falls. And I realized one other thing during all of this—being small can have its advantages. Nobody can hurt you if they can't catch you. I've heard he's in physical therapy still, and might be for months to come. I don't like writing his name, I've noticed. I wonder what that means? It's difficult not to feel some measure of satisfaction at his misery. Then I feel kind of guilty. Lainy says that's because I'm a good person, but that there is nothing wrong with feeling like he deserved what he got. I'm glad to be moving on because I want to write about good things. Like this oddly shaped family we are forming here at the Rook. Mom and Gran and Abel and Brigid. I'm going to make it my business to get to know these people and get them to like me. I think it's important for my mom that I get along with everybody. And I don't want her to have anything to be worried about. She's been very absorbed in her nurse training, but she's still drinking too much.

Gran and I had the longest conversation yet over the Christmas break because she stayed with me for a week, and I took care of her all day while Mom was gone. One late afternoon she saw the keys around my neck and launched into tales again, but this one was so much more detailed. It was all about super-human hunters in cloaks and werewolves and Scotland. They're a lot like fairy tales. I can only think that maybe she knows I love fairy tales. Maybe Dad sent her a letter before he died or mom told her at some point. But after our conversation Abel gave her some herbal tea and she was quiet the rest of the night.

I've not gotten anything out of her about the things I really want to know. I can't help but love her fairy stories, though, and she's always emotional when telling them, so I'm going to start writing them down. It would be nice if Mom would just tell me the stuff I want to know, but it's kind of cool having some mysteries to unravel, like Nancy Drew. I think all of the conversations with Gran are making us closer. I feel closer to her, anyway.

Lainy stopped by over the holidays for about half a minute. Her family was traveling to Southern California for the break. I told her I couldn't imagine leaving behind trees and the possibility of snow, and the smell of gingerbread and chimney smoke over the holidays. I don't want to be very far from so many comforts that help me feel close to my dad. We exchanged gifts, a Star Wars tee for her and a homemade Sex Pistols tee for me. I told her about meeting the neighbor and how I couldn't stop thinking about kissing him. She laughed and said she was glad I was feeling better. And added that maybe my imagination and hormones were getting the better of me. That's the truth. Still, I keep hoping to run into him in town. So far, no luck. Where does he do his grocery shopping, anyway?

Dad's ashes were transferred from the wooden box he was given to us in, to a handmade clay pot with knotwork all around it. Mom is considering laying Dad to rest in Scotland. She wants to plan a trip in the spring and I'm both excited and sad about it because other than moving to Maryland, I've never been out of the state of New York. Also, I don't know if I like the idea of my father being so far away. In the meantime, Dad rests in her bedroom on the fireplace mantle, with his portrait behind the urn or pot or whatever it's called. I've taken a small bit of him and put it in a locket he gave me when I was twelve, and tucked it into the secret window seat. When I need him, I just take the locket out of the seat and hold it in my palm and talk to him. I don't know if it's wrong to have done that. If it was, I don't think I care.

By the end of January, August had made herself much more familiar with Mahigan Falls. She and her cloak had become such a regular sight that people started referring to her privately as Red Riding Hood, until even her acquaintances in town began calling her Red. August didn't mind, especially since it reminded her of Halloween night, and the name her handsome neighbor had called her. And really, the name seemed to suit her, so it stuck.

At first August had been worried about running into Tanner or some of his friends, but the boy seemed to have completely disappeared, and if anyone missed him, they didn't mention it to her. She began to think of Mahigan Falls as her little town, and she found that one of her favorite places to drop into was Brigid's shop. The name over the door was Leigheas Apothecary, and August made a point of going by whenever she visited her gran. Inside it was a warren of narrow aisles and high shelves, overflowing with crystals and curios, strange old books and beautifully carved objects, while the unexpected aromas swirling around could, in certain aisles, produce an almost dizzying effect. At the back was a huge antique wooden counter with glass display cases and a wall of shelves behind it, rowed with glass jars and cubbies. August loved listening in as Brigid would talk with a customer, ask a few questions, and come up with a tea or an herb blend that would take care of whatever ailment had brought them in. August thought it would be a perfect place to work and learn all about what Brigid did, but it seemed that however many times she asked, Brigid had no need of her assistance.

Coming back from seeing Sorcha one particularly nippy Saturday, August stopped at the apothecary to warm up, and as she came in the door her heart skipped. Her handsome and mysterious neighbor was at the counter, taking a small bag from Brigid. There was something he needed, urgently, and she assured him she would do her best and call him when his order was in.

Then the man stopped and lifted his nose, as though he'd caught a scent of something curious, and turned to look straight at August. After a quick glance he looked away, tucked his head, balled up the bag and rushed by her toward the door. But just as he passed, when they were nearly hip to hip, he hesitated a moment, seemingly caught in some invisible force field. An impulse, a powerful urge to reach out her hand and touch him, washed over August. Time slowed, and she could smell him, even through the incense, and feel how hot her breath was coming out of her mouth, and how fast her heart was beating. She wanted to say hello to him, but she couldn't speak. Then his body leaned forward and away, escaping her orbit and plunging through the door, leaving bells pealing in his wake. A rush of disappointment coursed through her as she watched him disappear down the street.

"Hello, Red," Brigid said, bringing her back to earth and bestowing her usual warm smile.

"Hi. Wow, what was that about?" August offered by way of passing off her momentary passion. "Some people. Right?"

"Ah, he just needs something I'm out of. Some people come to rely on certain herbs and ingredients that are hard to find elsewhere."

"So, who was that?"

Brigid kept mum, though her eye twinkled and her brow furrowed almost imperceptibly.

"What?" August feigned innocence, though she knew Brigid wasn't buying it. "He's my neighbor. I met him at Halloween but I didn't get his name."

"My dear, it's up to him to give you his name. Wouldn't be proper for me to tell you. Names are sacred things."

August laughed it off, and thought it best to change the subject. "So, I see you've got some new crystals in. Are you sure you don't need some help making a nice display?"

~~Red Berries~~

Running into her neighbor, it turned out, had a much more lingering effect on August than just a few skipped heartbeats. She'd already thought about him more than a few times since they met in October. But now, since their meeting again, she couldn't get him out of her mind. At first she had just a few simple daydreams, almost entirely innocent. She would re-imagine the herbal shop encounter, but this time actually reaching out and touching him—just a finger, to the back of his neck, and then gently stroking down. That soon evolved into his face turning towards her, his mouth open as if to say something, and their lips softly meeting. And as August thought more about him, lying in her bed at night, it wasn't long before the shop melted away in her fantasies, and he was climbing into her bedroom window.

She lies in her bed as his lean form steps in through the sash above the window-seat, wearing only his kilt. He comes over to her, reaches for the blanket, and slowly uncovers her. She is wearing only her lightest bra and panties, and he gazes at her pale skin as he reveals it. His handsome chin is covered in scruff—rough and exciting. He is powerful and masculine, yet every move he makes is gentlemanly, ever mindful of her.

He whispers, "You're beautiful."

He leans over her and his fingers trace her collar bones, his hands pet her belly, and he bows low to press his lips against her bare flesh, peppering her skin with kisses. She feels the urge to wiggle, but tries to stay still as he climbs into her bed and stretches out alongside her. His woolen kilt scratches against her naked thigh, sending a thrill down her legs. The thin clothing she wears is little more than a breath, and her nipples swell and proclaim themselves under the fabric, bumping out an invitation to his hands, as they glide up and down her body. He cups first one breast and then the other, gently squeezing them and teasing his thumb around her urgent nipples through the wisp of silk as she sighs and gasps her pleasure to him. Then he slides his hand lower, cupping her mound like he's cradling a fresh peach, and she melts into his grasp. He asks her if she likes it, and she softly moans her want. "Open my bra," she whispers, "and put your mouth on me."

He straddles her and bows over her torso, and they are nose to nose. His mouth is warm and wet, his lips are salty. Their kisses are slow and deep and his hands gently pet her sides in rhythm with each slip of his tongue into her mouth. He sits back, unhooks the front of her bra and sweeps away the fabric, drinking her in and telling her what pretty, perfect breasts she has. "Perfect," he says again, and she is entranced by his desire. He puts a palm on each breast and rubs them gently, brushing his lips down the valley between before sucking each nipple into his mouth to tease it with the tip of his tongue.

She can't stop wiggling her hips as his lips taste her body, his kisses traveling down her torso to her panties. He inhales deeply, his nose brushing the lace, and he fingers the edging and looks up at her. His eyes are sly, almost begging for her favor.

"Shall I remove these?" He asks, his voice husky.

"Yes," she whispers.

"Do you want me to touch you there?"

"Yes," she manages to whisper.

He arches his eyebrow and grins, slips his fingers under the waistband, and slowly pulls down her panties. The thrill of her nakedness and how beautiful she feels shoots through her body, and she savors the sensation of his every breath on her. He pets her legs tenderly before he lifts her knees and gently parts them. She opens wider, welcoming him, and he stretches out alongside her, and she watches as he pets and explores the tender folds of flesh between her thighs. The tingling at the base of her spine travels up through her body as he rubs her wetness with his fingers. His breathing deepens and hers quickens. Her hips rise up again and again, trying to press against his hand.

She can feel his hardness on her thigh, pressed firm to her through his kilt, and she wants to touch it, though it's still a little frightening. Unlike the boys she's been with, with their smooth faces and chests, he's got hair all over his chest and whiskers on his face. She thinks of touching his bare cock and it makes her stomach quiver. It feels a little dangerous but so exciting and intoxicating, she begs him to keep rubbing. He tells her how much he wants to suck and lick the very center of her, whenever she's ready. She is so ready, she can barely speak the words.

By this point, the thought of him being so aroused and excited to kiss her between her thighs always brought August to the edge. When she reached her peak she could almost feel him pressed close to her. She would quake silently in her bed, yearning to say his name out loud, though she still didn't know it.

August indulged in these fantasies several nights a week with little variation. Sometimes he would be wearing a suit, and she would loosen his tie, and unbutton his shirt, and nuzzle his hairy chest. Sometimes she was wearing a nightgown, and couldn't wait for him to reach up underneath it. And sometimes, she made it all the way to the part where he finally climbed between her thighs and slipped his cock into her before she came. Eventually she started calling out "Wolf!" in gasping whispers during her peak.

Through the snowy winter weeks, her fantasies of Wolf began to include conversations, and interactions about other things, such as books and movies that August liked. She imagined him sharing his musical tastes with her, and that they were refined and intriguing. Eventually she was having an entire relationship with Wolf in her head. She realized that he might not be much like what she imagined, but she supposed it didn't matter, since he seemed intent on keeping his distance anyway.

And even though she couldn't get Brigid to divulge Wolf's real name, August's persistence paid off in other areas; by March, Brigid had agreed to let her work at the herb shop part-time.

In May, Abel began leaving bowls of bright red strawberries on the table, grown from an enormous patch behind the Rook, and before long August felt that she never wanted to do without them. They shouted their tart sweet flavor on her tongue, and sinking her teeth into their firm, just-picked flesh was a giddy, sensuous joy. She had liked strawberries before, of course, but these were different. It was as though something missing from her life had finally been fulfilled, and all the strawberries she ate before were fakes.

August was watching Abel carry them in one day, and noticed that he would scoop the bowls and baskets into his right arm, not using the left much, or keeping it tucked into his pocket. Thinking back to the holidays, she realized he even cooked that way, with his left arm by his side or his hand in his pocket, and she wondered why she hadn't been more aware of it before. She asked him how he grew the berries so large, and in such abundance, but in his usual way he took no credit.

"They were your grandmother's plants—she put them in the ground before your daddy was even born. I remember when he was little, he couldn't wait for those little red berries to pop out. I believe he could've eaten that whole big bowl right there without blinkin'. Probably ask me for another one."

Strawberries. Her dad loved strawberries. How could she have not known that? August realized in that awful moment how little she'd really known her father, and it was like losing him all over again. He seemed so far away, like a lifetime ago, and her throat tightened around her last bite of berry and tears slipped from her eyes.

"Oh, I'm sorry, Miss August! I shouldn't be goin' on like that about your daddy." Abel saw her wet eyes and put an arm around her shoulder and patted her. "But you think about this, too: the way you love those berries, it's like your daddy is still right here in this room with you."

She looked at him and blinked, like she'd never really seen him
before this moment, astonished at how clearly he understood just
what she was feeling, and knew exactly what she needed to hear.

"He's not really gone. None of 'em are."

"Them?"

Something crossed his normally tranquil face. A memory? She
couldn't tell.

"Uh ... I mean everybody. Everybody we think we lose. I'll tell
you what, I'm goin' to make you a milkshake just like I used to
make for your daddy. How's that sound?"

He didn't wait for an answer. She watched him as he dropped
vanilla ice cream, a double handful of strawberries, and a splash of
milk into the blender, and added a pinch of something he found in a
clamped jar. "That's my secret ingredient," he winked, and then
laughed. "It's jus' malt." When he was done he pulled a tall glass out
of the back of the cupboard—a real old-fashioned soda glass—and
topped it off with a perfect cloud of whipped cream and a
maraschino cherry. The final touch was a red-striped straw.

When he slid it across the counter to her, it looked exactly like a
picture from a soda shop menu. It was a thing of beauty. It smelled
like a strawberry patch, and when August sipped it every part of her
tongue tried to melt into the sweet smooth cream. She closed her
eyes and let the flavor sink into every taste of strawberry she'd ever
had. "Abel, that's amazing," she marveled. "But I can only enjoy this
if you join me for some lunch."

"I'd love that, Miss August. What're you havin'?"

"Well, I'm thinking burgers and fries to go with this classic diner shake. How's that sound?"

"Oh, I don't eat cows. Cows are my friends."

"Oh, right. I knew that." She paused a moment and thought. Abel remained politely silent while she thought about it.

"How about grilled cheese and French fries?" She offered.

"I love grilled cheese. We've got some nice hothouse tomatoes left. How about grilled cheese sandwich with tomatoes and basil? That tastes mighty fine without any meat."

"That sounds yummy," she replied, and felt a little thread between them complete a connection.

"I'm gonna sit here and watch you cook, if that's okay. I'm worn out today." His shoulders were slumped and he did look very tired. He was resting his arms on the counter. This was the first time August had ever seen him look tired or want to sit still for a minute.

"Okay, you rest, and I'll get you some lemonade and make you something tasty to put some pep in your step." She added, "And ... maybe you could tell me some stuff about my dad?" She tried to be nonchalant about it, but she felt transparent. She sliced tomatoes and regarded Abel from the corner of her eye, waiting for him to rebuff her in his gentle way, but he didn't. Instead, Abel wove tales of her father while she made their food.

He told her about some of her father's favorite things: strawberries, obviously, and also tree-climbing, archery, marbles—"I'll bet if you looked hard enough you'd find a couple dozen cat's-eyes rolled behind the furniture or under the radiators," Abel laughed. "And Robin Hood. I thought your daddy was gonna up and live in those woods one day!"

August took Abel's sandwich off the griddle, used the spatula to cut it diagonally, pulled the fries out of the oven, and sat down across from him at the island counter. She munched on fries and sipped on what was left of her shake. She couldn't help but rue the sound of gurgling from the straw as she finished off the last drops, despite the fact that she was now stuffed.

"You sure can pack in the food for a little thing!" He let out a hearty laugh and his eyes crinkled around the edges. "Where do you put it? Do you have a hollow leg?" August laughed too and they locked eyes for a moment. He blinked and looked at his plate to find one last cold fry and put it in his mouth.

"Abel, where'd you learn to make a milkshake like this?"

"Oh, well my dad used to run a drugstore, back when I was a kid. I worked there for him a number of years, and we had a lunch counter. Drugstores had 'em back then. Soda counters, lunch counters. And it was the only colored drugstore in miles and miles, so it was important, too."

"Oh, I'm sorry." August felt a flush of embarrassment. She didn't know what else to say. She'd never known anybody from the South and very few black people, even though she'd lived in New York. At least, not as friends. Not that she avoided black people, but everybody sort of clumped into their own groups at school, and August didn't fit into any of them.

"It's okay. Well, it's not okay. There were lots of troubles ... still are. I'll show you my family photo albums and scrapbooks sometime, and tell you about how it was, and how it is now, and what needs changin'. That is, if you want to understand it better."

"I do! I really ... I care about it. I want to know. Thank you." August felt relieved she didn't say the wrong thing, and a little guilty for the color of her skin.

"Okay, that's fine. We'll put it on the list of big conversations to have. Anyway, I wasn't planning on working at the drugstore, but I needed to stay a while, because it was important. After some time, too much time for my taste, I was more wanting to get some green under my feet, but I did learn to wrangle the best milkshakes this side of the Mississippi. Seems I had a knack for it. Still do, I reckon."

"Mm-hm, you do." August pushed crispy brown fry ends around on her plate. "Abel?"

There was an uncomfortable pause. After a couple of beats, he looked up. "Yes?"

"Would you please tell me why my gran is in that home across town?"

He took a deep breath and hesitated. Then he picked up her plate and put it on top of his. "Well, you know why she is." He made busy-work of the spent napkins and flatware and tidied imaginary crumbs from the counter.

"I know what people tell me, but I'd like to know the truth. I promise I can keep it to myself."

He closed his eyes. "I don't know that I'm the one to tell you about it." But August could feel his resolve crumble a little. There was a crack and she couldn't help but want to squeeze into it.

"I know. But I've lost my dad and I feel like I'm missing so many pieces of my own history. It's still too hard for Mom to talk about, and Gran can't remember things. Please Abel, whatever you think you can tell me?"

The old man sat quietly, his mind turned in on its own long memory. "Sorcha is a fine woman," he said finally. "And she is smart. Smarter than a lot of folks. But when your granddaddy died, she was in a lot of pain. She didn't have much cause or care to remember things, so she started letting 'em go. And then with her memory slipping away, it left her vulnerable to things."

"What kinds of things? Like leaving things burning on the stove?"

"That was part of it. But, your Gran Sorcha, she wanted to forget it all. She just wanted to join your granddaddy so much, and it worried your daddy a lot. So he came and had her put where somebody could keep an eye on her. And it's a nice place, they treat her good there. But I do wish I could have done more myself. You know, to keep her tied to this world. I do what I can."

"Abel, do you think Gran will ever get better?"

"I sure hope so."

"Thanks for talking to me about it."

"Well, I expect you have a right to know these things. If it's alright with you, though, I think it's about time I'm headed home."

She did have a thousand more questions to ask, but they would keep. For now. She hugged Abel as he sat. "Thanks for talking about my dad. It's been almost a year he's been gone, and sometimes I'm afraid of forgetting him."

"Memory is a funny thing, I guess. But I think it's kind of like telling stories: if you have a favorite, you tell it over and over, and you won't forget."

"I suppose the reverse is true for bad ones," she offered.

"That's where your gran lives. I wouldn't recommend it. It's best to acknowledge the bad ones and put them in a corner of the yard, keep 'em fenced so they don't ruin the rest of the garden. If they start to grow—get out the pruners."

On the one-year anniversary of Fletcher Evan Archer's death, August and Sylvia sat down to start work on a remembrance book—a scrapbook of photos, mementos, and notes, mostly about family vacations and everyday outings that turned out to be special trips. This project involved a sojourn up to the attic, where Sylvia had stashed away most of the Evan boxes, and August was surprised to find how many things in them were new to her, despite how often she'd gone exploring in her father's study and her parents' room.

"It's like a treasure hunt up here," August said while she cleaned off a cobweb from her neck.

"A lot of it was in storage. Do you have any idea how many people in apartments are paying rent for their stuff somewhere? It's a little nuts. But ..." She sighed and ran her hand over some of the boxes. "I'm really glad we have some of this stuff now."

August nodded. She was glad too, and started to poke through the piles. There was a packet of photographs, including a number taken years ago at the Rook, in rooms that August recognized. It was so strange seeing her father in what was now her home, looking no older than she was now, and more than once the discovery of an off-the-cuff snapshot had August and her mother weeping together even while they were laughing at Evan's antics. Some of these were snatched up for the memory book, as were some of her father's doodles, clipped from envelopes, bills, and any other pieces of paper that might have been too close to Fletcher Evan's pen. He drew leaves and trees, small maps, feathers, animals—Abel was right, August realized; her father truly loved the outdoors—and quite a number of cartoon faces. Some of them were strange, even monstrous, but none of them mean or cruel. Looking at those faces, August could almost see her father's smile.

There was also a small wooden treasure chest the size of a jewelry box, filled with old coins from all over the world. In there too were four tiny brass cannons, a fancy chrome lighter that sparked but didn't light, a souvenir penknife from Catoctin Mountain, a badge in the shape of a Scottish lion, a couple of medallions, a chunk of resin with a sprig of heather inside, and a photo of Sylvia looking like a teenager. She was smiling, her hair tied back in a bandana and her shirt knotted to reveal her midriff, and August saw that she looked very much like her at that age. What startled her, though, was to realize how much her father's collection reminded her of her own treasure box. Maybe Abel was right, about her father living on in her.

As they headed downstairs again, Sylvia pointed out one more treasure.

"Look, there. Your father's bow. It's been in his family for ages."

"It doesn't look like a bow, Mom. It's bent wrong."

"It's not strung, sweetie. You don't leave a bow under tension if you're putting it away. Why don't we bring it out of this stuffy attic?" She gave a side-nod and climbed over a pile of boxes, pulling out the bow and a hip quiver and grabbing a big shoulder bag.

"Look in here ... glove, bracer, points. Even his fletching knife."

Sylvia gazed at the bow for several moments. "I think this is going in my room," she said at last. August shrugged and reached out to help carry some of the items.

Once back downstairs they pasted photos into the scrapbook and drank strawberry lemonade and Sylvia told August the story of how she and Evan met in Scotland. It was a story August had heard many times, but she never tired of it. Sylvia had been there on a college-sponsored tour at the University of Edinburgh, excited to see where the great Joseph Lister, the father of modern surgical medicine—as Sylvia always identified him, and August always echoed her—had done his pioneering research into infection and sterilization a hundred years earlier. Dr. Archer was there too, conducting a seminar on Scottish oral traditions and lore at an anthropological conference.

"I'd never seen such a young doctor before. He'd finished his undergrad degree by the time he was 16 and got his Ph.D. by the time he was 22. You never met anybody so smart, and yet charming, in your whole life. He knew the answers to absolutely everything, but he never made you feel stupid."

"You're smart, Mom. No worries."

"Thanks sweetie." She chuckled and continued the story just as August had memorized it.

One glorious summer night, Sylvia joined a guided tour to Edinburgh Castle, overlooking the city. She stepped away from the group, intent on photographing a dramatic violet sky, and literally bumped into the handsome young anthropologist, trying to capture the same scene. He asked her out to dinner and they spent the rest of her visit talking "until the sun came up." The story always ended there, but August suspected that things heated up pretty quickly and went further than dinner and talking.

Between the stories and the bottle of merlot they later opened, with August sipping from her mother's glass, they didn't get much pasted into the scrapbook. At dinner time it still lay out, strewn with papers and photos. The smell of glue and construction paper hung in the air, with the faint chemical aroma of freshly clipped photo paper. Bits of tape were stuck to the edges of the table, and miniscule paper shreds littered the oak surface, where they'd fluttered every time one of the heavy pages was flipped. The two decided not to bother cleaning it up; they'd get back to it tomorrow.

Once she'd returned to her room, August took out the locket with Evan's ashes and curled up in her window seat. She imagined her father giving academic talks and gazing at faraway skies. She wondered what he, a true lover of books and classical education, would think of her skipping a couple of years of school. She squeezed the locket a couple of times, and whispered to him how she wanted to be there for Mom, and how she was going to pursue an independent research project, as soon as she had settled on a subject. Then she said, louder this time, directly to the locket, "I'm looking at colleges in the area, to be close to Mom." The locket glinted but didn't give any hints as to what Fletcher Evan would say. She imagined he would understand.

Two months after that solemn anniversary came August's seventeenth birthday, and her mother had an inspiration to present her with one of those new ice cream cakes.

"You can get any flavor of ice cream; they've got thirty-one flavors to choose from, and either vanilla or chocolate cake inside. And it's got real icing on top and looks just like a regular round layer cake," Sylvia gushed.

August pretended to ponder the choices, narrowing her eyes for effect.

"Well then, strawberry ice cream with vanilla cake."

That weekend they had a slightly better-attended birthday party than last year's, though not by much, since Sorcha wasn't feeling well and neither Lainy nor Brigid had more than a short while to stop by. Pastel pink and teal balloons were festooned around the bistro table on the front porch, with curly ribbons streaming all the way to the floor. After everyone else had left, Sylvia and August sat together in the summer heat, both of them wearing braids fixed with ribbons and gauzy, flower-printed summer dresses. Their tall lemonade glasses, filled with ice and topped with thick round slices of lemon, wept condensation onto the bistro table. The two nibbled at bits of still-frozen yellow cake and scooped up drops of melting pink ice cream while listening to the insects whirr and sing—a perfect summer day, if a bit hot.

"Mom, did you know Dad loved strawberries?" August scooped a frozen chunk of strawberry into her mouth. She winced with the left side of her face. "Oh, brain freeze!"

Sylvia grinned and nodded. "He liked blackberries too. He'd get scratches everywhere, climbing into wild blackberry bushes whenever we spotted them."

"See, why didn't I know that? I feel like there's so much I've missed. I should have paid better attention."

"Sweetie, it's okay, it's normal," her mom laughed. She put an arm around her shoulders and hugged her. "It just means you're growing up. You're coming to understand how important things are. And how precious. Growing pains, that's what you're having."

Lainy had given August a quartet of mix tapes full of Heart, Led Zeppelin, Pink Floyd, and King Crimson, their cases artfully decorated with Lainy's colored pencil drawings—rainbows, stars and butterflies. She and August together had polished off the first quarter of the ice cream cake. The rest of the gifts August received over the day consisted mostly of books: *Clan of the Cave Bear*, which everybody was raving about, and also *Cosmos* (her mother reminded her how Evan had insisted they all watch it together when it was on TV, and how fourteen-year-old August quickly developed a teacher-crush on Carl Sagan), and a fine hardcover copy of *Strange Case of Dr. Jekyll and Mr. Hyde* that was small enough to tuck into a coat pocket. There was also a beautiful antique edition of *Grimm's Fairy Tales*, which her mom explained had belonged to Evan, and to his father before. Apparently Gran had had it tucked away somewhere, and August opened the cover to find "Fletcher Evan Archer" written neatly inside. She laid the palm of her hand over his signature and closed her eyes. It was like getting a birthday gift from him this year after all.

The following Saturday August was working at Leigheas Apothecary, organizing herbs, hanging crystals in the window and dusting the Celtic, Viking and Native American jewelry. She had learned from Brigid that the name of the shop was Scottish Gaelic for something akin to "healing cure" and the proper pronunciation was close to "Layess," one syllable. Most of their customers, however, had Americanized it to "Lee-ahs," so for the sake of peace Brigid had long ago given up correcting them. Of course, Lainy called it "Leia's," as though her Star Wars hero had opened her own shop in Mahigan Falls, which always made August smile. Sometimes she just wanted to squish Lainy, she was so cute.

August was sweeping the dust bunnies from the corners of the front window when something made her look up, and she saw Wolf crossing the street, coming toward the store. Her heart leapt and she dashed to the back and crouched down behind the counter. The door bells rang as he entered, and she held her breath. She heard his voice calling for Brigid, and a shiver ran through her body. Then she heard him come back to the counter and stop.

"I know you're in here. Red."

And the sound of her name she exhaled finally, then stood up so quickly that she went lightheaded for a moment. "Hello, Mr. Wol— Neighbor."

He couldn't help smiling at the corners of his eyes. "Why are you hiding back there?"

August's brain was not quite ready to respond, but her mouth was more than capable of carrying on all on its own. "Why do you think? You've made it pretty obvious you aren't interested in talking to me. That doesn't feel so great, ya know."

"I imagine not," he acknowledged with a sympathetic expression on his face. She assumed it was sincere. He seemed the sincere sort.

"It hurts my feelings." It came out a bit more pathetic than she would have wanted, but to her surprise he seemed genuinely pained. He regarded her quietly for a few seconds, and she wondered with trepidation what on earth he was going to say next. She held her breath without even realizing it.

"Please forgive me."

"Well. Okay. How could I not forgive you with those big sincere eyes you have?"

"All the better to apologize with," he said with a wink and a smile. She smiled back and he gave a nod as if to say, *That's settled.*

"So what can I get for you?" she asked in her best shopgirl manner.

"There should be a package here for me."

"There are a few packages here that Brigid left for customers. What's your name?"

He hesitated and tried to peek around her at the bags organized on the opposite counter. August moved and swayed to block his view.

Her arms crossed and head tilted.

"Name?"

It was obvious he had to offer it up or risk offending her again, along with not collecting his package. She could feel the pressure of his gaze as he looked at her, studied her. His eyes turned to the floor. August swore she could hear the old wooden clock in the back room ticking, over the gentle Celtic shop music and the wind chimes swaying under the air vent. Finally he looked up again and straight into her eyes.

"Faolan. Faolan Conall," he said. With that hint of Scottish accent, it was like music.

August smiled congenially. Triumphantly. The wall was crumbling, at least a little. He smiled back and bowed to her, and when he rose he held his hand out expectantly. Unsure what was to happen next, she rested the whole of her hand and wrist into his. He immediately pulled it back as if he'd been bitten.

"Sorry," he said, a bit sheepishly, while rubbing his obviously smarting hand. "That wasn't very gallant, I'm afraid." He then shook the hand out. "That bracelet must be made of mistletoe. I'm severely allergic."

"Omigosh! I'm so sorry!" she said, pulling hard at the band around her wrist. "Here, I'll get rid of it." She jammed it into her pocket, then held her hand out for him again, barely containing a squeal of delight.

He lifted it gently and kissed her fingers, and August felt a tingle shoot up her arm and down her spine. He set her hand down again on the counter and stepped back. "Are you now satisfied, Red?"

"Well, I'm glad to know your name, Faolan Conall. I thought I was going to have to call you Wolf forever."

He eyed her suspiciously. "Wolf?"

"You know! Because of your Halloween costume? The night I was *accidentally* spying on you. Notice how I put the emphasis on *accidentally*?"

"Aye."

She almost melted when he said that. "Not that I mind calling you Wolf sometimes. So long as you don't."

"I don't."

Then she gave a playful scowl, "But I still wonder why you treated me like a virus. I'm just saying, maybe you could have at least told me your name."

"You know it now." His accent was so slight at times, but she could still hear a whisper of it. He shook his head. "Can't just let it go, can ya?"

She tilted her head again, and half-frowned this time.

His expression gave away the slightest defeat. "It's not you, dear girl. You are perfectly delightful."

August smiled. *Delightful.* She'd take it. But she could feel there was more he was not saying and she squinted a bit.

He sighed. "I can see you will have a hard time putting this down, won't you, Little Red?" His pale blue eyes sparkled.

She noticed that it both tickled and annoyed her when he called her that. She nodded, and waited expectantly.

He stepped closer and bent toward her with a conspiratorial look. She leaned in too, and felt his sweet-smelling breath on her cheek as he spoke low in her ear.

"Red, it is because I am fond of you that I do not allow you to become entangled in my life. It has been difficult to keep my distance, to say the least."

A thrill rushed through her at his admission, but the contradictory message pricked at her. This man was infuriatingly mysterious and tantalizingly beautiful. She could feel him closing the door on her, and her throat tightened and her stomach began fluttering. Her bottled-up longing filled her eyes as she spoke. "What harm could it do to just have a few conversations?" She wanted to say so much more, but she held her tongue.

His features softened, and her heart thudded hard at the glimmer of what she hoped would be his affirmation.

"Conversations? Just a few?" His gently mocking tone made it clear that he knew there was a danger that it would be much more than that. And that she knew it, too.

"Well, if we just kind of run into each other, then it won't be a big deal," she said casually, and traced a finger on the counter top. She was certain nobody could be cooler than she was being in that moment. "If I were perhaps reading by the stream at the edge of the woods tomorrow afternoon," she waved a hand in the air, "and you happened to stroll by around three o'clock, that wouldn't be a big deal, would it?" She paused here and gave him a brief glance then returned to tracing nothing on the countertop. "It'd just be two neighbors who chanced to meet at the end of their properties. Right?"

He peered sternly at her. "I'll take my package now. As to yards and streams and chance meetings, I imagine we'll have to see what fate has in store."

"I imagine we will." She almost choked on the words. Definitely not cool. She clutched onto a tiny bit of hope that he might meet her. Just to talk, of course.

He continued to look her in the eye and she held his look, as he tucked the small parcel under his arm, then turned for the door. She waited until his hand was on the handle.

"My name is August. In case you forgot ..."

He paused and then turned. He was trying hard not to grin. "August," he repeated. "I remember." Then he bowed once more, and slipped out of the door in one smooth step.

All that evening August thought about Faolan's wise and smiling eyes, which made it rather difficult for her to sit still through dinner. And all that night she stole glimpses of his house through her turret windows, and while she stretched out on her window seat she rubbed and rocked and imagined Faolan's kisses as they lay by the stream, his hands on her wet skin and his lips on her excited nipples as his lean body stretched out naked next to hers. She came more than once, and each time she called out Faolan's name. Spent, she finally passed out in her bed, and slept deeply and soundly for the first time in what seemed a long time.

The next day August woke up with no appetite and a fluttery stomach, thinking of Faolan. No breakfast today. She couldn't even look at the packages of powdered Hostess Donettes in the pantry, which were her absolute favorite quick breakfast snack. The weather was surprisingly mild for the end of summer, with a definite decline in the humidity. By two o'clock August was sitting at the stream reading *Strange Case of Dr. Jekyll and Mr. Hyde*, her bottom perched on a large flat rock and her feet down in the crystal water. The spot was perfect—the water formed a pool at the widest part of the stream, with shade trees hanging over the far bank and a drop in the stream bed that created a tiny, burbling waterfall.

If she were honest she would have had to say she was pretending to read about Jekyll and Hyde, since she was looking at the same paragraph over and over. She could not stop wondering if Faolan was going to appear, and if he did, what it would be like to finally have a full conversation with him. And, like a true gentleman, he did not keep her waiting long. Almost before she heard his step on the other bank, his baritone brogue slipped into her ears and gave her tingles.

"Good afternoon, Red. What a surprise to chance upon you here, at precisely three o'clock."

She cast him a sidelong glance. "You realize it's closer to two-thirty, don't you?"

"Is it? Imagine that. I suppose that makes it all the more coincidental, doesn't it?"

He leapt across the stream like it was a puddle, and August felt another zap of electricity as he came closer to her. Today he was wearing jeans and a tight sage-green tee. His face still had a couple of days of whisker growth, even though his damp mane of hair appeared to be freshly washed. They faced each other, she on her rock, and he just a few feet away, and he squatted on the sun-warmed grass and peered at her book.

"A fine tale, that. Monsters within us, light and dark at once. Each of us working at being our best selves, until something stirs the beast within. What do you think, Red? Have you a monster in you?"

August drank in his relaxed gestures and the cadence of his speech. She observed every tantalizing aspect, intending to hold the image of him close and keep it with her.

"I suppose we all do. I'm not so innocent as I seem," she teased, hoping he'd pick up on her none-too-subtle entendre. Ever the gentleman, he gave her no more than a wink for it—half a wink, really—and went on to talk about Robert Louis Stevenson's own life. He asked her if she'd read any other of his works, and wondered how August would compare him to modern writers of psychological horror, while he couldn't resist noting that Stevenson was Scottish, which might sway his own opinion a bit. August's heart fluttered that he cared what she thought on such matters.

For two hours they talked, and August was electrified by the way their conversation flowed and shifted, as though their perceptions were perfectly in sync. She couldn't get over how closely he listened to her, how he absorbed not only what she was saying, but also understood why she would think it. Never once did she have to explain herself. Her thoughts raced over ideas about human suffering, about love and the contradictory nature of man, both benevolent and savage, and she felt as though her mind was waking up after a year of hibernation. And perhaps in these moments, her grief receded just enough.

"When it comes down to it," he said in his musical lilt, "I think a monster is no more than a child, armed with a fierce power to take what it wants, and it's only when we learn to care about what someone else needs ..."

" ... that we truly grow up and tame the beast within," she finished, and he beamed at her. "Wow," she said a little too loudly, suppressing a grin.

"Aye. Wow." His face was radiant. If he'd been any closer she would have been unable to resist her impulse to kiss that perfect chin. August was somewhat crestfallen then when he rose, stretched his legs, gave a small bow and bid her a good evening. She mentioned casually that she would be at the stream again on Wednesday at three, hoping she didn't sound too eager.

"Well then, I hope I find myself on this path again," he replied chivalrously. He seemed to want to say something more, August thought, and she certainly did want to say more, though all she managed was an awkward goodbye, and after a moment he bowed again to her and turned away. She watched him pad off into the trees, a slight bounce to his now-dry black and grey locks.

They did meet several more times in that spot, and their

conversations continued to sparkle with ideas. Before their meetings August would fret over wanting to be graceful and ladylike; Faolan was so dignified, and it made her want to be his equal in manners, though she imagined she would only ever be klutzy and awkward, or say the wrong thing. And yet each time, once they began talking she forgot about those concerns, losing herself in the thrill of connecting with his mind. It seemed to August that there was nothing Faolan didn't understand. He had not read *Cosmos*, and yet none of the world's great astronomers or mathematicians were unknown to him. And with the tales of the Grimm brothers, he could quote them by heart and even embellish them, filling in details that he said had been left out. At August's request he had taken to reading them aloud for her. She loved the music of his subdued accent, which often revealed itself in a passage with a lot of Rs. His unintentional trill would inspire a blooming sensation deep in her body, and when his voice dipped into a low rumble, it sometimes gave her a shiver that rippled through her. A boy's voice had never had this impact on her before. Though, admittedly, he was no boy. He was a man, with a man's voice and man's chest hair, and facial stubble by dinner time.

Her mother had noticed an upswing in August's mood and started to ask oblique questions about what was making her smile all the time. After a few weeks of the reading sessions by the stream, she finally confessed to her mother what she'd been up to. To August's surprise she seemed unconcerned about her daughter spending time with their neighbor. "I've known Faolan for years. He's a good man. Just let me know if you want to talk," she had said to her, and didn't pry beyond that.

This revelation stunned August. Had she mentioned him to her mother earlier, she might have been able to tell her more about him—like his name, for example. August had harbored a sense that her mother wouldn't understand, or would think that Faolan was too old for her to be hanging around. She didn't want to have anything coming between her and her mother, or for that matter, anything coming between her and Faolan.

Faolan had promised that on their next meeting he would read aloud to her from *Alice's Adventures in Wonderland*, which he assured her would provide numerous opportunities to discuss logic, history, transformations, and the richness of language, as well as satire, comedy and "the pure joy of being surprised by something completely ludicrous yet utterly wonderful," as he put it.

He had asked her to come no earlier than three this time, and August could barely contain her curiosity about what he had in mind. She chose a cornflower blue sundress in honor of the book's heroine—and perhaps also because she thought it showed off her pale bosom nicely. As she approached their spot, with her well-thumbed *Wonderland* in hand, she could see fabrics fluttering in the gentle breeze. At the edge of the trees Faolan had set out a small table covered in lace and linens, flanked by wooden folding chairs. In the center of the table was a painted china teapot, surrounded by matching cups and saucers and several small dishes, some with neatly cut two-bite sandwiches and some with pastel-hued petits fours decorated with miniature icing roses. One plate was laid with a bundle of blue flowers. For the heat, there was also a tall glass pitcher of lemonade, with ice and slivers of lemon at the top, just the way she liked.

"This, this is amazing," she said at last. "It's just beautiful." She wanted to keep gushing about how special it was and how nobody had ever done something like this before, but she worried it would come out sounding like a bad soap opera scene. Her eyes were wet. She hoped he wouldn't notice, and then she hoped he would.

"I'm glad you like it."

"I love it! It's amazing. You're amazing." She knew she must sound like an excited child, but didn't care. She picked up the bunch of flowers and held them up.

"What kind are they? They're lovely."

"Forget-me-nots. They grow along the banks of the stream up closer to my end. They're abundant in our homeland as well. Do you like them?"

"Forget-me-nots." She smiled. "I love them. They just might be my new favorite."

"What was your old favorite?"

"Lavender. But I think lavender and forget-me-nots would look very pretty together, don't you?"

"Aye."

"Thank you." She went over to him and put her arms around him. After a few moments he put his arms around her as well, and they held onto each other for some time. She looked up at him, searching his eyes for his feelings, willing him to kiss her. She thought for a moment that he might, but then he smiled gently and dropped his arms, taking a step around her to the chair behind her.

"You're welcome. Now, please, sit," he said as he pulled out the chair.

With a sigh August sat down, determined to enjoy their time in whatever form it took. She spread an embroidered linen napkin on her lap, ate tiny cakes and sipped orange-spiced tea, and talked to the man she had come to believe she was in love with. She watched the sun catching the colors of his hair, strands of silver, black and steel, and the way his eyes crinkled at the corners when he laughed. He read the characters in different voices, the nervous Hatter, the sleepy Dormouse, the imperious Queen—which made August honk out her most embarrassing laugh—and the dreamy Cheshire cat. She listened closely to those fantastic words falling from his mouth, and she felt completely smitten.

The reading done and the cakes and sandwiches gone, they took to the rocks on the creek's edge. They dipped their feet into the cool water and discussed fussy white rabbits and giant top hats, curious little girls and words that turned themselves inside-out, and made each other laugh more times than she could count. She had been nursing a glass of lemonade while the sun dipped lower into the sky, slowly turning the clouds to sherbet orange, and as she drained the last of the liquid, end tilted high, the icy clump at the bottom of the glass came crashing down on her nose. She squeaked in surprise and the ice clattered out onto the rocks around her, leaving a sticky mess down her neck and on the dress. She felt a hot flush of embarrassment, picturing herself surrounded by mishaps and feeling like a disaster. But Faolan smiled in his gentle way, neither mocking nor judging, and through his eyes she was no longer the wreck she deemed herself.

She realized that his understanding and embracing of her, of who she was, was encouraging a sort of bravery within her. More and more she felt safe to be herself, disasters and all, and trusted him to never think less of her. She wondered if he even found it adorable at times.

On the last Friday in September August realized that she had a touch of nostalgia for school. Not Mahigan Falls High, certainly, but the air smelled like school time, and everybody else her age had gone back weeks ago. The feeling was only a fleeting one though, since school had many times been awful for her.

She relished the fact that she was instead sitting on a blanket by a stream at the edge of the woods, laughing with a handsome, intelligent man and talking about Jules Vern, and how some day soon everybody might be able to have tiny telephones in their pockets and could even call people in space with them. The creek was quite full and fast-moving from several recent thunderstorms, and though the water sparkled orange with late afternoon sun, August felt chilled by incoming evening air. She stood up to dust off her bottom, suggesting they go for a walk to keep their blood moving (and with the idea she might get to hold Faolan's hand), but as she straightened she slipped on the damp edge of a rock and fell into the water hole, whacking her elbow and twisting her ankle on the way in. She didn't even have time to think about how ironic it was that she'd been skillfully jumping rocks and climbing trees only the day before.

Faolan jumped in immediately and fished her out of the stream. August's dress, an airy cotton gauze that felt like feathers a moment ago, was now soaked and clinging to her. It wasn't long before her ankle began to throb.

"Red, dear, are you okay?" he asked with obvious concern. She managed a small, tight-lipped nod.

Faolan lifted her in his arms and carried her up the slope to his house. He kicked open the back door, grabbed a quilt that was draped over the back of a chair, and gently set her onto a red velvet couch. August recognized the library room from the night she was inadvertently spying on him. The wall was covered in books from floor to ceiling, which was nearly two stories high. He wrapped the quilt snugly around her, took another quick look at her ankle, and stepped briskly into the hall, pulling his shirt over his head and sending water spray everywhere. A few moments later he was back with a first-aid kit. He was wearing only a towel on his lower half, and August's heart nearly stopped at the sight of him. The throbbing in her ankle and her elbow pulsed hard with her heart while the rest of the world around her disappeared.

"Don't worry lass, we'll get you fixed up." He knelt beside the couch and examined her ankle. "Does this hurt?"

She winced. "Yeah. Not too bad, but yeah."

"I think it's just sprained." Faolan's accent had come on stronger with the urgency of the situation, and August wanted nothing more than to curl up against his chest. "We'll wrap it first and put some ice on it. Would you like somethin' for th' pain?"

"Just the ice, thanks."

When Faolan returned with the ice he was wearing a robe, and she nearly cried out with disappointment. Although, she acknowledged to herself, he did look cozy and domestic in that tartan wrap. She told him her ankle was already feeling better, and he was visibly relieved. But then he sniffed the air briefly and turned to look at her more closely. He opened the blanket and took her hands, and when he turned them over something warm ran down her arm.

"I seem to be bleeding."

For a moment it looked like he might lick her, but he only leaned in and wiped the blood away and peered at her elbow. "It's not bad. Just a little gash. I've got something for that as well, not to worry." He cleaned the wound with hydrogen peroxide, patted it dry, then taped a bit of sterile gauze over it. He bent forward and gave her elbow a little kiss.

It seemed at that one moment, with Faolan close enough for August to feel the warmth of his breath, they both noticed that her wet white dress now revealed all of what nature made of her. He looked away from her bosom and into her eyes. She was breathing harder, as was he, and the two of them hung there together as something passed between them. Then she leaned forward and gently touched her parted lips to his. They breathed each other in, slow and deep, just breathing, his sweet breath and his warmth swirling down the center of her. She rested her hand on his chest where the robe made a deep V, and tangled her fingers into the light and dark curls. A quiet moan rose up from her throat and she pressed her mouth tighter to his and slipped her tongue between his lips. She felt Faolan hungrily receive her, but he abruptly broke off the kiss and stood up away from her. There was a distinct bulge under his robe, but he quickly turned away.

"I'm sorry. I should not have done that," he said almost too low to hear.

August immediately attempted to protest but he shook his head and disappeared into the other room. She was too startled by what had just happened to call after him, and then he was back with pajama pants under the robe. He began pacing and running his hands through his hair, looking down at the floorboards.

"August ..."

Her heart was pounding. This was the first time he'd ever used her proper name, and she knew that couldn't be good. Was he going to say she had to leave? Or worse, that he didn't want her there? She sat up straight, pulling the blanket tight around her, and began to shiver, even though she was no longer chilled. He walked back to her and kneeled down, put his hands on her knees and looked into her eyes. She swallowed hard and held her breath.

"August, I think we've arrived at a dangerous place."

"Why? You mean ... because of my age?"

"No! Yes. Well, partly," he was clearly struggling to explain what was troubling him.

"Are you worried about getting in trouble? Because—"

"Lass, there are things more important than man's laws. Things that challenge our moral compass and encourage us down an uncertain path."

"But, if we like each other, what difference does it make?" August felt a lump forming in her throat. She knew that her voice was going to start catching and she knew what she was asking of him really might get him in trouble.

"I'm so much older than you. And—"

"I don't care! I have been with boys my age and they have never been half as wonderful as you are!" She could hear a childish whine rising in her own voice, making her sound even less womanly, and in danger of proving his point. Her face was growing hot and her eyes were scrunching up in an effort to fight off tears.

He made gentle shushing noises as he brushed a lock of hair out of her face. "Lass, don't fret so. You are very important to me and I want what's best for you."

"You're what's best for me. This is what's best for me. Can't you see how happy I am to be with you? Doesn't that count for anything? Doesn't what I want count for shit?"

"There are too many—"

"Don't try to tell me what I want," she interrupted him again, voice raised. "I hate it when people do that! They try to tell me I am too young to make a decision, or too vulnerable because I'm a girl. Or imply I'm not ready for a serious relationship. Well, I'm a serious girl, so a serious relationship is what I want to have. I can understand if you don't like me, or if a serious relationship isn't something you want, but don't tell me what I want. I know what I want."

He looked deeply into her eyes as the words poured out of her, and his open heart made her brave enough to say everything in hers.

"I think about you all the time, Faolan. About your brilliant mind and your smile and the crinkles next to your eyes. I think about the way your hair bounces when you walk and the way you squat down to talk to me when I'm sitting. How your voice is always gentle and you do such wonderful, thoughtful things. And yes, I think about sex with you. I think about it a lot. Why would I want a schoolboy who only thinks about boobs, cars, and Atari? Why would I want somebody whose big idea of a Saturday night is finding somebody to buy him cheap beer and having mediocre sex in his stinky, messy bedroom? Why would any girl choose that over—this? Book discussions, walks in the forest, tea parties by the creek ... and you know how to fix a sprained ankle. I mean, what could any guy my age possibly do to top that?"

If Faolan was going to say goodbye, August wasn't about to make it easy. He made a rueful half-smile and his head bowed forward almost into her lap. She had the urge to pet it, but thought it might be a mistake. When he spoke his voice was clear but his tone was somber.

"I am glad that I've made you happy. I've so enjoyed your companionship. It's been such a long time since I've allowed myself to get close to anybody. I can't tell you what it's meant to me."

"Why does this feel like a goodbye?"

He looked again at her. "I have to go to Scotland. I might not be back for a while." Before she could respond he stood up and walked over to a bookshelf.

He brought back a wooden box, and it immediately reminded August of the one she kept her treasures in. Even the carvings were similar, though this box had an archer on the top, ringed with an elaborate Celtic border, and more carving around the keyhole. He placed it on her blanketed lap.

"Take this home with you. It's very important to me. It will answer your questions."

"But, it's locked."

"You have the key. Let's get you home." He extended his hands to help her up off of the couch.

August was as much confused as hurt. "That's it? Just, 'I'm goin' to Scotland'?" she mocked his tone and accent. "I've bared my heart to you and that's all you can say?" She couldn't hold back the tears any longer. They began streaming down her face and she tried not to sound like a child when she said, "I know you must feel something for me."

He wrapped his arms around her and she buried her head into his chest, inhaling the scent of his skin and his robe and hints of spiced soap.

"Lass, don't cry. I do feel for you. But I need you to see that this urgency, it's dangerous. I have to go away for a while, I really must. If you still feel so strongly about me when I return, then we can pick up our book club where we left off."

Her sobs shook her body in his arms. "I'm afraid you'll forget me."

"Ah, no, I could never forget you. No matter what, I will be with you, and I will always be your Wolf. Besides, I have to come back for my box, don't I?"

He held her until her sobs subsided. He got her a glass of water, which she drank while he went down the hall to pull on jeans and a brown henley shirt, and together, slowly and quietly, he helped her back to the Blue Rook.

They found Sylvia there sitting on the porch, and she stood up with a look of curiosity and mild alarm.

"My goodness, what happened to you? You look like a little wet kitten," she fussed, and opened her arms to wrap August in a motherly hug. "Are you limping?" She eyed Faolan.

"I fell into the stream and hurt my ankle. And my elbow too, see? Faolan patched me up and gave me a blanket."

"Poor thing. Thank you, Faolan."

"We were talking about my Jules Vern book and I stood up and slipped on a rock and fell right in the stream. It was my own stupid fault. I feel very ungraceful right now."

"Nonsense, you're a swan," Faolan said in his most diplomatic voice, and they all laughed. "Her elbow does have a little gash, but otherwise I think she's fine. She may have a sight sprain. We elevated the ankle and iced it for a bit."

"August, go lay down on the couch and put that ankle up. We'll have a look at that elbow, too." Her mother opened the door and August smiled sheepishly as she headed for the living room. She thought she heard, over her shoulder, Faolan telling her mother he wanted to ask her something, but the door swung shut after her, and really, all she wanted to do was get off her ankle and wallow in self-pity, and maybe a pint of ice cream.

She lay there in the darkened room, her heart breaking, and yet still hopeful. She pulled the box out from under the blanket, which blessedly smelled of Faolan's home. She ran her fingers over the carvings and turned it upside down, probing for sliding panels or hidden buttons, but found nothing except satiny smooth wood. She poked her finger into the keyhole, but the box was locked tight.

Then the front door swung open, and August thrust the box

under the sofa as her mother came back in.

"Now, let's have a look at you."

"I'm okay, really. I think I'll just lay here and put it up and watch some television."

"I guess your friendly reading took an interesting turn today," her mother pried gently.

"Pfft ... come on, mom. Don't be ridiculous. Besides, he's not interested in me," August tossed back, trying her best to sound like she wasn't at all interested in Faolan.

"I had a huge crush on my history teacher when I was in tenth grade. Apple doesn't fall far, I guess." She grinned and petted August's hair.

"He's smart and yes, he's kind of attractive, but he's way too old for me."

Her mother looked directly at her and raised her eyebrows.

"Okay, maybe I have a teensy crush on him," August admitted. She couldn't suppress a grin.

"You're a smart girl August. And you've always been grown for your age, but you've also been through a lot of emotional turmoil recently. Just be careful how vulnerable you make yourself. Okay kiddo?" Her mom gave her the one-sided sympathy grin she did so well.

"Okay."

"I love you sweetheart. Here's the remote." She kissed August's forehead and headed to the kitchen for a bag of ice. In the two minutes Sylvia was gone, the exhausted girl fell into a deep sleep. She dreamt of keys and keyholes, rolling green hills billowing with pale purple heather, kilts and smiling eyes that crinkled at the corners.

August awoke on the couch with a numb foot and a dry mouth. Her mother was standing over her with a tray of toast and tea. She also realized that the memory of her father being gone no longer felt like a revelation when she woke, but was part of her existence as she now knew it. It was comforting to not to have that sense of suddenly remembering it when she woke up, and the flood of feelings that followed. But it also made her sad because it meant she was getting used to him being gone.

"Good morning sleepyhead."

August's tongue was thick and sticky. "My mouth tastes terrible, Mom."

"Here, sweetie, have some mint tea." She set down the tray and sat beside her.

August didn't feel at all hungry but she savored the fragrant tea as it woke up her mouth and sent soothing waves down her throat and through her body. She drained the cup and a minute later the toast too was gone. She was surprised to find her ankle and elbow seemed mostly healed. But soon her thoughts turned to Faolan, first as a flutter and then as a cold sinking damp that clung to her heart.

Her mother seemed to be picking up on it too—if not her daughter's thoughts then at least her feelings. "So," she said, brightening, "I have a surprise for you."

"Really?"

"Hang on, I have to go get it," her mother grinned as she hopped out of the room.

August craned her head towards the hall, and in a moment her mother returned with something furry and white in her arms. Then it wiggled. Her mother was carrying the most adorable ball of fluff August had ever seen, and it began to yip the moment it saw August.

"Mom, what on earth? Oh my god, he's a puff ball! He's so cute!" August's eyes were wide and when her mother dropped the wiggling pup in her arms August beamed and buried her face in the soft white fur.

"It's a gift, from Faolan."

August looked at her mother in disbelief. "What?"

"He asked me last night if he could give you a puppy. He said he knew you never got to have one because we were in an apartment. I told him it was okay with me. What do you think?"

"I ... I don't know what to think. This is okay with you?"

"Well I wouldn't have told him yes if it wasn't, silly! I think it's great. It'll be good for you to have some companionship. Look at that baby! I mean, who could resist?"

August cuddled the warm little creature to her face. "Hey, there. You're so pretty. Yes, you are!"

She found there was a scroll attached to the red satin ribbon around the puppy's neck. She sat the puppy in her lap and tugged the scroll free to unroll it.

Dearest Red,

I hope that I've not overstepped my boundaries. I thought that she would be good company, if not a wee bit of trouble. She is what is known as a "high-content wolfdog." She was already on her way to me last night from the wolf rescue when I spoke to your mother about making a gift of her, so I'm very glad she said yes! She arrived from Pennsylvania early this morning, and she will need lots of reassuring. Not just anybody can command respect from such a dog. Name her well.

And as I said, I will be back for the box, so please take good care of it.

All my love,

Faolan Conall—your Wolf

August nearly swooned at that one short phrase, "All my love." Her heart must have skipped three beats looking at the tender arching and looping of the script. She traced her finger over the ink, imagining her Wolf, writing those words at his library desk while thinking of her.

A yip brought her back from her reverie. "So you're a girl, huh?" She held up the puppy and took a peek to confirm, then kissed her on her furry little face. "I think your name is ... Snow White. But I'll call you Snow for short. Do you like that? Do you like that, girl?" The puppy scratched and wiggled and licked at her new mother and for a few moments August's heart was full enough that she didn't feel the empty spaces.

~~Red Autumn~~

It was October, there was a chill in the morning air, and August caught faint traces of woodsmoke on the breeze as she sat on the porch drinking lukewarm coffee and watching the sun creep higher over the tops of the trees. She remembered for a moment that something awful happened to her last October, and pruned it away— *Keeping it inside the fence, Abel*, she thought. She turned her thoughts to something about the air, and the light, and October itself that made her wistful and lonely for her father. He had loved this time of year, from the first turning of the leaves to Halloween and then Thanksgiving, and August remembered long walks with him through crisp air and whispering trees.

Now the man she was in love with was on the other side of the ocean, for some unspoken reason she may never be privy to. October belonged to Faolan as well, since it was Halloween night—or really the wee hours of All Saints' Day—that she first encountered him in his yard, wearing a mask, drinking from a bowl, and gazing at the moon. The unanswered questions and sudden endings hectored her thoughts. She was glad she at least had Snow to keep her company. Her fluffy white companion stood by her feet and pointed her nose into the wind, catching all the wild smells, sometimes losing her balance or chasing an early fallen leaf. *Life would be so much easier if I could be a dog*, August thought.

"C'mon girl, let's get you some breakfast," she said to the puff ball, opening the door and heading for the kitchen. As soon as she passed the living room, however, she remembered how she had stuffed the wooden box under the sofa. Faolan's box! How could she have let that slip her mind? She was dying to know what was inside of it, and she was determined to find out. She groped under the sofa and pulled it out, while Snow yipped from the kitchen. It didn't look any easier to open in the daylight. But first things first, as her father used to say; feed the puppy, then figure out how to open the box.

August put down some canned hash for Snow and waited more or less patiently while she slurped it up, then scooped up the snuggly pup, grabbed the box and headed upstairs to her room. With Snow tucked into the quilt on the window seat, August sat in the morning sunlight and prepared to do battle with the mysterious box. She pressed her finger to the keyhole again, then remembered that Faolan told her she had the key, which made no sense. How could she have the key to his box, and how could he know she had it? As she leaned over the box she caught sight of the keys resting in her cleavage, but she disregarded any idea that one of those keys would fit, since they had been with her for years, and before that they had been her father's. That would mean her father had the key to Faolan's box, which was ridiculous. Although, Faolan had seen those keys around her neck—what other keys could he possibly know about? The box was very similar to hers, after all.

"Okay, here goes nuthin'," she sighed, pulling the chain over her head. Her fancy two-toned copper and silver key was obviously too big. She then pondered the other key, the one that went to her own box, and rubbed the bow of it with her thumb. *It couldn't be that simple, could it?* She slowly inserted the key and turned it all the way around, 'til it came back to the top with a click. She held her breath to quiet her pounding heart and opened the lid.

On the very top there was an antique photo of a girl at a picnic. She sat on a blanket on the grass, backed by a tree and dappled in sunlight. She was wearing a simple dress and beamed at the camera with full lips and perfect teeth. Her long pale hair, though somewhat mussed with humidity fuzz, was crowned with flowers. There was a ribbon with a piece of jewelry, maybe a brooch, fastened around her neck.

August flipped the photo over, and saw written in disintegrating ink:

Issy, 1896

Something about the girl in the photo reminded August of the pictures in her own box, and she looked to the window seat where Snow was peacefully sleeping. Slowly she lifted the seat lid. The puppy slid back toward the corner, but, nestled into Gran's quilt, she only yawned and snuggled back in. August fished out her treasure box, set Snow gently back down, and put the boxes side by side. When she found her photo that reminded her of the Issy photo, she held it to the light and examined it closely. The same full lips, the same pale hair, though she wasn't smiling and her eyes were large and bright. The woman was beautiful, with a cinched dress that flowed to the ground and was neatly placed in a swoop at her feet. Her outfit was embellished with lace and a brooch at the throat. The same brooch. She was holding a nosegay in one hand, and the other hand was posed near her heart. Her hair was rolled up in the front and the back flowed long over her shoulder. While the one in Faolan's box was a snapshot, probably taken by a friend or lover, this was a professional portrait. She flipped the photo from her box over to find a faded scrawl that she had previously missed:

Iseabail A. Huntar, 17 years old, 1897
Engagement to Angus Archer

The mysteries only deepened. Issy and Iseabail could be the same girl, or twins, or cousins. But why would Faolan have a photo of a woman who belonged to the Archer family? Perhaps her family had known Faolan's family for generations, and the connection was somehow a neighborly one. It was a small town after all, as he kept pointing out to her.

After pondering the mystery for a few long moments she went back to Faolan's box to find a packet of letters secured with a green satin ribbon. She slipped the ribbon from around the stack and fanned them out in front of her. She could see that some of them were postcards from London, Paris and New York. The rest were letters, in envelopes about half the size of modern ones, the paper yellowed and the ink turned brown with age. The first few in the stack were addressed to Iseabail Huntar, and August was startled to see that a few were addressed to "Faolan Conall" in Scotland—evidently a distant namesake of Faolan's. The rest were addressed to Iseabail Archer, but were still sealed, with return remarks on the front. The postcards were all addressed to Faolan Conall and had nothing written on them beyond an address.

August opened the earliest letter, stamped April 19, 1896. It was written in a neat and graceful hand.

My Dearest Faolan,

How bitter sweet it is to miss you, my love. Mother dragged me off to France so she could enjoy another springtime in Paris. I should be happy because it's so beautiful here, but your absence casts a shade of sorrow on every beautiful sunlit thing. There are winding paths where we would hold hands and stroll between rows of meticulously tended gardens. There are oceans of grass and wildflowers where we would lay a blanket and hold each other under the shade of fat leafy trees. Have you ever stood beneath blossoming trees and let petals rain down upon you? Oh I would kiss you endlessly under such trees! All of these things seem somehow unreal without you here. As if your inability to see them and share them with me keeps them from fully manifesting in this world.

I have wondered what I could do to feel closer to you, my darling. What way could we feel close and ease our aches? I propose that each afternoon at three o'clock we should take a moment and think of each other and imagine we are enjoying the romance of Paris in the spring. I will send my love to you, and you can send your love to me. And each night, when the moon makes its appearance, let's say a tender goodnight, touching ourselves and rocking to sleep in ecstasy. I will imagine your strong paws, your soft fur against my flesh in the moonlight. You could imagine me finding every excited part of you with hands and lips, until your sweet howling cracks the silence of the night. I will have you in my heart these long weeks I am here and without your face to gaze upon and your hand to hold, or your mouth to kiss or your heart to embrace.

I think Mother drags me along to keep me away from you. She doesn't know we are married under the grace of the Gods, bonded through our hearts, bodies, and nature, in a way that is outside of man's law. Though not officially on paper, your name is engraved on my heart and you are my husband, no matter the proper entrapments that usually require such titles. I shall forever remain your Issy-Bel Conall for the rest of my days, I promise.

What wedding could be more sweet and sacred than a meeting of the souls? Our love is imprinted on the stars for all eternity, I am your wife.

I cannot wait to return to your arms and until then I will ache with a misty melancholy that only your touch can again make glad.

Love Always,

Issy

Issy was indeed Iseabail, it seemed. Paws? Maybe it's an old fashioned expression, she thought. August read all of the letters that had broken seals. The ones from that long-ago Faolan professed his love and devotion to Issy-Bel, and often his feverish desire to ravage her and bind themselves to each other. Yet he also expressed his wanting to be a gentle spirit, and to free her own spirit to follow its nature. He understood her to be his equal, and told her how he wished to escape the stifling, backward thinking of his family, and hers. Though the letters were few, some were many pages long, containing thoughts on music, philosophy, politics, loyalty and traditions. Most of it was foreign to August, both by time and region, so she didn't understand all of it. The strongest thread through them was the obvious love between the two, undimmed by Iseabail's mother carting her off to various parts of the world for weeks at a time. It seemed that whenever she was back in Scotland, Issy found herself back in Faolan's arms.

August would have happily ignored the rumbling of her stomach to keep reading, but Snow was getting restless, charging around the room and then stopping to look earnestly at the door. "What's the matter teeny bladder? You have to pee again, girl?"

While Snow scampered in the yard August pondered the connection of this woman to her family. Her photo had been in her father's box because she was an Archer ancestor. August seemed to recall that perhaps she was her great-grandmother. She really wished she'd paid better attention to everything her dad had ever said to her. Before Iseabail was an Archer she had been a Huntar, and she had been in love with a Conall, which explained why her picture was also in Faolan's box. And the way she spoke of him, it was clear August's own Faolan had taken after this fellow.

Equipped with an enormous apple, and with Snow at her heels, August returned to her room and settled back into her voyeuristic family history lesson. From this point, however, the story became considerably less romantic. The young woman became pregnant and her family could no longer overlook her carrying on with this outsider. Iseabail's reports about the accusations she endured, for herself and on Faolan's behalf, were wrenching. They called him an animal and said he was unfit for any woman to marry, and later that it was no wonder that her child—a "monstrosity," they called it—expelled itself from her womb. They thought it was "the will of the Fates." In one letter Iseabail told Faolan feverishly that no matter what her future writings might say, that she would always love him and be his wife, and that someday they would be together again, whatever came in the immediate future.

August felt horrible for the couple. *What the fuck is wrong with these people?* She rubbed her temples and kicked the base of the window seat. Snow picked up her head and tilted it, observing her master.

The last open letter was the worst. It was the young woman's goodbye to her lover. It was completely devoid of affection and written in such stodgy and proper language, August couldn't believe it came from her hand. "I am engaged to be married and will be moving to London," the letter said, "and only properly approved visitors will be permitted by the staff." She bid him farewell with a warning to keep his distance. It was all so cold, it must have been heartbreaking to young Conall.

The rest of the letters were from him to Iseabail Archer. There was one for every month over the next two years, and every one of them had been returned unopened.

August sat back, somewhat in shock from all she had just absorbed. She understood it was not for her to open those last letters, and she wasn't sure she was up to reading whatever that boy had written anyway. And what had happened to Issy? It was more like a sad story book. She really wished her Gran Sorcha's memory was better.

So she and Faolan shared an ancestral heritage, or at least family history. Maybe that had something to do with his Mr. Standoffish routine. And two different private chests held photos of the same mysterious woman. And the boxes themselves were not really so different, carved from the same wood, with some of the same decorations, and locked with the same key. August checked for a false bottom in Faolan's, and found it opened just like hers. Inside the hollow underneath was a silver and gold brooch—the same one Iseabail was wearing in both of the photos. August walked over to the mirror and held it up to her throat. She ran her thumb over the pearls and metalwork and sighed.

Snow began playing in the small stacks of letters so August shooed her away and collected them back up, slipping the ribbon around the bundle and replacing them and the rest of the artifacts carefully in their chests. Into the window seat they went. August scooped up the wiggling puppy, kissed her head and went downstairs to the kitchen. Faolan was wrong about one thing: she didn't understand. In fact, she had more questions than ever.

Lunch had come so late, the sun was already dipping into the western windows, and strong rays streamed into the kitchen. August noticed the suncatcher she and her grandmother made together at Sunnyvale during one of their many craft days. The glass beads winked in the window, scattering tiny rainbows all over the room. She decided she would get up early tomorrow and head over to the nursing home to see if Sorcha had any wisdom for her. Maybe she could stay at the Rook for a while, especially since Sylvia was going out of town. August fervently hoped it would be a good remembering day for her grandmother.

August was up with the sun. Her mother was off early to a medical conference in Florida and August had wanted to give her goodbye hugs and well wishes. After Sylvia drove off for the airport August fed Snow and let her out for a minute, then tucked her safely into her kennel and headed over to Sunnyvale.

The town was only just stirring so early on a Sunday, and as much as August didn't want to make a habit of getting up early, she did enjoy being one of the few people out and about. The building wasn't open for visitors yet so August fished her journal from her backpack and began writing and sketching while she sat on a bench by the entrance. She sketched out a quick drawing of the senior home on the hill above the old train station. Moments before the doors were due to open a familiar figure approached the building and August was somewhat surprised to see Abel, carrying a small package.

"Abel, hello!"

He seemed startled and took a moment to compose himself. He dropped his hands and held the small bag to his side.

"Oh! Well, hello there Miss August. My goodness, it's early for you to be here, isn't it?"

"I guess I could say the same to you. Did you come by to see my gran?"

"I did, actually. I'm here 'bout every Sunday morning."

"That's sweet, Abel. Is that package for her?"

"Yes. It's nothing really. Just her tea ... you know."

"What have you—"

The door swung open and a young female attendant stepped out to invite them inside.

"I see Sorcha has two guests this morning. How nice! Just go sign in." She ushered them in with a wave of her arm.

Abel signed in hurriedly while August inquired about having her grandmother come home with her for the week. When she approached the guest book herself she noticed that Abel had not only been there every Sunday, but almost every day as far back as the pages went.

"Excuse me," August said to the receptionist. She had never seen her before.

A mousy brown knot of hair swiveled around to reveal a sweet-faced young woman. Her name badge read Cheryl. "Good morning ... you're Sorcha's granddaughter, right? Can I help you?"

"Are you here every Sunday?"

"That's my schedule, yes," the woman's bushy eyebrows went up, and she waited expectantly for the follow-up.

"Does Abel often bring a package for my grandmother?"

"Every Sunday, Miss Archer. Her special tea from the apothecary, and sometimes food as well. I know she loves the scones from Wynda's Bakehouse. Have you had them? She's always in a better mood when he brings some. My favorite, though—and you have to try it—is a maple peanut butter waffle doughnut with bacon crumbles that is out of this world."

August couldn't help curling her nose up a bit.

"They taste better than they sound, I guess," the receptionist went on. "I just love their lemon meringue lady fingers too, if you like something more dainty. But, like I said, I think your grandmother likes the scones. She likes the shortbread, too. She's a classic."

"I did know she likes scones. Thanks for the suggestion. Am I clear to take her home today?"

"I think so. We have to double check with her doctor, but I can't think of any reason she wouldn't be able to."

"Thank you."

"You're welcome, Miss Archer."

August made her way to her grandmother's room, and through the cracked door she could see Abel and Sorcha engaged in heated whispers. Sorcha seemed surprisingly lucid and clear-eyed, but as soon as August pushed the door open Abel straightened up and his tone changed. He seemed to be talking about scones.

"I will bring you a ginger scone with lemon glaze tomorrow, okay? I'll go make sure Wynda's is making that one for tomorrow." He patted Sorcha's upper arm. She seemed confused and withdrawn, and didn't respond to Abel, but August saw her tucking the small brown sack down tighter into the space between her leg and the wheelchair.

"Thank you, Abel, for being so sweet to my Gran."

"Oh, you're welcome. You're very welcome. I will come by and check on the house later this week. The weather is supposed to be beautiful all week long. I have a new rocking chair for the porch that

I need to paint, and some work putting the garden to bed."

"Okay, Abel. I'll see you then."

"Goodbye then." He cast a thinly veiled look of concern towards Sorcha, made a gesture of dusting his cap on his thigh and lumbered out of the door with his arms heavy at his sides.

August went to her grandmother and tried to explain that she would be coming home to the Blue Rook for a couple of weeks. Gran remained detached and confused, despite August's suspicions that she was understanding things perfectly clearly. She found her grandmother's small suitcase and packed it with the essentials, talking cheerfully to her the whole time about books and her puppy and her mother's job and the changing seasons. She realized that Sorcha had surprisingly few medical needs despite her condition. She still had her own teeth and her hair was thick and healthy. Other than her being utterly swallowed by dementia, and atrophied from lack of activity, you might take her for a woman in her early sixties, instead of in her eighties.

August had finished packing and stood to face her grandmother. "I see Abel left his bag here for you, Gran," she announced, and tugged at the lip of the paper sticking out of the crevice. Sorcha didn't flinch. "Let me just put that in your bag, too."

August tugged the bag free as her grandmother stared blankly out of the window. She let the box inside slip out into the suitcase, and as she suspected, it had a familiar stamp on the flap, with the name "Leigheas" beside a crescent moon. She snapped the suitcase closed, slipped it under the chair, and wheeled Sorcha to the big white service van to take her home.

Once back at the Blue Rook, August wheeled her up the side porch ramp and into the kitchen, where Sorcha sat while she made lunch. They ate in silence together. August thought she might have to feed her, but she seemed to be able to do everything just fine, forking fruit salad effortlessly and taking dainty sips from her cup of Earl Grey. They exchanged one quick glance, both of them chewing, and August knew for sure that Gran was in there, understanding.

After lunch August read to her grandmother from *Sense and Sensibility*. She could feel Sorcha's awareness close to the surface, but couldn't draw her out. She thought maybe a stroll in her old garden might help, and took Sorcha out to the path under the trees, making one-sided small talk along the way. This didn't work any better, and August sighed and turned Sorcha back toward the house and wheeled her into her suite off of the kitchen. The room had been added by Evan once Sorcha began using a wheelchair, and had its own large bathroom. It was painted in a cheerful soft yellow and had white-trimmed French doors that led out to a small porch and a ramp into the yard. August parked Sorcha near the doors so she could look out onto the yard, and then she had an idea.

"I need to check on Snow," August told her grandmother. "I'll be back in a little while. Stay put, okay?" She parked the wheelchair, left the suitcase lying on the bed, and kissed her Gran on the head. She made plenty of noise on her way up the back stairs, then quietly slid down the front stairs and crept back around to the kitchen and peered around the corner into Sorcha's room. She saw Sorcha raised halfway out of her chair, reaching for the suitcase and craning to see the hall where August had disappeared.

"Gran," August said flatly. Sorcha flinched, then tried to ease back into her slumped state. "I know you can understand what I'm saying."

She rounded the wheelchair and knelt down in front of the old woman, whose eyes were actively avoiding her.

"Why are you pretending? Why don't you want to talk to me?"

The silence was long and a tear slid down Sorcha's sagging cheek. Her mouth was set in a thin hard line.

"Don't make me remember," she whispered low and deep.

"I don't understand," August said, and made her concern evident.

"You wouldn't want to either, child. Already they are flooding in. I am late for my herbs. And even if I took them right now, I am going to have to suffer for an hour before they are in effect again. Please give me my bag. Please take me back home." The woman finally looked at her granddaughter and August could see her face clouded with anguish.

"This is your home, Gran. And whatever it is that is hurting you, I'm going to help you." August petted the woman's legs. "Please don't cry."

Sorcha thrust out a hand. "If you don't give me that bag you will hear my screams for days as I will have to relive every horror of those years."

"What is in the bag?"

"Herbs. They go in my tea. They help keep the monsters asleep. Give it to me!"

August was torn. She didn't want Gran to forget, which was

obviously selfish. But besides that, she didn't know how crucial the herbs were to her health. She relented and gave her grandmother a dose of the herbs. Following the label she made a strong tea and gave it to the sobbing woman, who drank it down in less than a minute. It was an hour before her moans and fretting stopped, and August settled her in on the bed, where Sorcha fell at last into a long sleep.

August fed Snow and thought about her next step. She sniffed at her grandmother's herb mixture and looked in on Sorcha again before finally dialing Brigid and asking her to come out to the Rook right away. She was pacing the porch when Brigid arrived.

"What is it? What's happened?"

"It's my grandmother," August replied, and tears began rolling down her cheeks.

"Is she okay? Did something happen at the home?" Brigid was visibly concerned, but unflustered.

"She's okay. I think. I don't know, actually. She's asleep."

Brigid heaved a sigh, though her brow remained furrowed. "That's a relief. You really had me worried there for a moment. She's here, then? But what's got you so upset, love?"

August held up the box. "What is she taking?"

The medicine woman's mouth pursed and her eyes looked away. "You know I can't tell you that."

"I'm her family, Brigid. I have a right to know what's happening to her. My mother is in no position to take on Gran right now, so it's up to me and I need to know what this is and why she is taking it."

"Where is your mother?"

"She's in Florida at a work conference. Please, Brigid."

The wise woman looked into August's eyes. "I'm not sure you're ready for this, Red. It would be better if your mother was here."

"Would everybody please stop treating me like I'm a child?! I need to know what is going on with my grandmother. Look at me and tell me I have no right to know and I will not ask you another thing." August set her expression and waited.

Brigid sighed once more, setting down a burden she had been carrying a long time. "Get us some wine, girlie. We're going to need it."

"I don't need wine."

"You will after this," she replied, with a look that made August wonder what genie she'd just let out of its bottle.

August pulled two glasses out of the cabinet and handed the first bottle of wine in the rack to Brigid, who gave an appreciative nod. "Get me a corkscrew, and get comfortable," she said, and after filling her glass she downed it, and poured another.

"Your grandmother is taking a special herb combination that I make for her. It helps her forget."

"But why does she need it? Why does she check out like that? It's not right, Brigid." August's voice took on an edge of outrage and she began to pace. Brigid stood calmly and let her spill out. "She's my grandmother. She should be here with us, and it's like she's already dead. I want it to stop. I want her off that stuff. Is it safe? I mean, will it hurt her if she stops taking it?"

Brigid put down her glass and sighed. "No, it won't hurt her *physically* if we taper her off of it. Make the tea weaker and weaker over six weeks or so. But emotionally, I can't say. She has reasons that she wants to forget, legitimate reasons. I don't like it either, but my place is not to judge. I'm a healer, it's my job to help the people I care for, and for your Gran her memory was a constant misery."

"Gran's not healing. This can't be healthy for her. I may be young but even I know if you stop growing and learning and feeling things you're not really living."

Brigid gave her a smirk. "That's true enough. When did you get to be such a wise woman, darlin'?"

August softened a bit. She could see this was a sore subject for Brigid, and one she wasn't happy about having a role in. "What is it that Gran wants so badly to forget?"

Brigid drained her second glass, and gestured to August to take a drink herself. "I will tell you what I can, but understand, some of it is going to be difficult to believe."

There was a soft scrabbling noise and then Snow began yipping from the doorway. Brigid turned to see the small creature.

"You've got a puppy. I'm more a cat person m'self, but who can resist a pup? Especially a fluffy little teddy like that. Come here, you wee baby. Ah, she looks like a tiny wolf."

August picked up Snow and Brigid scratched her under her chin. "This is Snow."

"She's awfully cute. When did you get her?"

"Just yesterday. She was a gift from Faolan."

Brigid's eyes widened, "Faolan?"

"Yes. Why?"

"Dearest girl, why would Faolan Conall be givin' you a pup?" She wasn't hiding the note of concern in her voice.

"I guess because he figured I would like her. He asked my mother first. She's fine with it."

"Red, that is not what I mean, and you know it."

August did know, or thought she did, but she wasn't at all sure she wanted to admit her budding romance to Brigid, for fear she would say something awful about him or tell her it was wrong. She knew that if Brigid wasn't happy about her and Faolan it wasn't going to be easy to just carry on in the fairytale way she had been.

August's hesitation told Brigid all she needed to know. "Darlin', you need to be careful. There's things at work here you don't understand. There is a long history you don't know about."

"Well, nobody will talk to me about it! Don't you think it's about time somebody explained all these dark family secrets?" She and Brigid locked eyes and August did not flinch from the woman's gaze.

"Yer a hard-headed girl, at that," Brigid sighed. "Well, I suppose you'll have to be, when you hear some o' this." She closed her eyes, composed her thoughts, and gazed at August with gentle but firm purpose.

"Your family is made up of hunters. Did you know that, love?"

"Just recently, yes. Archers. We are literally archers."

"Yes, that's right. But not just archers. Your whole family is made up of a long ancestry of hunters. Collins, O'Connell, Huntar and Archer, those are some of the ones in the Celtic lands. Your mother is from a different line, a Germanic one. But that's a story for another time, aye?"

"How do you know all of this, Brigid?"

"I know because I was there for a good bit of it myself."

"You mean you've met some of my other family?"

"I mean, girl, that I was there for much of what has transpired since Iseabail Ayrshire Huntar was born. I suppose if you're gettin' to know Faolan, you've heard that name?"

August looked at her, waiting for the punchline. None came. She then screwed up her face and said, "Come on. Brigid, be serious. It's not like you to tease."

"You're right, it's not. I'm not teasin'."

August paced nervously, wondering if she really was ready to hear what the woman was about to tell her, but also knowing there was no way around it. She felt her stomach knot up and wished her mother was home.

"Brigid, that's crazy. If that were true you'd have to be over a hundred years old!"

"One hundred and twenty-nine this past February," she raised an eyebrow and fixed August with her pale gaze.

August drained her glass in a gulp and poured another. Brigid emptied hers as well and poured the last of the bottle into it.

"Okay Brigid, let's pretend for a moment that all of that is true. How would you know Iseabail?"

"I delivered her. I was a young midwife in Perthshire at the time. Ach, look at yer face, Red!" Brigid laughed like a girl with a secret. "Drink up, love, an' stay with me. I served all manner of families with my herbs and midwifery, but Iseabail was a favorite for me from the moment she was born. Ah, me, but that was a long time ago. A crown of strawberry curls atop that fat little head of hers. She was a grand child, she was. She didn't cry a bit—normally that's a bad sign with new babes—but she stared at me as if she knew me, and she cooed an' held my thumb tight 'til I put her to her mother's breast. You favor her, you know."

August had long admired Brigid's silver tresses. Now she regarded her hands and skin more closely: strong fingers, hardly knotted; a little jowly in the chin, and laugh lines of course, skin a bit thin and veins showing underneath, but the woman doesn't look anywhere near a hundred years old, let alone over a hundred. Or at least she didn't think so, since she'd never even seen a hundred-year-old before. She turned down a corner of her mouth and shook her head.

"How is any of this possible? How can you be over a hundred years old? C'mon Brigid—this is crazy. Seriously, stop teasing." August was now uneasy.

"I know how it sounds. But I'm not like other people. I'm a Herne, from the auld sod, and we're a long-lived bunch t' start with. Plus I've studied the old ways all m' life, and I have a gift for the herbs an' potions, if I do say. What to eat and what not to eat. What to drink, of course. How to get the mind and the body listening t' each other. These things work together to make for a long life."

"Are you saying you aren't human?"

"Oh, I'm human, right enough. Or at least mostly," she winked. "I won't last forever. I'm just special. Good stock. Very good at the healing arts, too. You're special, too. Hunters live a long while. And have keen senses. Smell, sight ... and the like. Quick healing, too. You've not noticed?"

August blinked and then stared for a long moment, then downed her glass of wine.

"So ... I'm not human?" August was both incredulous and inexplicably hopeful.

"You're part human. But yer mostly hunter, with some other stuff dashed in. Ye could live to be two hundred yourself, maybe more ... depending."

August tried to absorb it all. Brigid had never given her reason to doubt anything she said before now, but this was all just too incredible to fathom.

"Wait. Then why haven't we heard about people living a long time like that? What about science? I'm just ... I don't ..."

"There are many mysteries of this world. Even mysteries that aren't hidden can be hard to discover; mysteries that are hidden, and closely guarded, are near impossible to expose."

"Wow. Okay ... when you put it that way. So, I have photos of Iseabail." Brigid nodded and picked up her wine glass. "My dad gave them to me years ago. The strange thing is that Faolan has a photo of her too, and letters."

"How do you know that?" She sipped her wine slower now, focusing on August's words.

"Hold on a moment." August disappeared upstairs and returned with the two wooden boxes. She opened them on the counter, and it wasn't lost on Brigid that she used the same key. Brigid held the photos and stroked them with the tips of her fingers. Her eyes misted over.

"Beautiful, wasn't she? Your great-grandmother, on your father's side of course. Ah, I wish you could have known her. She was so full of life and so bright. She loved books the way you do. Your eyes are so much like hers. See how much you favor her jawline ... and there, around the nose and brow. Faolan gave you this box?"

"He told me it would answer questions. Really, it just created more. I had the key to it. It's obviously been locked up a long time if I've got the key. And I've had it for years and my father must have had it a long time before that. Seems odd, doesn't it? That my father would have the key to his box?"

"That's because this box, the one with the bowman, once belonged to Iseabail, so of course she had the key originally. They probably each had a key. The families go way back. Ach, it's too much to explain in one night! I think we should talk about your grandmother, while I still have the strength to do that."

"But I have so many questions."

"I know dear. In good time." She heaved a sigh. "Now your grandmother. She lost everything, some years back. All of her children, excepting your father, almost twenty years ago. Then she lost her husband."

"Wait—wait a minute! My dad had, what, brothers? Sisters?"

"Aye," Brigid nodded.

"And they all died?"

"You mean no one had told you that much, even? Oh, Red, no wonder yer so determined to have yer family! Aye, love, Fletcher

Evan grew up with two brothers an' two sisters, an' he was the youngest o' the bunch. All o' them gone, and then Bryan, her husband, all in a year. With all of that, and then you came into the world, she was terrified of getting fond of you or anyone else ever again. But that didn't sit with her either, and the woman's heart was so battered, it was either die, or go numb. Abel begged her not to take leave of this world. He's always loved your grandmother, and I think he might've hoped that one day, perhaps if her heart had healed, they could be together."

"Abel loves Gran?"

"Very much. But quietly. It's not his way to put himself over anyone else. He does what she asks and never wants for anything in return, other than to be near her. He's a gardener, it's his way. I know it hurts to watch her remove herself from this world. He reads to her, an' does what he can to keep her mind sharp. The herbs calm her and help her to forget, but there's still a mind in there and she still needs some exercise. So he keeps this house for her, brings her by most holidays and he does anything else she needs of him, without question."

"God, Brigid. I can't believe I've never heard any of this before. And Dad had two brothers and two sisters, and so I had aunts and uncles." August was feeling the wine now. "Oh, poor Dad! He must have been living with so much hurt and I never even knew it. But I don't understand why this has all been such a big secret from me."

"Family and love is a messy business, dear. I know your father wanted to protect you from the dark parts of his family lineage, at least until you were old enough to make up your own mind about things. He still had the pride of an Archer, but that legacy is a strange one and sometimes dangerous. He wanted to shield you from the history, and all of the dangers that that entailed.”

“How did they die?”

Brigid’s eyes clouded for a moment. “That’s a tale for another night. I just want you to know that your grandmother has good reason for wanting to forget.”

“I want to take her off of these herbs. I want her to come back to the world. I want to get to know her.”

“Sorcha doesn’t want to be a part of this world.”

August was undeterred. “She chose to stay, didn’t she? It’s been a long time—it’s time to wake her up. It’s time for her to heal. Isn’t that what you do? You heal people.”

At this, Brigid gave her a sharp, but thoughtful, look.

“Is there some way we can wean her off of the medication while also keeping her calm?”

“Ah, well, I can add something to relax her anxieties, an’ cut back the herbs that make her forget. I’ll have Abel come by the shop and pick it up. Wait until next Sunday to begin giving it to her. I’ll put instructions in the package. Once Sorcha is with us again, if she can function, I think she’ll have the answers for you, darlin’.”

August nodded emphatically. “Thank you.”

“But understand, that if she wants to forget again, I must do as she asks. As her *healer* it is my duty to relive her suffering and obey her wishes.”

“I understand.” August felt an undertow of disappointment tug at her, but she knew it was the right thing.

Brigid polished off her glass and August walked her to the front door.

"I'm afraid you've a lot of your own suffering ahead, my girl. Also, much joy." She put her arms on August's shoulders and regarded her with tipsy affection. "I think once Sorcha lets you into her heart, she's going to be very glad she came back to this world."

They embraced and Brigid stepped off of the porch into the darkness, none too steadily. "Whew! If it's all the same t' you, dearie, I think I'll come back for my truck tomorrow. Nice night for a walk."

The next morning was cloudy and August, sleeping off the night before, didn't open her eyes until she received a check-in call from her mother. Though she told her about picking up Sorcha, and updated her on the adorableness of Snow, who was stretching and yawning at the foot of the bed, August left out the visit from Brigid and anything that hinted at the mysteries she was uncovering. Those were conversations for later, after her mother was home and August could gauge her emotional state.

The week inched by slowly without much interaction from Sorcha, despite August showing her the Fletcher Evan memory book she and her mother had made. At times it seemed that the woman would flicker with recognition, but the flames died quickly, smothered by her implacable will to forget. Most of their time together was spent on the shaded porch, curled up in cozy sweaters and sipping hot cocoa. August read to her, or played record albums with the living room windows open, so Sorcha could enjoy some of her old music collection breezing through the screens.

Abel came by on Friday with the new herb package, though he didn't say anything to August. He simply handed the bag to her, nodded and turned on his heels. August thanked him and didn't try to stop him, figuring there would be time for talking later. She rolled up the previous bag of herbs and tucked it into her window seat. When she made Sorcha her tea at lunch, she thought her grandmother might have noticed something different, but she drank it down without comment.

August spent Friday afternoon writing and sketching in her journal—she drew Snow sleeping and the view from her windows, and Gran in the late sun when it slipped below the clouds. She also read and re-read the letters in Faolan's box, and spent some time in the mirror comparing herself to the young woman in the photographs. She wished she could have met her.

Saturday was all bright sunshine. Sorcha's new herbs were beginning to work and moments of recognition flashed in her eyes. August read to her from *Sense and Sensibility*, and she thought she heard Gran quietly chuckle. When the mail arrived that afternoon August saw an airmail envelope and her heart raced. It was from Scotland.

October 1, 1983

My Dearest Red,
Knowing what a curious and clever young woman you are, no doubt you have already unlocked the box and gone through the

contents, maybe several times. I sincerely hope that some of your burning questions have been answered. If not, we will talk more when I return. Also, I hope that none of what you are learning pains you too deeply. Indeed, I hope that in time, some of it might bring you joy in ways that are unexpected.

Of course I came to realize that you may have more questions than ever now, but we should pace ourselves darling girl. Trust that I have a thought to how this should unfold, as much as any man could know such a thing.

I hope the puppy is as much joy as she is trouble. I trust that you named her well and I cannot wait to hear your thoughts on raising such a fierce and adorable little beast. Don't forget to howl with her. Lay back, put her on your belly and howl to the moon—she soon will do the same. I know you will be a good mother to her.

I intend to return in a couple of weeks, but things here are unpredictable.

Have you thought of picking up your father's bow?

With Love,

Faolan

August hugged the letter to her chest. She read it twice more immediately, felt warm and wistful, and she could barely wait to pen a response. She knew it would be wiser to keep some of her cards close to the vest, yet she yearned to pour out her heart to Faolan. She wanted to give him every bit of feeling and thought in her; if he had been there with her she would not have been able to stop talking.

August sat down at her desk in her room and went through

eleven sheets of paper, some with only three or four words on them, before she completed a letter that felt right.

October 8, 1983

Dearest Faolan,

Thank you for writing. I might have been a little excited when I got your letter. I did manage to figure out the key and the box, and I looked through the things inside of the box, and I have to admit that I don't understand much. In fact, I have many questions. Was the Faolan who wrote the letters to Iseabail your great-grandfather? Iseabail is my great-grandmother, according to Brigid. It had occurred to me what a huge coincidence that would be. Not only that you and I have strong feelings for each other, but that you ended up being the neighbor to my family. Is that what you were trying to show me? Also, why would I be hurt? Those are just for starters. I guess I will have to wait for your answers at the pace you set.

At first I wondered how you knew about my father's bow, but of course you seem to know more about my family than I do. I have, in fact, thought of picking up the bow. I have some things to learn, but I think that Mom can probably help me figure out the basics. She's been away this week, but she returns tonight. Fingers crossed I don't hurt myself, or worse, somebody else. I hope that when you come home you can fill in many of the blanks that my story is suffering from. I would be eternally grateful for that!

The puppy is the best thing ever! I named her Snow White, but call her Snow for short. Whatever trouble she is I haven't noticed, because she's so wonderful to cuddle to, and play with. I promise we will practice howling and give you a demonstration.

There are many more things I want to gush to you at this moment. I'm missing you. I would love to curl up on the porch and have you read a book to me. I want to listen to music with you, and play with Snow together. And I know this is strange so don't laugh, I want to make you a sandwich. Isn't that a strange thing to want to do for somebody? I don't understand it, but I guess you're getting a big sandwich when you get back.

I hope to see you in a couple of weeks.

Love,

Your Red August

She wasn't sure that writing "love" was the right thing to do or not, but she couldn't help herself. She wanted to allow that indulgence since she didn't even say a tenth of what she wanted to. She was actually pretty proud of herself for keeping it short and sweet.

When Sylvia returned that evening August welcomed her home with long hugs and fresh apples and endless questions about her father's archery equipment.

At first her mother was resistant, trying a variety of excuses that didn't ring true. But eventually August's persistence won out and Sylvia brought down Evan's bow from its corner of honor in her bedroom. She showed August how to string it and told her how to care for it.

After breakfast on Sunday—the first meal to be shared by the three generations of Archer women since the New Year—Sylvia took

August out to the backyard with the bow and quiver. She went over basic safety precautions and gave her daughter a quick rundown of the equipment and how it worked, as well as strict instructions to wear her arm guard.

"And no dry-loosing, because pulling and releasing the string without an arrow could damage the bow and possibly the person holding it." Sylvia made it clear she wanted no emergency room visits. "Archery is about doing the same thing over and over again," she emphasized finally. "You must get your form down, and repeat it."

Sylvia had cut the foot off of a thick cotton knee-sock and August slid the tube of fabric over her forearm. She laughed about the variegated green stripes, but had to admit it looked quite woodsy once she got it on. Her mother gave her an approving nod.

"Above all, be careful. Don't shoot towards a building or anywhere that people might walk. I'd use the berm at the edge of the woods just past the barn; that's where your father used to practice. There should be targets in the barn—just set up a bale of hay and lay the target over it."

August nodded, though her head was swimming with all of the information.

"You look confused, sweetie. Have you got it?"

"Yes, Mom—I've got it!" August sighed, and scooped up the equipment.

"I think I'm going to walk over there with you and shoot a few, just to set you up. I don't know what I was thinking. You can't just tell somebody how to use a bow."

August huffed again, but she knew it was probably best.

Out by the barn they found some old hay bales—there hadn't been a horse or even a pony on the property in years—and they hauled two of them over to the berm at the northwest corner of the property, setting one on top of the other. Sylvia threw a burlap target over the top bale and they stepped back thirty paces.

"I'm rusty, but this is how you do it."

Sylvia explained her actions as she set up her form, nocked an arrow and shot it off, quickly followed by a second one. They both landed near the center of the target.

"Well, how about that? Not too bad considering! Remember, just set your form up exactly the same every time, like this, pull that back to the corner of your mouth, like this ... and ... release." The third arrow struck the bullseye soundly. They both let out with a "Hooray!"

"Okay, you try." Sylvia observed and corrected while August got her form down and the proper sequence of pulling the string to the corner of her mouth, then ear, and release. "Okay, I'll leave you to it sweetheart. If I were you, I'd stretch your arms after. You're gonna be sore!" She headed back to the house, but August could see the dot of her head in the kitchen window, watching over her.

August turned to face the target and lifted her father's bow, and marveled at how right it felt in her hands. She gave the string a few more gentle stretches, being careful not to release, and then slipped an arrow from the quiver she'd fastened to her hip. She ran through the steps in her head, not necessarily in order: hold the bow correctly, make sure the cock feather is up, nock the arrow into the string, pull back.

She undershot at first, but the twang of the string was exhilarating. It sent an electric charge up her arm and down her spine, and she quickly nocked another arrow. *Pull harder, pull cleaner,* she told herself, *and release. When you get it right, do it the same every time.* The second arrow struck the burlap with a satisfying thunk. It felt totally natural to her, and her third arrow came up out of the quiver and into the target in less than ten seconds. She put seventeen more arrows into the hay, and her arms were beginning to shake a bit, but the feeling of stretching them like that was thrilling. She would have gone on all afternoon if she could. No wonder her father had taken up the family sport. August wondered why he had never taught her how to do this. She guessed he must have abandoned it for his books. It's also not so easy to practice archery in the city, she supposed. So many unanswered questions. She promised herself to come out at least twice a week and practice until she could consistently hit the center of the target and her arms wouldn't shake anymore.

August went back to the house with the quiver slung over her shoulder and the bow swinging in her left hand, feeling closer to her father and also to Faolan, having taken up this activity at his suggestion. It eased the ache of missing him, if only for an hour. The next morning, despite the sock, she had an angry purple and magenta bruise on her inner left forearm. She showed it to her mom, who went up to the attic and dug out a couple of leather arm guards they'd missed the first time around. One in a reddish color, and one in brown. The brown one was huge and obviously meant for a man's burly arm.

"The red one was mine," her mother said with a sigh. "You can have it now, sweetie."

August was touched by this gesture, and hugged her mother and thanked her.

October seemed endless without Faolan's return. He sent a letter each week, with August sending back two or three responses each time. If she'd had any worry about seeming too eager or clinging, her joy at sharing and bonding with Faolan far outweighed it.

There were many restless nights in her room, with the moon beaming down on her, that August caressed her body and yearned to be naked with Faolan. At times her ecstasy was so profound, she fell asleep feeling as though he really had been inside her. Sometimes she even worried that when they finally did come together, her imagination would have ruined it for her. Perhaps his touch would be too strange to her. Or he might make a weird face or strange sounds during lovemaking. But her romantic nature made her sure that love could overcome all of these things. She knew that she was absolutely in love with him, and she was just as certain that he must be in love with her. Or at least some aspect of her. Why else would he sign his letters "with love?" Why else would he write to her about coming back as soon as he could, and that he missed her? Even though he was never very forthcoming about what he was doing in Scotland, August got the sense there was some kind of serious family business he was dealing with. She made the effort to not pry him too much for information, choosing instead to trust that he would reveal things to her in the best way possible.

Sorcha was coming out of her haze with the new herb regimen.

August thought she still seemed a bit too placid and detached, but she was definitely more tuned-in to what was going on around her, and more likely to leave the wheelchair parked and move about on her own. Sometimes they carried on talking for an hour or more, and though she didn't always remember the conversation the next day, Sorcha had been able to come up with a few pieces of the puzzle here and there, and August wrote it all down in her journal. More importantly, she could feel Gran warming to her. When she was practicing with her bow, she caught Sorcha at the end of the garden, watching her. And when it was time to hand out Halloween candy, Gran not only helped August set out the bowls, she began telling family stories about Halloweens past, and some of the things that Goose (as she sometimes called August's father) would do to scare everybody. It was the first time August ever heard her grandmother's laugh.

"Gran, why Goose? I'd never heard him called that before."

"Oh, he was a dead-eye with the arrow. We always teased that he'd win the Prize of the Goose." She said it as though August should know what that meant.

"The Goose Prize?"

"No, dear, the Prize of the Goose. He was good enough to be in the Royal Academy of Archers."

"Oh. Okay, Gran." August still didn't understand what she was talking about, but jotted it down in her journal anyway.

Sorcha was exhausted from the excitement of all the little visitors that night, and August helped her into bed. Then she fed Snow, and the two of them practiced howling a bit in the window seat. Later that night, in honor of the anniversary of their meeting, August penned a long and lusty letter to Faolan. She wasn't entirely sure how he would take it, and she wondered if it was even a good idea to put those particular things down on paper, where somebody could one day find them. But time apart from him had not taken the edge off her urgency. Nor could she bottle it up and cork it, for all the sensible reasons. If anything, it seemed to roll over her at times, like a tsunami. It was a force of nature, and she had to let it out.

October 31, 1983

Dearest Faolan,

My sincerest wish is that this letter finds you well and that your troubles may be lessened, even for just for a few moments, while you contemplate the tender things I am writing to you here. Though you've not been specific, I do understand you are having some difficulties while visiting your homeland. Your letters are full of worries, but are careful not to be burdensome. Know that I am sending wishes out to you each night that these troubles right themselves. Know also, that my desire for you has not waned and my urgency, if anything, has only increased. I will be here, waiting, to talk and listen and be whatever my heart can be to yours.

I want to share some things I think of each night, before falling asleep, with your face indelible in my mind's eye.

Since the night we first met I have imagined your mouth on mine—and, I confess, your mouth has been other places on me as well. As mine has been on you. A mutual worship of bodies and souls, caressing, confessing. Your hair has been tangled between my fingers more times than I can count, your head bowed between my breasts, between my thighs. And as I imagine these things ... a tangle of limbs and spirits, of sighs and pressing flesh, we embrace and rock together, and I touch myself as if you were here, touching me.

If we were together, on this, our balmy anniversary night, we would lay down a blanket at the edge of the creek. We'd stretch out, hand in hand, and whisper promises and truths beneath the moon. We would share a glass of wine and begin with slow, soft kisses, inhaling each other, embracing and pressing as close as we could with our clothing still between us.

I would stand and undress for you while you watched. Moonbeams would light my shoulders, my breasts, and I would watch your face as your eyes filled with desire. Oh Faolan—I hope this is something you want! I want to show you my body, and to see yours, and feel your hands caressing me in the glow of a moonlit night. I want to show you my breasts, small though they are, and I believe you would think them beautiful. I want to entice your gaze and feel your desire for me even though I am uncertain of it because of the distance you keep. Could you want my small breasts, my thick thighs, and my large bottom? Could you love how I look ... between my thighs? Is that something I can ask you? I could never bear to ask you these things if you were here with me. If you were even on this continent! I hope you understand, I am being vulnerable right now for you. Naked, emotionally, in a way I realize we can't be physically, now ... maybe never.

Think of my body, naked for you. Ready for you. Think about what you would do to me if you were here now. My knees go weak at the thought of your hands cupping and petting me—my pale, cool flesh pressed into your strong, warm hands. To feel your mouth exploring every hill and valley of my landscape—I am drunk with the want of it all. Dizzy and aching all at the same time. Tingles and gooseflesh. Musk and sweat.

Your smiling eyes that crinkle at the corners would gaze upon my nakedness and your desire would grow long and hard. So many times I have imagined you without your clothes, erect and above me. The long, lean lines of your body tensing and relaxing in rhythm with mine. Pressing against me, pressing into me, until I am shivering with pleasure.

I am writing this letter in my room so that I can lay down and think of you once I've finished it. When I reach my peak I will say your name out loud. Faolan! A name—a song—I have called into the darkness for many months now, and before I knew it, I called you Wolf. After my tensions are released I will hold my pillow close and imagine laying across your chest, tracing the curls of your hair with my fingertips.

You see, we've already made love dozens of times in my room. You just didn't know. Perhaps, some day, we can take a long afternoon alone together, just for tasting each other.

Please take care of yourself and please let me know that my feelings are not one-sided. Don't leave me wondering if my desires are foolish or unwanted.

I hope to see you soon. I miss you.

All My Love,

Red August

It was the most wildly sensual thing she'd ever written, she was sure of it. She worried it was like a bad romance novel, purple as cheap grape bubblegum, but she didn't care. It was as she wanted it to be—too much. She read and re-read the letter, whispering the words across the ocean to him again and again, and she lay back naked across her bed and put her hands on her body as if they were his. Her climax came so quickly it left her dizzy and breathless, and though it was a relief, somehow it only added fuel to her desire. She knew it would be unquenchable until they really were Faolan's hands on her body. Before her fingers had even dried, she added a drop of lavender and vanilla oil perfume and dotted the letter with the mixture of scents on her fingertips, then tucked it into the envelope and sealed it. She pulled on a robe and bounded down the stairs to the mailbox on the porch. August kissed the letter, closed her eyes, and tucked it under the lid.

Once upstairs she washed up, brushed her teeth and then lifted Snow onto her bed. With the dog's sleepy warm body curled up next to her, she soon fell into sleep.

On Saturday morning it was not the sun that woke August but the sound of dishes clattering downstairs. She could smell coffee, maple syrup, bacon and other irresistible scents wafting up from the kitchen. Her first thoughts were queasy wonderings about Faolan, then her father's waffles, and how she wished he were downstairs making breakfast or reading his paper.

She slipped on a tee-shirt and robe, scooped up Snow and shuffled down the stairs, her stomach now awakened. It fluttered with concern whenever she thought of Faolan, and each time it did, she nuzzled into Snow's fluffy neck. With her mother out of town again, she had expected to find Abel at the stove, and was already preparing her thanks, but to her amazement it was Sorcha at the counter, lifting eggs out of the skillet. The old woman looked completely at home, humming a tune that sounded familiar to August, though she couldn't place it.

"Grandmother?"

Sorcha spun around with a smile on her face, spatula held high.

"Good morning little dove! I've just about finished cooking breakfast. Sit down, sit down! How about some eggs, tomatoes, baked beans, bacon and coffee? Oh, and toast of course. Here, I even made tattie scones! How'd ya like that!" Sorcha didn't wait for a reply, she flipped the food onto a plate while putting bread into the toaster. She moved easily through the kitchen, shutting a drawer with her hip and whipping out a dishtowel with a crack.

"Hurry and eat the bacon in case Abel shows up."

"Thank you," was all August could think to say. She wrinkled her nose. "Baked beans? For breakfast?"

"Of course baked beans for breakfast!"

With some hesitation she asked, "How do you feel?"

"Oh darlin' I feel fantastic! As though I were Sleeping Beauty after the prince's kiss."

"Well, that's wonderful, Gran."

Sorcha cast an eye on Snow and knitted her brow. "I don't like dogs. Why do you keep that little beast around? Put it down and eat up!"

August meekly complied, still too stunned to do much else.

"You've got to get some meat on your bones sweetheart. Look at you," Sorcha tutted. Then for the first time in her life August felt her grandmother's warm arms around her as she gave her an affectionate squeeze.

August nibbled at her food at first, though she was soon eating with gusto, all the while regarding Gran and imagining what next to say to her, and wondering what could have brought on such a transformation. She dropped the occasional bacon bit to Snow, who sat alert beside her chair. Sorcha pulled up a chair next to August and buttered a triangle of toast, and proceeded to break her over-easy yolks open with the pointy end. It looked to August as though ten years had melted away from her overnight and her sallow, waxy skin was now glowing and pink.

"This is really good Gran. Hasn't it been quite a while since you cooked?"

"It has." Sorcha munched on crisp bacon and spooned sugar and cream into her coffee. She held the mug under her nose. "This smells glorious. They try at Sunnyvale, but that stuff is watered down grocery brand swill. And look at this bacon—almost black. Fantastic!"

"You certainly managed to pick it right back up again. Not a broken yolk in the lot."

"Honestly dear, you really don't forget how to cook once you've done it enough years. And I missed it. I just lost the will to do it for a while. For a long time, I suppose."

August put on her most serious face and looked into her grandmother's eyes. "Are you okay, Gran?"

Sorcha put down her fork and toast and laid her hands on August's. "Darling girl, I was not okay. Part of me is still not, and never will be. But in these past days it's been harder to retreat into my fortress. And the miraculous part is that I don't want to anymore. At least, not right now." She smiled radiantly. "It's you, lassie. You are the miracle. I thought at first I was seeing ghosts, but I woke up and saw it was you, my own dear little granddaughter, and I had been sleeping away my life without you." She pulled August forward and planted a gentle kiss on her forehead. "Oh, and then last night I dreamed of your grandfather, and he was fit to be tied. I don't believe I ever saw him so mad. He said it broke his heart to watch me leave the world the way I did, but to leave you here alone, and you trying so hard to find me, well that was just selfish and spoiled, he said. He also said I needed to stop being such a bloody bitch to

Abel or he was going to leave my grouchy ass and then I'd be sorry. And he was right! When family needs you, everything else is put aside, and that's all there is to it!"

August blinked. "Wow. Okay then. That's ... wonderful." She put her arms around her grandmother and squeezed, and it felt so good to feel her squeeze back.

"I saw your father last night too. My little Goose. He told me you needed me. He said I would have to tell you all the family stories. Well, when I remember them I will. Oh, Goose. I lost so many years with him." She seemed about to dissolve into sadness again, but waved it off with an impatient arm and scolded herself.

"Oh, enough, Sorcha! Come on, let's eat our breakfast and then go for a walk. I probably won't get far, but I've not been on a good walk in years."

The pair traced a slow circuit around the house, Sorcha pointing out tell-tale signs of the Blue Rook's history whenever she spotted them, and naming all of the plants that were still hanging on in the chill. Then they hiked through the yard to the creek where Sorcha plunked pebbles into the pool by the waterfall, and then back again. August read and Sorcha dozed, and later they made dinner together. August was delighted by her grandmother's tart wit; she imagined she would have been quite a handful in an argument. They avoided big topics. For now, the two of them simply wanted to enjoy each other's long-missed company.

When Sorcha retired to her room August wrote down all that she could remember was said. Then she opened up the small stack of letters from Faolan and re-read them. She penned him a flowery letter full of desire and hope, and, unable to wait for the morning, she trotted downstairs to tuck it into the mailbox. She imagined him opening the letter, and his heart, to her. The night was moonless and the stars scattered like glitter across the sky. The smell of far-off snow from the mountains danced around the old house, and August shivered and went to bed. It was difficult to rest thinking of her love so far away, so she imagined him close, the two of them wrapped around each other in the ether, and she drifted between the starry glitter and the hidden moon into sleep, cradled in his arms.

Tuesday morning, August found Sorcha walking slowly through the back yard, kicking at a pile of leaves under the sharp November sun. She brought coffee to her, Snow bounding at her heels, and they sat at the bistro table under one of the largest trees. The iron mesh seat was cold under her rear, but it warmed quickly. Sorcha was wearing a seafoam-green shawl around her shoulders, holding the mug in both hands. She thanked August and they watched Snow plowing through piles of leaves and dragging around sticks twice her size.

"Why did you have to get a white dog?" Sorcha muttered. "I hate white dogs. I hate all dogs, but white ones in particular." She peered at her granddaughter. "You're going to ask me a lot of questions today," she said, with a hint of resignation. Then looked up, squinting against the sun.

"Why don't you like dogs?" August studied her face and waited patiently as her gran looked away and sipped again.

After a long pause August began again. "I'd like to. Ask you questions, I mean. Besides the one about the dog." She adjusted her chair so that the sun was no longer behind her.

"Well it's a bloody good thing Brigid put something in that tea to keep me happy or I'd tell you to go to hell."

August thought perhaps her grandmother's flinty nature could be a two-edged sword—ready to defend, but also quick to wound.

Once past the flash of hurt, however, she thought about what sort of life made Sorcha so quick-tongued, and what sort of family would have loved her despite it, perhaps even because of it. There was something vulnerable hiding behind that temper, and she spoke thoughtfully. "Grandma, I realize we don't know each other very well, so tell me what you're thinking, okay? I know losing my dad must have been horrible for you. No parent should lose their child."

"It's worse than you can ever imagine. Unbearable, really."

"We have each other, now. We can remember my dad together and keep him alive in our hearts." August felt lighter just thinking of sharing memories of her father to keep his spirit close.

"Oh, child! My heart is a knot of scars. Most of the joy that it's ever known is sliced through with misery and pain. I lost all of my children and my husband." She sighed. "But I know you need this, and I know Bryan, your grandfather, would never have let me wallow in my own self-pity all these years. Ah, you would have loved him. He had such a keen sense of humor. He was a lean and capable man. Handsome as the day is long. And he could outwit just about anybody, but he didn't show it off. Hell, I miss him."

"Do you have any pictures you could show me later? I want to hear all about him." August watched her fidgeting with the edge of her shawl. "Until Brigid told me last month, I didn't even know that Dad had brothers and sisters."

Sorcha looked momentarily horrified. "Indeed he did! My first sons, twins they were. And you never knew them! Oh, child! Fat little beauties, my boys, with pale curls. We named them Tavish and Thomas. Lyrical don't you think?"

August smiled gently and nodded.

"Then my girls came next. First Ceana, with her strawberry hair and freckles. You've never seen a more beautiful child born to a human. Like one of the fairies. Then Blair, ah, she was the feistiest little thing. Quick with a bow and arrow, as well. Took after me, most said—my hair was once a fiery auburn, you know—and she could be a handful. Your father, he was the baby. Those girls looked after him like he was theirs." She laughed, and August laughed with her. "They would dress him up and put him in the pushchair and strut around with proud smiles, showing him off to everybody. Oh, they adored little Goose. I wish you'd had a chance to know them. They surely would have loved you."

"Thank you."

"For what?"

"For talking to me."

"I'll probably regret it. Ah well, life is full of regret, anyway." She watched a squirrel gather some acorns and scamper off. Her face darkened.

"But not only regret? There's a lot of good, too." August prompted.

"I suppose."

The doorbell rang, and though it should have been inaudible from the back yard, Snow woofed an alert, and August caught it too. "I think that's the bell! I'll be back in a bit!" She sprinted to the front door and signed for a small package. As she had hoped, it was from Faolan. She hugged it to herself and ran up to her room with Snow on her heels. She flopped onto her bed, scattering dust into the sunbeams, and ripped open the package.

There was a card under the brown wrapping, taped to the box inside. August ran her fingers over the hand-laid blue-gray paper, and noticed flecks of pale blue flower petals in the fibers.

Red, my darling,

I just received your letter, so full of want and the scent of you. Of course I feel for you, my sweetest, never you worry about that. It is beautiful that you trust me with your confessions. I hold dear each letter you have sent. And this most recent, I admit, inspired a restless night for me as well.

Inside the box you will find a family heirloom meant to bring good luck. The chain was my great-grandmother's and the pendant is decorated with river pearls from the Tay, here in Scotland. The larger pearl is actually one of the biggest ever found in the river. It was once a gift for a loved one who has long since passed away. I'd like you to have it. Wear it for me, please, and I'm sure the charm will bring me safely home. If all goes well I will be returning home on Friday, the 18th. What do you think of having Thanksgiving together?

All My Love,

Faolan

August shook the lid off of the cardboard box and found a pink velvet clamshell jewelry box inside. She opened it, and resting on a satin bed was a pendant that resembled a cluster of gold ivy hanging delicately from the chain, with tiny odd-shaped pearls dotting it, and a large pearl at the bottom. She'd only ever seen pale, smooth, round pearls before—these were cream-colored, almost gold, and a bit lumpy. The pendant was mounted on a filigree bale and strung on a gold chain. She felt like royalty holding such a beautiful, valuable antique in her hand. Knowing that Faolan wanted her to have it made her heart swell.

August jumped up from her bed and set the chain and box down on the dresser. She slipped the keys from around her neck, and peeled off her clothing down to her underwear. She picked up the necklace and turned to face her full-length mirror. She regarded her body in the mirror and imagined what Faolan would think if he could see her standing there in filtered sun rays, hair loose around her shoulders. Would he call her beautiful? She imagined him there fastening the necklace around her throat, as she hooked it into place. Her flesh bumped up and a chill ran through her as the cool weight of the pearls settled on her breastbone. She luxuriated in the moment.

August slipped on tights, Peter Pan boots and her V-necked burgundy jersey dress and went back downstairs, the pearl bumping lightly against her chest as she bounced down the stairs. She went back outside to re-join Sorcha, who had by now taken the entire carafe of coffee outside and nearly emptied it. August sat back down.

"Where on earth have you been? I think I'm done strolling down memory lane today, darlin'. Let's go shopping. I haven't been shopping in too many years to count. I think I'll actually buy some holiday presents this year! Yule and Hogmanay aren't far around the corner, you know." She put a third heaping teaspoon of sugar into her coffee and dumped in what was left of the cream as well. Then she looked up and squinted at August. She dropped her spoon and pushed her cup aside and leaned forward to squint at the necklace. "Where did you get that? Is that what I think it is? It can't be."

"It's a pearl, Gran."

"For God's sake child! I know it's a pearl! A river pearl, too. I mean is that the Conall pearl?"

"You know this necklace?" August felt her stomach flop in alarm.

"Then it is the Conall pearl? I haven't seen it in years, but I know that necklace, yes. It belonged to that son-of-a-bitch Faolan Conall. And what are you doing with it? Take it off!" Sorcha's face was fixed in a stern grimace. She crossed her arms. "Explain, August. What is that thing doing 'round your neck?"

Snow was alerted to the tenseness of the discussion and regarded the two women. She trotted over and sat next to August's chair.

"Um, Gran, I ..." August felt a sting of panic, unsure what to say or think now that she realized her grandmother thought Faolan was a son-of-a-bitch. "Wait. Okay, wait. Before I tell you how I came to have this necklace, you tell me why Fao ... why the person who this belonged to is a son-of-a-bitch."

"I'll tell you why, because his father tried to kill me. Then Faolan killed my little Blair!"

August shot out of her seat. "That's not true!"

Snow stood and gave a little whine at Sorcha, looking back and forth between the two women.

Sorcha pointed an accusing finger at August. "The hell it's not true! And keep that beast back!" Sorcha held her walking stick out in front of her.

August could feel her face getting hot, she gnashed her teeth and flexed her jaw. "Snow, sit!" Snow barked once, then sat.

Sorcha's eyes narrowed and she stood up too, then lifted up the bottom of her sweater, revealing a sinewy tangle of scars on the side of her torso. "It was almost two years before it healed, and it opened up sometimes for years after that. This is the legacy of the Conalls. This is what they are capable of. Now where did you get that bloody necklace?"

August's tone shifted to concern. "What? Oh my god, what?"

She stepped in closer to look at the scars. Sorcha looked away from her granddaughter, but kept the sweater pulled up.

"Looks like some kind of cuts, or gashes." August gently brushed her fingers over the plastic-feeling flesh that rippled and wrinkled across her Gran. August could feel tears welling up. Sorcha pushed her sweater down in irritation and sat back down.

"Animals. Every last one of 'em."

August blinked, not knowing what to say. She sat down and stared at her grandmother and clutched the pearl in her hand.

"What did you mean about Blair? What do you mean he killed her?" Her gut knotted as she forced the question out, even though she was afraid to hear the answer.

"When Banning Conall tried to kill me it set off a terrible battle between the wolves and the hunters. During that battle, Faolan Conall killed my Blair. Your aunt. Your own blood, girl!"

"The man who gave me this necklace is our neighbor. And he is a Conall, but he can't be the one you are thinking of. It's just a coincidence. Mom knows him. She said he's a good man."

"Sylvia ought to know better, damn her. Of course she's always been soft on those ... those ... kind. What are you doin' spendin' time with the likes of a Conall? Don't you know anything? Don't you know your history? Didn't your father tell you?"

"Tell me what? Mom said we come from a family of archers. Brigid said hunters. That's it. What has that got to do with *my* necklace?"

Her grandmother's eyes grew large, then squinted hard and she took August by the shoulder. "August. Listen to me carefully. That's not *your* necklace. And a Conall cannot be trusted. That neighbor of ours murdered your Aunt Blair, I tell you. He murdered her and he moved into that house to stalk and terrorize me because his father didn't finish the job. Those wolves don't want any of our kin to be happy."

"Grandma, this story ... well, look ... I don't mean to be disrespectful, but it's so far-fetched."

"You think I don't know that? Why the hell do you think I went to sleep for so long?"

Family feud or not, August couldn't believe that Faolan could kill anybody. It crossed her mind that Sorcha must be having some kind of breakdown or mixed memory from her new medicinal treatment. Brigid needed to adjust her herbs. She'd have her come out and assess the situation.

How could all of these people have been killed and she'd never heard about it? Battles and archers and wolves and hunters? What does it all mean? And why does Sorcha dislike sweet little Snow? Maybe she needed stories about monsters to cope with all of her loss. But why would she recognize the necklace? It had to be a coincidence.

"Grandma, I'm sorry this necklace is upsetting you. I'll take it off for now, but we're going to have to talk about this some more, later. Let's just have some lunch and I'll read some more Jane Austen to you. How's that sound?" August lifted the chain over her head and dropped the necklace down into her bra.

Snow whined and crawled on her belly across the gap between the chairs to Sorcha's feet. She nudged the old woman's ankles and rolled onto her back, exposing her belly and panting.

"Oh, you bloody beast," Sorcha fumed. She got up and went into the house and retreated into her room. August cleared the cups, washed the dishes and fed Snow while she tried to make sense of all the things her grandmother had said. She decided she'd better call Brigid.

From the phone extension upstairs, August explained to Brigid what Sorcha had told her and asked about herbal adjustments. What Brigid gave her instead was a rushed and enigmatic request to discuss the matter at the shop the next day. When August hung up, the phone rang almost in her hand. It was her mother.

"Hi sweetie! I just wanted to check in with you. Also, I have some great news!"

"Wow. Hi mom. You sound really happy. What's the exciting news?" August picked up a pen and wrote "Mom - Tuesday" on the pad by the phone.

"First, how is Sorcha?"

How does she always know to ask about exactly what is on my mind? marveled August.

"Um, she's good. In fact, she's had a change in medication and now she's way more awake. She actually made me breakfast a couple of times. With baked beans … for breakfast." August began doodling a flower.

"Well that's kind of amazing."

"She does keep telling me some crazy stories, though."

"Oh yes, she's full of those."

August teetered on the edge of telling her mother what her grandmother and Brigid had told her about the Archers and the Conalls and Blair. And she wanted to recount the conversation about Brigid being over a hundred years old and how she was from a race called hunters, which her mother must know, and how Iseabail was her great-grandmother. In fact it only just then occurred to her that her mother must know all of that stuff. Why wouldn't her mother want to tell her these things herself? She wanted her mother to be home and to hug her and clear up all of the misunderstandings. But Sylvia sounded too happy and August didn't want to worry her about what might unfold while she was away. "So, Mom, what's this great news?" Her flower doodle began sprouting a tree from one of its leaves.

"Well, I've been offered a traveling RN position. I would be traveling all over the country and they even have stint for me in Edinburgh."

August put down her pen. "Wow. Mom—I don't know what to say. What about the house? What about me and Gran?" *What about Faolan?* A prickling feeling rose at the back of her neck.

"Oh, sweetie," her mother laughed. "You can take care of the house and it sounds like you're managing fine with your gran. It's just for a six-month run and I will be home between assignments. You sound worried. Why do you sound worried?"

"I guess I'm just feeling like I've barely had time to adjust here and things are changing again."

"Nothing is changing except I'll be traveling. You're a capable girl ... I mean woman, you're a capable woman. You are managing fine. You've got Brigid and Abel. And you can visit, if you want. I think you'd be fine. Don't you think?" There was an edge in her voice. August understood that, despite her mother being a competent professional, she was still very fragile and needed August to be on board with this. And though August hated the idea of her mom being so far away, it certainly seemed that she maybe needed it. So if August could help by letting her mom go, then she was going to try. But she didn't have to be happy about it.

"Mom, I think if it will make you happy, you should do it. I'm not going anywhere. The house isn't going anywhere. But I would like to talk to you about some other things when you have more time." August slouched against the wall. She was happy for her mother, but she could feel a lump in her throat and the sting of tears.

"I think it really is for the best, sweetie."

For you, you mean, August thought, suddenly feeling a burn of agitation at her mother's selfishness. "Yep," she replied flatly, half hoping her mother would notice her irritation.

"I'll be home the day before Thanksgiving and we'll spend some time together and talk about it. Then, I have to be off by the second week in December. Hey! I'll be in Edinburgh for Christmas and Hogmanay! Sweetie, do you want to come to Edinburgh for the holidays?" Sylvia sounded like a teenager on the verge of discovering the world, all hyped up and way too cheerful, rather than a widow trying to run away from her sadness. Or maybe it was a combination of both. August understood all of that, even if she felt a bit abandoned. The idea of Edinburgh during the winter holidays did sound exciting, but she had too much here she was in the middle of connecting to. Faolan would only have been back a few weeks. And even though things might never really turn into a romance with him, she still wanted to be near him. And then there was Sorcha. She didn't think she should leave Sorcha just now, after practically forcing her to open up a lot of old wounds.

"Who'd take care of Gran?"

"I guess she's not well enough to travel, huh? I'm sorry, honey."

"It's okay. You go, enjoy the holidays and Edinburgh and we'll have a cozy Christmas here. You can buy me something awesome and send it, okay? None of that crappy touristy stuff. Okay, maybe one bit of crappy touristy stuff."

Her mother laughed, and she did, too.

There was a short pause on the other end of the phone. "Thank you sweetheart. Let's look forward to Thanksgiving together at least. Let's make a real feast of it, okay?"

"Yeah, let's do that. Oh, and Mom?"

"Yes?"

"I don't mind it so much if you call me 'girl' most of the time. At least when it's just family."

"Okay sweetheart."

"See ya soon?"

"Yup! Bye. I love you August!"

"Love you too, Mom. Bye."

As she hung up, August realized that maybe the best thing to do would be to write all of the troubling things down in a letter. Then she could say it all quickly and her mom could read it when she had time to think about it and respond.

Faolan would be returning home next week, and her mother the week after. Then she thought about how violently Sorcha hated the Conalls. She had imagined Faolan was going to be more welcome at the Rook, and now everything was in doubt. She pulled the necklace out of her shirt and gently rubbed it with her thumb. How could such a beautiful thing be at the center of so much anger and hate? She had to find out what was at the root of Sorcha's ill will and fix it.

Abel came over that night and made a lovely dinner, but despite his attempts to be charming and make conversation, Sorcha was in a foul mood and having none of it. At least in front of August. She ate very little and then headed off to her room in a huff. He followed her, and August caught a glimpse of them hugging and could hear Sorcha making cooing sounds while in his arms.

When Abel came out of the room August busied herself with clearing the table and pretended like she hadn't noticed anything.

"That mac and cheese was amazing as usual. You've got to

teach me how to make it," she said in a cheery tone.

"Thanks. It's a pretty easy recipe." His tone was somber as he loaded the dishes into soapy water.

"I have a feeling it will always taste better when you make it." She gently patted his shoulder and then grabbed a dishtowel. "I'm sorry she's so mad, Abel. I'm afraid it's my fault."

"It's not really your fault." There was a long pause. August didn't know what to say.

"Do you know about physical therapy?" he asked, seemingly out of the blue.

August shrugged and dried a dish. "Well ... yeah. Mom's a nurse. I know what it is."

"Do you know that it's very painful? You have to stretch your hurt parts, make them flexible, make them strong," he said, without looking up from his washing.

"Okay." August stopped her work and put an elbow on the counter, focusing her attention on him.

He continued slipping dishes into the rack with a steady rhythm, plunk, plunk, plunk. August noticed again how Abel favored his right hand, to the point that his left arm was practically just hanging there. He stopped and awkwardly dried his hands, the towel low, she supposed so he wouldn't have to lift his left arm too high. He fixed her with a look after he hung it on the hook by the sink.

"Think of what Sorcha is going through as physical therapy for her heart and soul. She's got a lot of healing to do now that she's aware of her surroundings again, and I'm afraid even at her best she's never been known for her manners."

August sighed. "Why do you ... well, I mean ... what makes you stay around, Abel? It's not like she's sweet to you."

"It's a long story. Complicated one too. But what it comes to is that I love her. And, I owe her. You're gettin' a very one-dimensional view of your grandmother. She's smart as a whip, and she has a big loving heart. She is actually sweet to me in private, but it's like she has to put on her armor when anybody else is around. I already had feelings for her before your granddaddy died, but I was never going to interfere ... you understand? But, I was kind of hoping her heart would heal and maybe I could ask her to marry me." He regarded her out of the corner of his eye, testing the temperature of his remark.

August smiled and nodded, afraid to speak and interrupt this rush of information.

"I've spent a little time with some other ladies over the years she's been at Sunnyvale, but nothin' took. It was like ... like I was already attached to her, the way a man is. Bonded, you could say. Her being sick, and being turned in on herself, didn't mean I stopped lovin' her, so I took it as my duty to keep on, the way a husband does. Sickness and health. I know she'd have done the same for me."

"That's ... it's very sweet. I do wonder, Abel, where do you live?"

"Nearby. Only about a block from the nursing home. It's a small place, but I like it that way because it gives me more time to devote to Sorcha and the Rook, which really feels more like home than my own place does."

"It's hard to get a feel for family around this big house. There aren't any photos up, for starters."

"The photos were too much of a reminder for your gran. Brigid and I took them all down for her."

August put down the towel and hugged him.

"What was that for?" he asked.

"For being totally awesome," she said and dabbed her eyes with the neck of her tee-shirt. With his right arm he returned her embrace.

Impulsively she said, "Can I ask ... what's wrong with your arm?"

Then she felt it again—that same hesitation, as though Abel were trying not to tell her something, but unable to lie. "It acts up in the colder months. I got maimed some years ago. That plus getting older, it's just catching up with me is all."

"Would you like something for the pain? Can I get you a heating pad maybe?"

He kindly waved away her concern with his good arm and asked, "What set Sorcha off today?"

"A pearl."

"Come again?"

"Look, here." August pulled the necklace out from inside of her shirt, revealing the pearl and nestling it in her palm.

Abel's brow furrowed and he bit the corner of his lip. He let out a deep sigh. "What are you doing with that?"

"Then you know what it is, too?"

"I do."

"If I tell you, you can't get all mad at me like Gran." She held her breath, and Abel nodded. "Faolan sent this to me from Scotland. It's one of his family heirlooms."

He looked grim and it made her stomach tighten.

"I see," he said after a thin-lipped pause.

"I think ... we're in love." It was the first time she'd said it out loud, and her throat tightened with the declaration. "He's also the one who gave me Snow."

Now Abel looked worried and August wondered if she was ever going to get off of this emotional roller coaster. He glanced over his shoulder towards Sorcha's bedroom door and took August by the elbow and nudged her toward the living room. He lowered his voice and said, "August, your grandmother has seen a lot of bad things. Some of those bad things are directly related to the family who owned that pearl."

"So it's true, then? That there is some kind of feud between the Conalls and the Archers? Wow, that sounded weirder than I expected it to."

"It's true."

August was crestfallen. "What am I supposed to do? Faolan couldn't have had anything to do with that. He wouldn't." August was searching Abel's face for any hint of answers.

"I'm afraid that he did. But not the way Sorcha thinks he did. Faolan's not bad, he's just caught in the middle of a lot of hate and history."

"Abel, are you telling me that you know about these crazy stories my gran has been telling me about dogs and killings?"

"Wolves. Yes, I know these things. And I know your man Faolan, too. But I'm thinking maybe you don't know him so well. It's no accident he's your neighbor."

"What does *that* mean?"

"I think it's better if you talk to Faolan about that."

"Oh my god! Seriously? Why can't—" Her voice rose and Abel signaled her to quiet it down. "Why can't anybody just give me a straight story?" she rasped, gesturing wildly. What is with all the 'go ask so-and-so' stuff? It feels really weird to be upset with you, but I can't help it! I'm about to lose it."

Abel was a bit taken aback by August's sudden flash of anger, and he turned his head and regarded her from the corner of his eye.

"I'm sorry. I'm just so frustrated." She was choking a bit on the emotions now.

His stance softened. "I understand. Maybe try takin' a deep breath. Like this. Now, slowly breathe in, and hold it, then slowly breathe out. It tricks the body into thinking you're calm."

August did feel some of the tension leave her. "I just want somebody to sit down and tell me the whole story. I have to keep piecing things together, but I can't upset this person, and I can't ask that person. I've been through a lot, too. I mean, it's nothing like what Gran has been through, but it's my family and I love them. It's like everybody's got this big secret and I'm the only one who's not in on it. How is that supposed to make me feel, being left to twist in the wind like that?"

Abel let out a long sigh. "I hear you, Miss August, I do. You know, you're a lot more like your grandmother than you might think. When does Faolan get back in town?"

"Next Friday."

Abel took another deep breath and leaned in. "Alright, I'll tell you what—I will tell you everything once he's back in town. If you arrange for us to meet at his house, and let him know that you want to know everything. If he agrees, then I will meet you both there and we'll talk. I reckon Brigid ought to come, too."

Ten days sounded like an eternity to August. But what choice did she have? She also wasn't sure she could get a letter to Faolan and have an answer back in time. The only way to find out if he would agree was to call him. She got a knot in her stomach just thinking about it, both from excitement at the thought of hearing his voice, and from nerves that some things might come to light she really didn't want to know.

August nodded. "Okay. I'll call him and let you know what he says. And I'll tell Brigid about it tomorrow."

Abel nodded and put his hand on her back and gave it a rub. "Good. I'm going to head home now. I have a lot of thoughts to gather myself. I recommend you don't wear that necklace around your grandmother and don't tell her about you and Faolan just yet."

"I think she's onto us, but I will avoid the subject." She smiled and inhaled deeply and held her breath for a moment. "Thanks, Abel."

She saw him to the door and gave him another hug. At least he had given her something, some reassurance that Faolan wasn't the monster that Gran imagined. But August was not about to put away the necklace that he had entrusted her with—it was practically her duty to wear the charm that would bring him home safely.

She went upstairs, changed from her dress to a sweatshirt. She paused to look at the necklace in the mirror again. Then she kissed the pearl and dropped it into her top, hiding it completely. Sorcha would never have to see it—if she even planned on coming out of her room again for the rest of the night. August dug through the letters to find the one with the phone number. They'd only talked briefly on the phone, once. It was impractical with the time difference and the inability to know the other's schedule and the unreliable long distance that the little town he was in seemed to have. Besides, there was something romantic about writing letters and sending thoughts—and scents—through the mail.

August closed her door and dialed the number, but all she got was a fast busy sound. She then called the operator for assistance. After several tries, the call went through but would go dead. She began to pace, feeling very restless. She took Snow outside and they walked around the property. At one point August thought she caught sight of a figure at the edge of the property near the tree line, and she caught a whiff of something dank. Snow did growl, but nothing was there when she inspected the area. Probably a deer or something, she figured. August and Snow played some fetch before closing up for the night. Sorcha's light was off and the house felt very lonely. She needed to do something to keep her mind busy, so she dug up some of her grandmother's cookbooks and started writing down Thanksgiving recipes. Then she thought of her father telling her that the way to make things happen was to act as if they were going to. She got out her stationary supplies and listed everybody she wanted to have around the table:

Sylvia

Sorcha

Abel

Brigid

Lainy

Faolan

After thinking about it for a few moments, she also wrote, "Evan." She couldn't bear to leave him out. She folded paper into place cards, wrote their names in pretty script, and drew fall leaves and pumpkins with colored pencils.

She sighed. This would be a very interesting holiday.

~~Faolan's Return~~

On Wednesday August couldn't resist trying to call Faolan a couple more times, with the same results. She decided it was too late to write a letter, so she just paced and worried over it.

She called Brigid to ask if she could skip work, and spent Wednesday and Thursday trying to cheer up Gran. It seemed to be working, a little. August even caught her throwing a stick for Snow, and she smiled as she watched the pup wiggle and bound with excitement. This was a good sign. Maybe things would turn out okay. After two more tries on Thursday to reach Faolan by phone, she gave up on the idea. Brigid stopped by with some more herbs, and a faux complaint about things falling apart at the shop for a lack of help. She also suggested that August try adding a little nip of Scotch to Gran's coffee in the morning, and give her a little warm milk and Scotch at night.

August balked at the idea of giving alcohol as medicine, but Brigid just clucked at her.

"I suppose givin' her pills is the answer? I'll have you know there's a fine tradition for using spirits as tonic. And y' don't need a prescription for whiskey, my girl. All things in balance."

"I get it. Doctor's orders. Are you coming to Faolan's on Saturday?"

"I am. And you'd better be ready for quite a tale, assuming he's ready to tell it." She raised her eyebrows as if waiting for a response.

"He will be." *Why wouldn't he?*

August spent the following week writing lists of questions and clues in her journal. Sorcha at least pretended to forget about the pearl and focused most of her energy on organizing old recipes, talking to Abel about his daughters and what they were up to (running the family business, and raising children), and flipping through family photo albums, until she'd get emotional and tuck them away.

The following Friday morning August woke to Snow licking her face before the sun was even up. Her first thoughts were of Faolan's arrival and she was filled with a confusing sense of both joy and dread. *Boy do I need some therapy*, she thought. *Dead father, crazy grandmother, absent mother, distant boyfriend with a mysterious past, attempted rape, murdered ancestors, random dog attacks, and a boss who claims to be over a hundred years. Yup, definitely need some therapy.* She'd have to shelf that for now, though. Who was she going to tell this to, anyway?

August threw on some comfy jeans and a cozy clinging sweater, and peeked out of the windows trying to see if there was any commotion at Faolan's. It looked quiet, but it was hard to tell from this far away. The pearl shifted on her breastbone, safely hidden under her top. She quickly made up a breakfast of French toast, sausage and coffee and took it outside to where Sorcha was sitting with Snow, the pair of them facing out towards the property and the tree line by the barn.

"Thank you, darlin'," Sorcha greeted her cheerfully. She picked up the mug and cupped it in her hands.

"It's pretty cold out here Gran. You sure you don't want to go inside?" She watched Sorcha sip at her coffee and drop her other hand down to rub one of Snow's ears. The dog, now several inches taller than a month ago, leaned in with a small groan of satisfaction.

"I love the chill," she finally said. "Reminds me of home."

"I need to go help Brigid for a few hours," August announced, and wondered if her grandmother could see through her ruse. She had given Faolan's home phone a try, but there had been no answer. She was somewhat concerned he might turn up on her porch, and she didn't want a big upset with her grandmother at this point, so she figured it was better to wait for him at his place. She also couldn't wait to see him, but wanted to be cool about it. She knew he was expected home in the late morning, but that was it.

"Do you need anything before I go?"

Sorcha set down the mug and twisted around in her seat. "Well, I don't know what. Abel is coming over later to make us lunch. I told him I was feeling homesick and he teased that if I kept it up he'd make me haggis." She laughed, as lighthearted as August had seen her. "In truth I think he's planning to make potato soup. That man is as good a cook as he is a gardener."

"He does seem to have a way with—"

"Did you know that he has degrees in horticulture and pharmacology?"

"No, I—"

"He went to Howard University. You know, in D.C. That's how we met. Well, not exactly. That's how he and Brigid met. Meeting me came a bit later, you know. My goodness this coffee is so strong—not that that's a bad thing, dear. Good and strong. I enjoy good strong coffee. Thanks for the nip, too." Sorcha winked a twinkling eye at August and gently poked her with her elbow.

"Brigid said you would enjoy that. Well, I'm going to head off. Save some soup for me! I'll be back in a couple of hours. I'm just going to take my bike." August turned to leave as her grandmother settled back into her chair, facing the other direction.

"August!"

She halted in her tracks, her heart gave a few hard thuds. "Yes, Gran?"

"I love you, child."

August was so startled she hardly knew what to say. "Well, I ... I love you, too, Gran."

August turned to come back towards her but Sorcha held up a hand. "Don't make a fuss! Go on now." She picked her mug up again and reached back down to rub Snow's ear.

August put on a red knit cap that Sorcha had just made her a few days before, picked up her bike and pedaled up the road and around the curve, to the long unpaved drive that led to Faolan's house. She got excited when she saw that his vintage sports car—a dark green convertible that said "Tiger" on the fender—was parked there next to his big black truck.

She hopped off her bike and knocked on the door. No answer. She went around the house twice and when it was obvious nobody was home she sat on the front step, jiggling nervous legs and wondering how the day was going to play out. It wasn't long before she saw dust plumes as a taxi made its way up to the house.

August shot up and her heart pounded and her stomach flopped. She pulled the pearl necklace out and laid it over top of her sweater. She kept shifting her weight from foot to foot, and generally felt like she would jump right out of her skin.

The taxi pulled alongside the front step and the driver got out and rounded the car to the trunk to retrieve the luggage. There was a reflection of sky and trees on the windows and she couldn't see into it. She clasped her hands together and held her breath as the rear door of the cab opened and Faolan stepped out.

He stepped toward her and she closed the gap quickly and threw her arms around him. When she leaned back to look at his face, she felt like her whole body was smiling at him, and he beamed back. His arms were still tight around her as she reached up and touched the crinkles at the corners of his eyes.

The driver cleared his throat. "That's thirty-six bucks."

Faolan let go of her reluctantly and fished out his wallet. He held out a fifty to the man. "Keep the rest."

"Thanks, mister. Good day to ya."

"Yes, good day indeed," he said, smiling down at August. She was already back in his arms as the taxi started down the drive.

"You look ... amazing, Red," he said, his voice husky and low, and she felt it reverberate in his chest. Every part of her skin was tingling. Each place he touched her sent little shocks through her system. "You sure are a sight for sore eyes."

She could feel his energy swelling toward her. This was finally the moment. It was going to happen, their first real, intentional kiss. No excuses or accidents. No apologies. He tilted his head down to her and she pushed up on her toes, and their lips met. His arms were wrapped around her and she melted into him. His mouth was hot and his skin smelled like spice. She felt at home in his arms. Their tongues tasted and explored for a long while, their bodies pressed and swaying together on the front patio, enshrouded by evergreens in an impromptu bower. The chilly air bumped up their flesh but did not make them cold.

Faolan scooped August up into his arms and took her into the house. He took her to the library and set her down on the familiar velvet couch, where she curled her legs up behind her. He knelt by her side, stroked stray hairs away from her face and looked into her eyes. She searched his face and dissolved into his touch.

"I wore your necklace." She grasped it and displayed it in her fingertips. He smiled gently.

"It worked. Here I am, safe and sound." He touched the pearl with his finger and rested it there on the warm orb and a memory flashed behind his eyes. "I'll have to tell you the story behind it, some time."

"I'd like that. And ... that sort of brings me to something."

He regarded her with a hint of concern on his brow.

"I'm supposed to arrange a conversation."

"Oh? What kind of conversation?" He seemed unruffled as he continued to stroke her hair, and gave her a kiss on her forehead.

"I tried calling you. I tried a bunch of times. Why didn't your phone number work? I was so frustrated." She recognized the sound of her own whining—*not very attractive*, she thought.

"I told ya, lass, it's a tiny town on an old piece of land. I'm afraid the phones are rather fickle. I should have called and checked in again. I'm sorry." Genuine, as always.

"It's okay. I just really wanted to set it up. It's a meeting. Abel and Brigid say they will tell me all I want to know about my grandmother and my family history if I can arrange a meeting here, tomorrow, with you."

Faolan's hands paused and he leaned away.

"What? What's wrong?" August swung her feet around to the floor and took his hands, which were now hanging stiffly at his sides.

"August, I don't know if that's such a good idea." He gently took his hands back, stood and began to pace. "I don't know if we're ready for that yet."

"What do you mean, ready? Why not? They said you had to agree to it. Please agree to it."

He stopped and faced her. "You don't know what you're asking. There are things you can't un-hear once you've heard them."

August stood, her heart beating faster. "You're scaring me. Why shouldn't I know things?" She stepped closer to him and put her hands on his chest. "Faolan, I know there's been trouble between our families. There is nothing you can tell me that I won't understand. There is nothing you have done that I can't forgive you for." She thought of Blair and knew it had to be a misunderstanding.

He took her hands between his, his expression softened and he kissed her fingertips. With a resigned tone he said, "You're right. I guess we can't really move forward if you don't know what we're dragging behind us. I knew we'd have to talk about it. But for now, can we just forget all of that and have a few moments of peace?"

She nodded and nestled against his chest. "My grandmother thinks I'm out running errands. I have to get back soon." She burrowed into him, trying to make herself as small as possible.

"Your grandmother's at the house? With your mother?"

"No, Mom's still gone, but she'll be back soon. I didn't fill in all the details in my letters. Brigid had been giving my grandmother a tea to help her forget ... though, I guess you know a lot of that stuff. Anyway, she changed it for a new tea that sort of ... well, it woke her up again. She's been with me pretty much since you left."

"I'm glad to hear she's feeling better. What has she said to you?"

"Oh, all kinds of stuff. We've talked about my grandfather and my dad and recipes and books. She told me about my aunts and uncles being killed ..." She paused here for a moment and held her breath.

"She told you that? You didn't already know?"

"Nope. And she showed me this big scar on her torso where something cut her all up. Also, she really didn't like Snow at first, but they have been thick as thieves lately. Gran pretends like she doesn't like her, but she's always sneaking her sausage and rubbing her ears."

"Is that all?"

August untucked from him and looked at his face. "Is that all?"

"I just wondered if she gave you any details. Or had anything to say about anybody else."

"Well, as a matter of fact she got upset when she saw the

necklace you gave me."

He shook some thought away. "Let's save that for tomorrow, too." He sat down again at the corner of the sofa, inviting her to sit beside him. "How about you tell me about how Snow is doing and what sorts of things you're going to cook up from your grandmother's recipe books? And I think you owe me a sandwich," he teased.

August snuggled in next to him under his arm. She apprised Faolan of Snow's adventures and the pup's transition from chubby teddy bear to leggy runner. She asked him about helping her practice her driving and rattled off a list of the foods she'd learned to make.

"I nearly forgot," Faolan piped up. "I've brought something I think you'll like." He reached into his bag and pulled out a small flat box. Inside was a finely tooled green leather book. "I had it made. It's a journal, for the both of us. We both can write in it, to each other, for each other. Or press things into it, or write poems or drawings, whatever means something to us."

August was speechless. She took the journal and examined it, feeling the buttery soft doeskin cover, tracing her finger over the knotwork edges. The leather was rubbed to a shine in some spots. A flap wrapped around the end of the pages and the whole thing had a length of thong that wrapped around the book and fastened to a copper button with some writing. August squinted and she could just make out "Perth Leatherworks" stamped onto it in tiny letters. *For us,* he'd said. Which meant they were real, the two of them, together.

"It's beautiful," she finally managed after a hard swallow. "Can we write something in it right now?"

"Of course. Let me get a pen." He went over to the desk and set out a long stem of ebony and gold and opened a crystal inkwell. "You'll want to come over here," he winked. "It's easier to use the ink that way."

August rounded the monstrous desk. She settled into the writing chair, the chilly buttoned leather creaked under her bottom, but soon warmed to her body. But now the thought of an empty book and a strange pen seemed daunting.

"I've never used this kind of pen before," she confessed, feeling like a child.

If Faolan thought this made her less womanly, he didn't give a hint of it. "Here, practice on a sheet of paper, first. You'll figure it out soon enough," he reassured her. And he was right. The ink seemed to flow from her hand, as it made graceful loops and crosses. The pen made her handwriting look beautiful and old-fashioned.

She opened the journal to the first page and wrote:

The Story of Faolan and August
Once upon a time there was a girl named Red who walked through the woods from her Grandmother's house and met a Wolf...

"An auspicious beginning, Red." He kissed her again on her forehead. She started to close the book but he quickly caught the cover. "No, you have to let it dry first. You can blot it with a tissue if you're in a hurry, but it's best just to give it a moment."

She flushed, feeling utterly unsophisticated. "Guess I'm not used to fancy pens."

He looked into her eyes and laid a hand on her cheek. "Na don't trouble yourself, darlin', we all have things to learn. I don't mind teaching you. You'll teach me things, too."

He stroked and petted her back with his warm hand, and she leaned into his touch. There was nothing more she wanted to do at that moment than take her clothes off and watch him take off his, but she knew the timing wasn't right, and besides, she had to get back to the house and check on Sorcha.

She stood and turned to him. "I have to go look in on Gran. But I would love for you to hold me, for a few minutes. On the couch, maybe?"

He took her hands in his and gave her a tender kiss. "Come," he said, and led her to it, sitting down in the corner and pulling her into his lap. She curled up against him like a kitten, her arms around him and her face buried in his neck.

"You're spoiling me with all of these presents. This is probably going to sound silly, but I love how you got *us* a present ... like we belong. I feel like I belong with you." She lifted her head again and looked into his eyes, and her desire to taste his kisses filled her so completely that she herself became the kiss she pressed to his lips, melting against his body and pouring her whole heart into him through her lips and her tongue and her breath. And she felt him respond, felt the electricity moving through his body, felt his muscles tightening around her. His hips began to move and stir beneath her bottom as he grew hard against her.

"Red," he gasped at last, "if you're off to see your grandmother, I think you'd better do it now."

She wanted to straddle him there on the couch, right that moment. She wanted to feel his hands moving over her body, wanted to feel them take possession of her, her breasts, her thighs, her hips. She wanted to feel them slipping up under her sweater and then into her jeans, caressing the swells of her thighs until his fingers met the cleft of her mound and eased her desire. But she did need to go and she didn't want to keep trying to entice him when he was trying hard to develop the other parts of their relationship, ahead of the calls of their bodies. She groaned as she imagined his touch, though it turned into a small sob of bitter disappointment. Of course he was right.

She looked into his rough, beautiful face, and bumped her forehead against his with a sigh. "Dammit." She gave a little frown.

"I know. In time." He held her face and nodded until she did, too.

"I'll see you tomorrow." She said it almost like a question.

"Of course."

She stood up, and so did he, with an awkward jiggle of his leg to set things straight. They both laughed. She could barely walk herself, her gait a bit lopsided as though her underwear were on crooked.

She could feel the words she wanted to say rise up in her, that urgency nipping hard at her. But she was afraid. If she said them and he didn't say them back, then what? She'd already said it in letters. And so had he. But that was different, wasn't it?

"I love you," she blurted, unable to stop it, though it barely came out in a squeak.

"I'm sorry, what, lass?"

"Oh, nothing ... I was just saying I can't wait to see you. You know, again ... soon."

"I can't wait to see you, too." He gave her a final squeeze and she headed out the door.

Her heart soared. She felt like the starry universe itself were blessing her, and she couldn't stop grinning. She imagined even her father would have approved of this gentle, wise, book-loving man. She threw her arms over his shoulders and gave him one last joyful kiss and dashed outside. When she hopped on her bike she felt the fullness of her womanhood and beauty gliding through the trees and under the sky. "I love you Faolan!" she shouted into the sky. Her heart was full of joy and wonder, and the sun washed her with hope as she pedaled back to the Rook.

Faolan watched her go, her long dark hair waving behind her and her heart-shaped bottom wiggling as she pedaled. He took in the vision of joy and beauty that she was, and stood there for a long while after she was gone, wondering how she would feel about him after tomorrow, once she knew who he really was. Wondering if he even had the right to love her. Too late for that, he sighed to himself. He already did.

Once back home August tucked the pearl back inside of her sweater and found Sorcha in the corner of the porch, reading a book with Snow at her feet. The music from one of her collection of Celtic albums was drifting through the open window. If she had any suspicions about where August had been, she didn't let on.

"Did you help Brigid, then?"

"I did, Gran." She walked over and gave her a half squeeze.

"You certainly seem cheerful today," she said, barely looking up from her book.

"Hey, you want to come with me while I practice with my bow?"

Sorcha snapped her book shut and hopped onto her feet, "I thought you'd never ask!"

That afternoon they walked out to the archery set-up. Sorcha didn't even need her cane anymore because of her daily circuits around the property with Snow. She watched August shoot and made suggestions about her form and talked about Goose while August hit bullseye after bullseye. At one point Sorcha did go off on a tangent about how some relationships are unnatural. August was kind of shocked, since she'd never sensed any bigotry in her family and while she cleaned up her equipment and put it away she asked, "What did you mean, Gran, about unnatural relationships?"

"I just mean some relationships are wrong—goes against nature is all."

"I know you can't mean ... you don't mean black ... what I'm trying to say is that I know you're not a racist."

Sorcha turned and looked at her as though she'd just said the most ridiculous thing in the world.

"What on Earth—*no,* I'm not a racist, child!"

August was feeling at a loss.

"Gran, do you mean gay people?"

"Oh heavens me, no! That's perfectly human."

August wrote the comment off to a long day. For having been asleep so long, Sorcha had been doing a lot. Sometimes her thinking was so crystalline that August would forget she ever was impaired.

"Unnatural," Sorcha said again and then pulled a knife out that had been hidden somewhere in her clothing and threw it at the bale, hitting it, though not dead center, but damned near. "Still got it!" the old woman boasted and walked over to pull the knife out of the hay and tuck it back away.

August stood there with her mouth hanging open.

"Close your mouth, darlin', you'll let in the flies!" she cackled and they walked back to the house, Snow trotting behind them.

Sorcha knew something was going on when neither Abel nor Brigid were available for a visit the next morning, particularly after August threw on her cloak and left with an excuse of running errands. The old woman decided not to pry, even if she could feel tension in the air, hidden beneath a layer of uncomfortable smiles. Whatever it was, she had had enough of secrets and she wanted no part of it; instead she took a moment after her medicinal tea to pray to her ancestors and to the trees and stars that everything would turn out for the highest good of all concerned.

Abel and Brigid arrived at Faolan's home with platters of food and found August already there, and looking a bit nervous. Faolan too seemed to be on edge, but they set out coffee and tea and sweet rolls as though they were about to have a pleasant little tea party. The four of them sipped and stared at each other for several minutes, until Brigid finally broke through the din of clinking saucers. "Well, we might as well get to it."

Faolan looked as though she had announced his doom, but they all set their cups down and he led them to the library where he'd laid out a number of things. One of them was a large leather-bound book, tooled with a scene of a wolf hunted by a figure in a cloak. The scene on the cover reminded August of the transom over the front door of the Rook. There were also some tincture bottles and herbs in a ceramic bowl, which looked like the one Faolan had been using the night they met. There was a box with a collection of odd items, including smashed bits of silver, a large claw on a leather thong, and some antique coins, as well as a stack of ancient letters and photos and a lock of strawberry blonde hair tied with a faded green ribbon. Propped up behind the box was a large, dusty, cobweb-covered painting of an animal, a werewolf, with shining white fur. It looked like a movie prop from something that Vincent Price would be in, or an episode of *Night Gallery*.

"What *is* all this? Looks like Halloween decorations, most of it." August was somewhat amused as she fingered the items in the box, touching the claw necklace and examining the hair and its pale orangy-pink hue. She ran the palm of her hand over the cover of the embossed leather book, and swept away a web from the frame of the painting, before dusting her hands off and looking up at the three of them. They were all standing in a row, staring back.

Brigid's fingers where dancing together in front of her stomach and she swallowed hard and looked to Faolan. Abel examined the floor for a moment and scratched behind his ear and then also fixed his gaze on Faolan.

"This is to help us tell you the story of my past ... and yours, too." Faolan looked at August intently and waited for a response.

"Um ... okay. So, tell me." She arched her eyebrows high and turned up a palm, *what are you waiting for*? But they were being so weird she started to feel uneasy again.

"It might be ... difficult ... to, well ... to accept some of what I've got to tell you, unless I show you something first," Faolan said, shifting his weight a bit.

Now August's brow furrowed and she waved a hand in the direction of the collection of oddities. "This isn't what you have to show me?"

"There's more. But ... I just wanted to warn you that it might scare you."

She straightened and her face was awash in both concern and rapt attention.

"Should I be scared?" She searched their faces for some hint at what the mystery could be. She certainly felt safe with this group, and in this house. Though it did occur to her that neither her grandmother nor her mother knew where she was—nobody but these three.

"Well, no ... not exactly. You're safe. I promise you're safe. But there's something I can do that's ... special. I can do it whenever I want to. But sometimes I can't control it and I have to take special medicine to keep it from happening. But right now, it's safe."

"Well, if you promise, then I trust you." Her face was open and she tried to stand firmly on the foundation of trust she'd built with this group, who had become like family.

A nervous wave of exchanged glances between the group again made her stomach tighten. "I can't stand the suspense. And you all are being so weird right now. Could you please just show me and get it over with?" She crossed her arms and set her jaw.

"Okay, then ... here it goes. But remember, you're safe and ..." he looked at Abel and Brigid and took breath, " ... and, I love you." Abel and Brigid looked at each other with concern.

August softened at the words and felt her heart soar. "I love you, too," she said, a hypnotized smile spread across her face. He stepped forward and reached out his hand, she reached out hers too and he gave it a kiss, then let go and stepped back.

August watched in quiet shock as Faolan took his clothes off. Brigid and Abel didn't look away, nor did they seem at all surprised. But here was the man she had wanted to see naked for all these months, stripping in front of them. August felt her face get hot and parts of her body get warm and swollen, which made her uncomfortable, particularly mixed with the anxiety of the previous hour and the fact that there were others in the room. Then he began to twist, and stretch. Strange grunts came from him, and then with some crackling and snapping sounds, Faolan's body began to change. He grew taller by almost a foot and thick gray and white hair began to coat his back, his neck, crowning his head with an unbelievable mane. His handsome face stretched into a muzzle and his teeth lengthened into points. He stretched his arms out and they transformed with cracks and pops while his hands became massive paws. His cock became erect and pinked, while a protective sheath grew around it. August was transfixed with horror and wonder. What she was seeing was impossible, yet there it was.

The creature in front of her that had been the man she loved reared back his head to let out a deafening howl that sent a surge of adrenaline through her entire body. Brigid and Abel quickly shut the double doors to the library. She realized that the dark burgundy wallpaper covering the walls and doors was actually padded leather, and with the thick curtains closed, the room was apparently sound-proofed. The sound was terrifying and August felt it in her bones, as her heart pounded with fear and excitement. She stood firm and let the howl wash through her, neither flinching nor giving up ground, trusting the beast would not hurt her.

After the howl, the wolf dropped to all fours and then sat, like a gigantic, harmless pet. He panted and put a paw up.

August looked at Brigid and Abel, both of their eyes wide and they nodded. She approached the beast and cautiously petted his giant head. "Faolan?" She looked with wonder at him, then gave questioning glances to Abel and Brigid.

The wolf let out a gentle bark and then a bit of a whine and nudged her with his muzzle. She put her arms around the great furry neck and hugged tight. The creature smelled like Faolan's spices, but also like pheromones and fur, it was an intoxicating chemical elixir.

"But how?" Her words were muffled by the creature's pelt.

"He's a werewolf," Brigid offered. August shot her a look. "Eh, I guess that's probably not helpful at this point."

August let go and stepped back and spoke to the wolf, "I understand why you had to do this. You can change back now. He can change back now, can't he?" Abel and Brigid nodded and after a moment, a reverse of the procedure took place, though this time much more swiftly. Abel threw a blanket over the naked man's shoulders and he pulled it around himself. "Wine, please," Faolan said as he sat on the couch, looking a little exhausted. Abel handed him a large globe of garnet-colored liquid and August stared in astonishment.

Faolan looked up sheepishly at her. "Well Red, what do you think of the Big Bad Wolf?"

"How is this even possible? It's like something out of a fairy tale."

Brigid opened up the library doors. "Well, I think now that we've gotten that out of the way, we should all go sit around the table and eat a bit, and we can tell you about the Conalls and the Archers." August and Abel followed her through the large main room, past the long dining table and into Faolan's kitchen. Floor-to-ceiling windows looked out onto the back yard, fringed on all sides by woods that thinned a bit where the creek led away from the property. Faolan pulled on his clothes and caught up with the group.

Brigid grabbed trays from the refrigerator, crackers from the cabinet, and bread from the drawer, and set the food out on the table. August realized that she must have been at Faolan's house many times, and wondered how long they had known each other. They all took seats at the table and Brigid and Abel began filling their plates with fruit, cheese and bread. Faolan, however, piled his plate with cold chicken and slices of roast beef. August pushed her chair tight against Faolan's. She sat down and draped a leg over his. He petted her thigh with one hand, as if they were old lovers, and with the other he fed himself, gobbling up great bites from the meat on his plate. "It makes one a bit famished, the transformation," he offered by way of apology.

Brigid inhaled deeply and composed herself then looked at August and said, "I'm going to tell you the story because I've been around to see most of it. More importantly, I'm aware of both sides of the story."

August nodded and tried to appear relaxed and ready to calmly listen by sipping her tea and plucking fluffy bits of bread from the tray to pop into her mouth. Like this is no big deal, August thought to herself. Hardly worth batting an eye.

Brigid began with Celtic fairy lore, explaining that many of the fairytales August knew were grown from a seed of truth. There once were unicorns. There are families in the woods so hairy they look like bears, and they seclude themselves in rough cabins far from others. There are huge sea creatures in Loch Ness, and there are mermaids and water nymphs—though very few left. "And, as you now know, there are werewolves."

August reached up to brush Faolan's cheek, and pushed a stray lock from his forehead. She looked lovingly at the side of his handsome face.

"Their condition is somewhat like a cross-species infection, but one not well understood. Neither is the DNA that allows them to perform the seemingly impossible process of transformation."

Brigid explained that she had been studying the phenomenon since she was a young woman and there are others who have spent their lives studying the condition as well.

"It is actually rare for someone bitten to acquire the infection, though it has happened. Nor are werewolves totally helpless to their transformation, as you just witnessed. They can choose to transform. Though the full moon does exert a certain power, a 'call of the wild' if you will, that can be hard to resist without the aid of certain herbs. And it seems older werewolves have a harder time returning to their human form. Faolan here is one of only three lycans I know of who have even been interested in totally controlling transformations,"

Brigid noted.

August laid her head on Faolan's shoulder. Faolan gave her head a pat. He seemed more at ease now. Brigid's voice was lulling; it was like listening to a bedtime story.

"There is a certain culture within the lycan community called the Veritas—it means truth—that devoutly believes they are a superior stage of evolution. Better than humans, better even than hunters, and dedicated to remaining true to their traditions," added Brigid with a note of disgust.

August looked at Abel for some kind of confirmation, as though he was an authority on such things, and he gave a solemn nod.

Brigid continued, "They celebrate their primal urges with ceremonies and hunts—and not always of animals. To do anything to repress those urges they consider treasonous and insulting to the others of their species. Of course there are a number of them who use the suppressing herbs if they want to mingle safely among the humans for a bit, but you won't find them admitting to that."

"It sounds like a religion," August offered.

"More like a political movement," Abel said, arms crossed. Faolan and Brigid nodded in agreement.

Brigid explained how lycans and hunters had remained at relative peace for centuries, even living symbiotically at times. The hunters, who were the lords of most of the lands, would round up animals near places werewolves were known to hunt, as an offering to them to satiate their bloodlust, thereby reducing the risk of human victims among their subjects. But some lycans—those who would later form the Veritas—viewed anyone providing for them as a slap in the face. Most everybody else could see the advantages of the cooperative relationship, but these few held their ideals about prowess and purity, and their power to transform, above all else. Even above the prosperity of their own kind.

"Things came to a head in 1965 for several reasons. Urbanization was putting pressure on the lycan community, and they were increasingly marginalized as their hunting grounds shrank. It was also becoming more difficult for them to hunt humans without being detected. They were forced to blend in. That happened to be right around the same time I perfected my herbal combination for suppressing their transformations. The resentment of the Veritas lycans for needing to assimilate, along with humans and hunters encroaching on their sacred spaces, touched off a battle that began when Sorcha was attacked by Ban." This is when Brigid paused to look at Faolan, who had finished his meat and was drinking ale. He tipped his cup once more, drained the glass and pushed it aside.

"Who is Ban?" August asked during the long silence.

"Ban was my father, August. He is responsible for the deaths in your family. If not directly, then by starting a war that never needed to happen." He gently lifted August's now-numb leg off of his and went back to the library, returning with the large painting of the white werewolf. "This is my father, Banning Conall."

They all stood up. August walked a bit stiffly over to the painting and touched the textured brush strokes near the muzzle of the beast. "This thing attacked my grandmother?"

She wanted to smash her fist through the painting, scream at it, tear it to shreds—anything to destroy the reality of something that had already come to pass and she could do nothing about.

"Aye," Brigid said.

"And me," Abel said. He stood and peeled off his plaid flannel shirt. He wore a sleeveless tank underneath, and August could now see that his left arm looked as though someone had dragged glass shards down his shoulder and bicep. His dark brown skin was striped with long, shiny scars past the elbow, not so different than the ones on her grandmother's torso.

August was piecing other things together. Her father had been killed by an animal, "possibly a wolf," someone had said. But a wolf in Central Park? Highly unlikely. If anything like that had been living in Central Park the authorities would have found it. It must have been this creature. August's face twisted in pain and tears began to roll down her cheeks. She looked at them all and began to step backwards. Faolan reached out to her hand, she recoiled and moved away from him. She pointed at the painting and shouted, "Did that animal kill my father?"

Faolan set the painting aside. "No darlin', no. My father died before you were even born. But ..." he hesitated and looked down. This made August feel sick to her stomach. He was going to tell her something terrible. He's going to say he did it. She's going to have lost her father and Faolan, because she could never forgive him if he hurt her father.

She set her jaw and narrowed her eyes. "But what?" She had backed herself against the wall.

He looked at her. "It was your Uncle Thomas who killed my father, after he attacked your grandmother and Abel. In the battles that ensued your uncles and your Aunt Ceana were killed."

"Then who killed my father?"

"It was my brother who killed your father." He broke eye contact again and looked away.

"Your brother? Why? Why would your brother do that? Because my uncle killed your father?" August held her breath.

"I'm afraid so, lass. After that battle, it was chaos for months. Blood and deaths and threats of vengeance for anybody who escaped the fighting. Madness."

August gasped as the weight of loss and knowledge pushed against her. "Wait. What about my Aunt Blair? Gran said you murdered her. Please don't say that you did. Please tell me that's not true. Please Faolan, tell me that's not true."

His face sagged, his brow worried and wrinkled. "I can't blame your family for coming after mine when they did, after what my father did." He looked older than August had ever seen him.

"Gran said you killed Blair. I didn't believe her. She's been telling me all of this in bits and pieces since I got here. I thought she was just senile, or reacting to her meds. It's no wonder she didn't like Snow, and why she got so upset when she saw the necklace. I mean, look at that fucking thing, who wouldn't be terrified after being attacked by that."

He moved closer to her, but kept his hands at his sides. He looked positively beaten down. "I didn't kill Blair. I did hurt her—pretty badly. But that was an accident and I'm ashamed that it happened."

"I think I'm going to be sick." August felt woozy and staggered sideways. Abel caught her before she hit the ground and Faolan scooped her up and took her to the living room sofa.

"I'll get you some tea, darlin'," Brigid said, and put the kettle on in a flash. "I think that's enough of a history lesson for one day."

Abel got a blanket and covered her up while Faolan crouched next to the sofa and petted her arm and hand and whispered comforting things.

August looked out of the wall-sized windows around her and considered the naked branches against the bright autumn sky. The blanket Abel covered her with was soft and fuzzy and tickled her nose. She could hear the tea kettle whistle and in five minutes Brigid was giving her a steaming cup.

"Passion flower. I'd give you the valerian, but it smells dreadful, like cheese in old socks. Drink up."

"I'd like to go look in on Sorcha," Abel said.

"I'll go with him," Brigid said. "Are you going to be alright?"

"I think so. Thanks for the tea."

"Just try to relax. We'll see you at the Rook," she came close enough to pat August on the hand, then she and Abel left.

August finished the tea quickly so she could snuggle back down into the couch.

"I feel stupid," she told Faolan.

"Shhh, don't you fret. It's been a hard day."

He pulled a chair next to the couch and stroked her hair, then began singing, low and sweet. Something about a boat and hair and parts of it were in another language.

When I've done my work of day,
And I row my boat away,
Doon the waters of Loch Tay

When she woke up it was dark outside, and there were only a few lights on in the house. Faolan was sitting in the armchair perpendicular to the couch reading a book, with reading glasses perched on the end of his nose.

"Glasses, huh? I thought canines had excellent vision," she gave him a sleepy smile.

He closed his book and laughed softly. "Hello sleepyhead. I'm sure there are many ways canines are misunderstood."

"Sorry, I was just being funny." She wiggled until she was sitting upright.

"Me too. They're mild reading glasses and I only need them in low light. To tell the truth, I think certain other things take their toll, too. My eyes change ... when I transform ... is it okay to talk about this? Are you feeling at all well?"

"I think so. What time is it?"

"A little after seven."

"I'm starving. Maybe you can explain werewolf eyeball technicalities while I have a bowl of ice cream or something."

He laughed and got up from the chair and picked up the phone. "Why don't I order pizza?"

"That sounds fantastic. Mushroom and onion, extra cheese and thick crust. I mean, if that sounds good to you, too."

"Aye."

She snacked on grapes while they waited for the pizza and watched Faolan setting up plates, napkins and glasses on the table, which was soothing. Despite all of the trauma of the day, she was calm and comfortable.

The pizza arrived and they tucked in at the table. Faolan poured himself a glass of ale and offered some to her. It had been a tradition in her family to drink some ale with family meals since she was fourteen, even though nobody else her age was allowed to. In fact, it was strictly prohibited—not that that stopped them. As a result she never felt the need to gorge herself on cheap beer at parties.

"Sure, why not?" she answered his offer. "Half a glass, though. I'm a lightweight." He poured precisely half a glass and put a glass of water next to her plate as well.

"Where we come from ... where your ancestors come from, even today, ale is a regular part of dinner starting as soon as a body crosses into the full-moon phase of life."

"That's a fancy way to say puberty, I think."

He laughed, "Aye, it is. Or an ancient way."

"I don't suppose there are different rules about sex, too, are there?"

"There are. And, no, our age difference wouldn't cause an eyelash to bat, at least not among our clans."

August felt a little jolt of excitement, but tried not to let on.

"Don't go gettin' yourself all in a titter. I told ye, there's more to the question than that. Times are different now."

"You said 'titter,'" she said playfully. She bit into the gooey pizza, savoring the mingled flavors and texture, and tipped back her ale.

"You're incorrigible," he teased.

"That's right, you should encourage me."

He smiled and shook his head, then swept aside a stray clump of hairs that were stuck to her eyelashes.

"In time, if it's meant to be," he said.

August's throat went dry. She tried to pretend she didn't hear the note of uncertainty of their future in that statement.

"You're pretty darn old, aren't you?"

He nodded.

"Good lord, this pizza is amazing. I thought New York had all the best pizza. And this ale tastes a little different than what my family drinks. Is it ... flowery?"

"Aye, elderflowers. I brew it myself. I have a hard cider, too, but I think the ale pairs better with pizza."

"Wow, I didn't even realize you could do that."

"Pair ales with pizza?"

She laughed and snorted, almost inhaling a chunk of mushroom.

"Easy, love! Sorry, I'm being a bit of an imp. Many of the things we buy now were crafted in the past. No different than anything homemade, when you think about it. I'd be glad to teach you."

"Sometimes, when they were just grabbing something from the grocery store in a hurry," August remembered, "my parents would get the Newcastle Brown Ale, which went great with pizza. But the stuff they preferred was bitter and heavier than this—like, a lot. I'm actually kind of surprised. This is so ... so ..."

He gave a hearty belt of laughter. "Light, is it? I'm not too feminine for you, am I, lass? I like delicate things, too. Layers and subtleties are a joy in life."

"I'll drink to that." She held up her glass and he gave it a clink and they tipped them all the way back. He tidied up as she watched and thought about all the things she wanted to ask him.

"You know, Gran hates you because she thinks you're the one who killed Blair."

"Aye."

"You could have told her the truth. She might not have hated you all this time. She thinks you're living here to torment her."

"For a long time I didn't even realize that she knew who I was. It's not like I talked to her. She's been living in the nursing home since I moved here. Sylvia and Evan came by whenever—"

August sat up straight, startled at the mention of her parent's names.

"You knew my father?"

"Well ... yes. We knew each other. August, I'm not sure you need another flood of information at this very moment. Our families have known each other for centuries. There is so much to tell and we'll have time to talk about all of these things."

"Okay, so my dad knew you and he knew ... what you are. Right?"

"Aye. He is the reason I moved here. Well, he's the reason I offered to move here and watch over Sorcha."

"Wow. I'm just ... wow. You do realize how some of this stuff makes no sense, right?"

"I realize that it must be confusing, with what little you have to go on, yes. Look, darlin', after the battles were over and cooler heads prevailed in our world, what was left of the Veritas retreated deep into the forests of Perthshire. Sorcha insisted on coming back to her home here, where she had raised her family, even though Evan was the only one of her children left, so far as she knew. It was risky because we didn't know if the Veritas could find her and Bryan, your grandfather. So, your father and mother tried to get them to move to New York where they could live together with little concern of being found. But then Bryan died, and it only renewed Sorcha's resolve to stay put. It did strike me a bit odd, that she didn't want to leave because of her memories here, but then she set about numbing her mind so she would forget. Your father and I, we became friends in Scotland, after Sorcha's attack. I offered to move nearby and keep watch over her. I also vowed to keep the secret about Blair."

"My family moved to New York to hide?"

"They did. And with Abel and Brigid here, your grandmother got very good care and your family got to raise you like a normal human girl. At least that was the plan. I think your father had hoped that one day the Veritas would get over their vendetta and he could introduce you to your heritage without fear. Perhaps even move back to Scotland. But as years went on, and their numbers dwindled, they only became more threatening and hateful."

"Why is your brother part of this Veritas movement?"

"My father was a violent, vicious man who nurtured vengeance in my brother as though it were a blessing. They hated everyone that wasn't their own. Your Uncle Thomas and my father killed each other, in the end, but my brother just couldn't let the dead bury the dead. Even though it was our father's fault to begin with. He wanted to avenge our father's death, which to him meant wiping out every remaining Archer. My brother Ciardha is actually the head of the Veritas now. It's his excuse to seek vengeance."

"Keery-ah ... what?"

"It's spelled C-i-a-r-d-h-a, but it's pronounced Keer-ya. Hopefully you'll get a feel for the languages of your homeland."

"I wouldn't count on it. Okay, so all of that stuff was almost twenty years ago. Why start shit back up now?"

"No grudge was ever too old for them, but I assume this is how long it took him to find your family."

"Do you know how my grandfather died?"

"Heart attack. It happens, even to archers. Even to werewolves. The heart is imperfect."

Then a sickening thought occurred to her. "Wait ... where is your brother now? Does he want to kill me, too? What about my mother? Oh my god! My mother! What if he—"

"I believe he is still alive and that he will try to come after your family. Including you. I have somebody watching over your mother, though she doesn't know it."

"Mom's not going to like that when she finds out, I'm guessing."

"Maybe she won't find out."

"I wouldn't count on that, either. Take it from her child, she's got eyes in the back of her head. But, thank you in any case."

"Evan was a good friend. I'm sorry my family took him from you. It was the least I could do for him."

"Why would you leave here knowing we might be in danger? Without at least telling me, or warning me ...?" It sounded more hurt than she'd intended.

"Abel and Brigid are always watching and they know who to ask for help, if they need it. And I'd believed I had found my brother, which is largely why I went. Though now I believe he never left the States. He is most likely still in New York. I do know that he was in Arizona, chasing a false lead. I've planted a few of them over the years." He could see how hurt she was and continued with, "I never would have left unless I thought you were safe."

"I think in the future, you'd better tell me when I'm in danger."

"Aye. August, since we're on the subject, you need to train harder on your bow. You must always be prepared to use it."

"Always prepared to use it? How am I supposed to do that? It's not like I can lug it around on my bicycle or carry it around the grocery store."

Faolan took a deep breath and nodded. "Aye, that's true. It's more in case the situation should escalate and we have to go back to Scotland, where you would be a hunter ... with your people. I want to train you on the knife as well, which is a bit more practical for defense. Truth be told, your grandmother is a bit of an expert with a knife."

"Yeah, I got a hint of that recently. What about a gun?"

"We tend to avoid guns. They announce themselves to all within hearing. And unlike bows and knifes, they can kill easily by chance as much as protect you from harm."

"Right. Accidents. I understand. Lots of safety training, I

guess."

August took a deep breath and exhaled with resignation. What is this life? Her grandmother once fought with a knife, and now she herself would need to be trained on a variety of weapons. Last year she was just a horny, over-imaginative teenager living in a New York City apartment, and her biggest nemesis was a pack of bitchy cheerleaders. Now she lived with knives and archery, werewolves and war. Magical things that are real.

"Do you have a gun?" she needled.

"I do. But we'll revisit that subject later."

"Does it have silver bullets?"

"That's a myth, actually," he said. "There is no special effectiveness of silver. Werewolves can be killed with steel, lead or silver, same as any large beast. Not that it's easy. When we've transformed we're very powerful, and swift, with keen senses. Due to our small genetic pool, however, we do develop certain defects."

"Like your mistletoe allergy?"

Faolan rubbed his hand in memory. "Indeed, like that," he said, and August smiled sympathetically.

"Wait ... hold on a second. My mother told me she has a mild mistletoe allergy. She said her grandparents were very allergic to it."

"Your mother is part lycan, yes. Mostly human, but part lycan."

"My father is a hunter and my mother is part werewolf?"

"Aye."

"I need a goddamned diagram or chart or something. This is getting complicated."

"We'll write it out in our journal. Okay?"

August nodded slowly. Though she felt a seed of fear stirring in the pit of her stomach, she wasn't nearly as afraid as she thought she should be. Perhaps she was just numb from all that had been thrown at her. Or perhaps she hoped she would find Ciardha after all and make him sorry he hurt her family.

"This is all so insane. Nothing makes any sense to me anymore." She began shaking and felt the hot choke of tears stuck in her throat.

Faolan's phone rang and he got up and took the receiver from the kitchen wall. August listened as he rattled off a line of one- and two-word answers and returned to the table.

"What is it?"

"That was Abel. Brigid and he had a long talk with Sorcha. About you, and about us."

"Oh God, what'd she say?"

"Well, she was upset. And she wants some time alone with Abel, to talk. Brigid gave her some sedative tea and they think it's best if you stay here for the night."

August jumped up and pizza crumbs went everywhere. "Is she mad at me?"

"It doesn't matter right now, she just needs time to think."

"Maybe I should go talk ..." August turned to leave, but Faolan caught her by the shoulders.

He shook his head gently. "Some people need to be left to their thoughts. It does no good to chase them into their thinking space. Let her sit with it."

August relaxed a bit, nodded, took her seat, and picked at her pizza.

"Faolan ..."

"Yes?"

"Would you lay with me and just hold me?"

"Aye lass, I will."

Faolan scooped her up into his arms and she embraced his neck and tucked her head into him as he carried her up the stairs to his bedroom. It was opulent and uncluttered at the same time, and the smell of spices, leather and polish hung in the air. There was a pair of walnut chairs next to a simple yet ancient-looking cherry table. On the other side was a stack of chests in teak and mahogany with brass corners and fittings, some carved with Celtic symbols and some with what she thought was Chinese. There was an array of glowing lamps that dotted the room, some shaded, some stained-glass or with amber globes. Of course there was another bookcase, and many of the books here were laid on their sides, and looked as though they were handmade. Medieval-looking weapons hung on the wall near the bed, and the bed itself was an enormous piece of furniture, with carved chestnut posts and a massive headboard, spread with a burgundy coverlet and piled with velvet and silk-covered pillows.

Faolan set August down onto the bed. The downy bedding half swallowed her, and she pulled off her sweater and jeans as he watched. She curled up like a cat, wearing only her panties and tee-shirt, and reached out for his hand, pulling him down to her.

"Pet me," she cooed while wiggling down into the bedding. "You would never hurt me, would you?" she asked in a sleepy voice.

"I would never hurt you," he said.

He stretched out next to her, curved around her back side and gently stroked her arms and her hair, occasionally leaning forward to place gentle kisses on her shoulder.

"Tell me a story."

"What if I tell you the story of *The Mermaid Wife*? It's a Scottish folktale."

"I love mermaids," she said as she wiggled tighter to him.

"The story is told of an inhabitant of Unst who, in walking on the sandy margin of a voe, saw a number of mermen and mermaids dancing by moonlight ..."

"What's a voe?" she asked with a yawn.

"It's a small bay, lass."

He had not gotten ten minutes into the story before August was breathing deep and slow. He kissed the back of her head and inhaled the lavender and vanilla scent of her hair.

"I love you," he whispered to her shoulder, then quietly got out of the bed. He covered her up and clicked off all but one of the lamps, leaving a soft halo over August as she slept. He sat in a tufted armchair near the window and pulled a small blue blanket over himself and watched over her until sleep took him.

~~The Howl of War~~

Faolan bolted up from the chair, faltering on a numb leg, and shook the blood back into it. He staggered over to a window and threw open the curtains and opened the panes, letting in a cool night breeze. Ignoring the pins and needles in his leg, he focused all of his attention on sniffing the night air and strained to listen. He had heard a howl—a war cry. August blinked awake in the bed and looked at his alert face. Another howl came and the crack of a bullet, and now August was sitting up too, her heart pounding.

"What the hell is that?"

"Get dressed," Faolan answered. Without another word he grabbed a gun from his dresser drawer, gave it a quick check and then tucked it into the back of his jeans. As she extracted herself from the mounds of bedding and pulled her jeans and sweater back on she repeated her question, "It's three in the morning! What the hell *was* that?"

"Howl. Gunshot." He took down a short sword from its display on the wall, and tied the scabbard to his pants. He pulled out a large knife in a sheath from another drawer and handed it to August.

"A howl? Oh my god! Is my Gran okay?"

"I hope so. Grab your cloak. Let's go!"

August put on her cloak and put up her hood, as Faolan grabbed her hand and led her to the edge of the property, where they both ran faster than she thought possible, making almost no noise and maneuvering easily through the darkened woods towards the Rook.

They hovered silently in a cluster of trees nearest the front of the house. Brigid's car was still there. Maybe she'd come back. Or maybe she decided to stay over. It didn't mean anything bad, August assured herself.

"Stay here for a moment. Crouch down and take your knife out and wait here while I get closer. I'll signal you when to move forward."

August's heart pounded. Every sense was tingling and vibrating. He ran up to the porch and signaled to her to follow. The front door looked as though it had been kicked open. She felt sick as she looked at the explosion of wood splinters from both the door and the jamb.

"Oh my god!"

"Just stay behind me."

They silently moved past the living room and around the corner to the dining room, Faolan's eyes alert as she had never seen them, his nose sampling the air. She noticed his ears were starting to point and fur was bristling out at the back of his neck. As they made their way towards the kitchen she saw the wreckage. Dishes and pans everywhere. Some dark liquid drops that August quickly realized were probably blood.

August whispered, frantic, "Is that blood? Faolan, oh my god."

Faolan stopped suddenly and halted her. She could feel the hairs on the back of her neck prick up as he made a low growling sound deep in his throat and it stirred something wild in her, somehow making her want to growl too. The room was chilled. The back doors were open to the yard.

He called out to Sorcha and Brigid and Abel. As they carefully made their way through the kitchen they could see a bloody handprint on Sorcha's door. As they moved past the kitchen island August blanched at the sight of a disembodied arm laying on the floor in a pool of gore. It looked like it was Abel's arm and August wanted to scream.

"In here," came Abel's strained voice. "Hurry!"

They rushed to the room to find Sorcha lying on the bed, her sweater shredded and soaked dark. Brigid lay on the floor with her eyes closed. Abel was standing to the side, leaning on the wall, shaking and holding a stump where his left arm used to be.

August's eyes widened in panic. "Shit! Shit! Shit!" Without thinking she pushed past Faolan, grabbed a long silk scarf from the wall rack and tied off the stump.

"What happened?" Faolan asked him as he felt the women for their pulses. He picked up the phone extension and was starting to dial when he heard sirens already approaching. He quickly grabbed linens to press into Sorcha's wounds. He couldn't see where Brigid was hurt.

Abel's voice was low as he spoke through gritted teeth. "He's here. Your brother is in Mahigan Falls." Faolan's face hardened and his eyes narrowed as he exhaled sharply.

"I know. I could smell him."

Faolan directed August to go to the porch and meet the medical team. "Jesus, where's Snow?" she asked, feeling fresh panic rush over her.

"She may have run after him," Faolan said. "Just go to the porch and get them back here, okay? Snow is smart and fast, she'll be alright."

The EMTs were unable to enter the house until the police checked the premises because of a reported gunshot. August tried to contain her frustration, but she didn't have to wait long for the police to give the all-clear, and in the meantime another ambulance arrived.

"You're going to need a third ambulance," August shouted at them.

One EMT was a short but strong looking young man barely out of his teens and the other a stocky middle-aged woman. The young man looked to the woman for an answer. She explained, "We only have two ambulances in this town. Let's have a look and see how we can help, alright?"

Something about the woman's appearance made August think she would be bossy and rigid, but she actually had a very calming demeanor. August led them back to the room while the police were scoping out the yard and trying to make sense of the scene. The woman EMT asked Abel questions about what had hurt them and how long ago it had happened while she, along with the other EMT, touched and squeezed various parts of Sorcha and Brigid. August heard Abel tell them it was a big wolf. One of the police officers packed Abel's arm in a cooler and he and a third EMT drove Abel to the hospital while the others loaded Brigid and Sorcha into the ambulances; from the demeanor of the medical crew, August couldn't tell if they were going to be okay or not. She almost couldn't tear her eyes from the horrific scene that remained, but she joined Faolan with the police outside.

They told the police as much as they could. They'd already collected a gun that Abel had turned over to them, telling them that he hadn't managed to hit the animal, it was too fast. The full story would be collected by the sheriff at the hospital once everybody was stabilized.

August kept herself together, answering questions and doing everything she thought would help, but once the house was empty of officials August threw her arms around Faolan and began to sob.

"I only just got my grandmother back, I can't lose her! I can't lose another person I love! I can't! I can't!" She was trying to sound fierce but nothing could dilute the anguish in her.

Faolan was anguished, too. "I should have been here. I should have been watching closer." They hobbled to the couch where he held August's shuddering body until she regained her composure.

"We'd better get to the hospital," he said, and she nodded. He took her hand and helped her to her feet. "I'll make some coffee. Go wash up."

August dragged herself to the upstairs bathroom where she washed the blood off of her hands. She noticed a smudge of Abel's blood where she must have swiped away a stray hair. She scrubbed her face so hard it was bright pink. She changed her clothes and put down some food for Snow in case she returned home, and felt queasy at the thought of coming back later to find a full dish of food and no Snow. Faolan put coffee in two travel mugs and they headed to the hospital in his car.

She could feel herself going numb. The coffee was warm and strong, and she focused on how normal it was. Part of her felt wrong for not having jumped into the ambulance to accompany Gran to the hospital, but she couldn't make herself do it. She didn't really want to know how bad they all were—as if not knowing they were dead meant they were still alive.

They sat silently on the ride. Whatever was going through Faolan's mind, she could tell it was grim. The radio announced a local-area warning to be on the lookout for an unusually large rabid wolf or possibly a bear. She thought about Abel and Brigid, about her grandmother and her dog, and she fixed a picture of them in her mind, all well and okay, and made it a prayer.

"They're not going to mistake Snow for the wolf and kill her are they?" she asked, barely able to attach emotion to it.

"I told them what she looks like. They promised to bring her home, safely, if they found her."

"Can't you bark or howl or something to get her to come home?"

"August."

"I'm sorry. I'm just so fucking upset right now. And then I don't feel anything. Then I do. It's confusing, okay?"

"Okay."

The sky was lightening with pinks and purples as they pulled into the emergency room lot of the hospital. On the other side of the sky the full moon was just slipping beyond the trees. The lights on the road and on the building twinkled harmlessly, almost beautifully, August thought, giving no hint of the life-and-death dramas that had occurred within the walls. The chilly air bit at her nose and she shivered. She pulled her cloak tighter as they walked to the entrance.

The ER's waiting area was bright and not very busy. A child was cuddled up next to his mother, looking feverish and tired. An older gentleman was standing at the counter with a rag wrapped around his hand, only a small amount of blood visible. August felt detached, as though she were in a movie—watching herself, her small hand inside of Faolan's big hand—and stared off at the pastel colored abstract art on the walls. He led her to the reception counter and inquired about Brigid, Sorcha and Abel. The woman directed them to a waiting room further into the hospital and there they sat for the next four hours. It seemed like an eternity. Police came back and forth through the automatic door, the radios on their hips squawking intermittently. One of the officers told them that the sheriff was trying to make it back to town to examine the scene and that they didn't really need much more information anyway, since Abel told them what had happened.

Finally a set of doctors came out to speak to them. One was a black woman in her thirties, her hair slicked back into a barrette, with small diamond earrings on each lobe. Her name tag read Dr. Schaffer and her hands rested in the pockets of her long white coat. The other doctor was tall, tanned, and lean, graying at the temples, looking to August like an aspirin commercial. *He must have to buy his coat special for the length*, she thought, still directing the movie she felt like she was in. His tag read Dr. West. He had a paper cut of a mouth that was neither grim nor friendly. She searched both of their faces for some clue as to how bad the news was. She realized she'd been holding her breath.

The physicians introduced themselves and explained their roles in the care of Brigid, Sorcha and Abel, all three of whom were alive and recovering. August began breathing again. While Brigid was in stable condition and Abel was in good condition, despite the gravity of his injury, Sorcha was in critical condition and the next several hours would be key to determining her prognosis.

Brigid had had a small heart blockage that caused her to lose consciousness. She was on medication and was actually awake and speaking, and would be having a procedure to clear the blockage. They were assured that the operation was minimally invasive, had a relatively low risk with typically good results, and Brigid had agreed to allow it.

Abel was on pain medication and under observation for the next couple of days. His arm was too damaged to be saved, and the previous scarring would have made re-attachment near impossible. Schaffer noted that the early damage may have saved his life, as the reduced blood flow to his bad arm helped keep him from losing too much blood. If he didn't develop any clots or infections, he would be discharged on Tuesday and given orders for outpatient physical therapy.

"Somebody will obviously need to drive him to get a prosthetic made," Schaffer said.

"Of course," Faolan replied. "Can we see Brigid?"

West chimed in, "I think it's best to let her get some sleep for the night. She's had an awful shock and the police have been questioning her. She really needs her rest. Oh, one last thing, we are giving them all a rabies vaccine series. We recommend one for you also, just in case."

"Why? I didn't get bit," August protested.

"Well, it really only takes some saliva getting into an eye or some broken skin. The shot series isn't as bad as people make it out to be," West replied, then patted her on the shoulder. "We can do yours first before you leave."

"Fine," Faolan conceded.

They got their shots and headed back to the Rook. Faolan gave it a thorough inspection, house and grounds, before letting August out of the vehicle.

"Good news," he said, as he opened the splintered door and Snow bounded out to greet August, licking her and wagging. Her fur was matted with dried brown blood, but she seemed unhurt. August kneeled down to hug her.

"Snow! I'm so glad you're okay, girl! I love you! I love you!" Scooping up the dog she walked towards the kitchen, avoiding the blood drops. "She must have used the new pet door. I didn't know she even knew how."

Faolan scratched the puppy's head and kissed August on the forehead. "She's not going to fit through it much longer. I'm going to clean up this mess. Then we're going to my place. It's more secure."

"I have to tell my mom what's happened. I don't know what I'm going to say."

"You'd better tell her that there was an attack at the house and that everybody is okay, but that Sorcha is in a coma."

"You don't think she's going to put things together? She knows, doesn't she? About Dad and about all of this. She has to know Dad was killed by one of you."

Faolan looked stung. His bright eyes turned sullen.

"I'm sorry, I just meant one of your kind. I'm new to all of this, I don't know what words to use."

He nodded grimly. "It's okay. I was just concerned that I ... well, I don't want you to be afraid of me."

"I don't ... I mean, I'm not. I know you aren't your brother. It's like any other family. Only you can shape-shift into a giant wolf." They both smiled a little and leaned into each other.

Faolan rubbed his face and took a deep breath, "Look, I didn't mean to start a whole other discussion. We're both tired. We really should get this done as quickly as possible, and then eat and rest. I'm about beat, myself. Sylvia does know, but don't let on that you know, yet. She'll probably put it together, eventually, I just don't know what she'll do about it."

"Okay."

"Go ahead and call her. I'll clean all of this up. Then pack a bag." He turned and grabbed the mop and bucket.

August gave Snow a quick bath, turning the water a pinky red. The puppy squirmed and yipped as August scooped her up into a fluffy towel and cradled her tight to her body. Back in her room she ruffled the puppy fur to almost dry, then brushed and blow-dried her to a puff. Snow curled into a ball on the bed and immediately fell asleep as August packed a bag that would last her a few days. She also grabbed the boxes, quilt, and locket from her window seat.

No longer able to put off the inevitable, she perched on the edge of her bed and picked up the phone extension on her nightstand, dialing her mother's room number at the hotel, then gave up on the eighth ring. Maybe she was having a late lunch. August left a message at the desk to return her call and gave Faolan's number.

It took longer to leave the Blue Rook than they had planned. Faolan wanted to repair the door well enough to secure it, and they kept thinking of other things to take along, not knowing how long it would be until everyone could return to the house.

Shortly after they had unloaded everything at Faolan's, the phone rang. He picked up the kitchen extension, said hello and turned to August. "It's your mother."

August cupped the receiver in her hand. "Hello?"

"Hi honey. I got a message that you called." Her voice was unconcerned, even slightly distracted.

"I have some bad news. First, I want to say that everybody is alive."

"What? Oh no, what happened?"

"Gran and Abel and Brigid all had to be taken to the hospital. Abel and Brigid are recovering, but Gran is still in critical condition."

"What? How? Why?"

"Apparently there was some kind of animal attack. The police are investigating. The shock of it all caused Brigid to have a sort of small heart attack or something. We're all okay. Well, except Gran. I'm going to call and check on her before I go to bed tonight. Then I'll be at the hospital first thing tomorrow. I'll call you."

"No! I should come home now. I should be there. You're too young to have to deal with all of this."

"Mom! Listen! Listen, I'm okay. Faolan is with me and I'm

staying at his place for the night so I don't have to be alone. There's nothing you can do here right now. You might as well stay until your work conference or whatever is over, Mom. Really."

She let out a breath. "I don't know if I could concentrate knowing that Sorcha is in the hospital."

"She'd want you to. She'd want you to keep on with your things. You know she hates a fuss."

"That's true. But I should at least call the hospital and get an update on her condition."

"No, don't. What I mean is, they don't want to have to update a dozen family members. I'm down as the contact person. I have been handling things fine and I feel fine. I promise as soon as I visit her tomorrow, I will update you. Okay?"

"Okay, honey. Please, take care of yourself. I'll check for messages on my lunch break. Just leave the number where I should reach you. Also ... August ..."

"Yes?"

"Promise you will stay right with Faolan, okay?"

"Um ... okay. I will, I promise. It's been a long day. I'm going to eat something and get some sleep. I'll talk to you tomorrow."

"Talk to you tomorrow. But let me talk to Faolan before you hang up."

"Oh ... sure ..."

"Love you Button."

"Button? You haven't called me that in a long time."

"I know."

"I love you, too, Mom. Goodnight." August held the receiver

out to Faolan. "She wants to talk to you."

He shrugged and mouthed, "Why me?" August returned his shrug.

He took the phone and said things like, "yes" and "of course" and "I will" and then bid her goodbye.

"She wants me to stay near you. She knows something is up."

"I'm not surprised. My mom is clever."

"She is at that. Soup's on. Well, nearly."

She padded over to the stove in her fuzzy socks. "Soup's almost done?"

"It is. Where's your cloak? I thought you sat it on the sofa over there."

She shuffle-walked across the smooth tiles in her stocking feet, which always made her feel like being silly. It was something she and her father did to make her mother laugh. She did more shuffle-walking towards the living room, then did frog hops when she reached the carpet. She scooped up her cloak, which had been hanging on the armchair where Faolan couldn't see it, and then did a duck-walk back. She locked eyes with him as she did her silly walk, daring him to laugh. He wrinkled his brow gently, then grinned and let out a small burst of laughter, showing white teeth and the glory of the years he carried on his face. August smiled too and threw her arms and the cloak around him. "I love soup," she said.

"It was just an expression. I actually made roast beef sandwiches." He hung the cloak on a wall hook at the end of the kitchen cabinetry. "I don't want it to get musty. Always hang it up."

She nodded. "Musty." She gave a small giggle. "You sound like a granny sometimes.”

He shot her a look. “I reckon you don’t feel about grannies the way you feel about me, though, do ya?”

They both laughed. August cut hers short. “I shouldn’t be laughing, or smiling, or probably even eating while Gran is in the hospital. It makes me feel like I don’t care about her.”

“Aye, I understand that Red.” He finished assembling the food onto plates.

“I love sandwiches. Are there any potato chips? I am starving.” She slid over to the table and plopped into a chair, hooked the corner of one of the plates with her fingers and slid it in front of her. “Wow, chips and pickle already on the plate. Wicked. Is that rye? I haven’t had roast beef on rye since we left New York.”

“Straight from the bakery,” he assured her. Then he scooted a bowl full of meat trimmings across the floor for Snow to dive into. He settled into the chair nearest August and sidled his knee up against hers.

“I’m glad you feel well enough to eat. I wasn’t sure you would be able to.”

“I’ve decided that worrying isn’t going to help. I know she’s at least being kept on pain medicine and sleeping, so she’s comfortable. I can live with that for now. That and the absolute faith that she’s going to be better tomorrow, and your brother is going to be hit by a very large bus.”

She raised her eyebrows and bit a large chunk out of her sandwich and smiled as she chewed. “Milk please,” she said through her muffled mouthful. He poured. He smiled. He leaned forward and kissed her forehead. She blushed.

"Do you know what the deal with that is?" She waved her hand towards the cloak.

"With the cloak?" He looked confused.

"Mmm-hmm." She worked her way through the sandwich quickly.

"It's a hunter's cloak. You don't see them much anymore. They're sort of ... traditional."

"Oh?" Bite sandwich. Crunch chip.

"They're very old-fashioned—though they were effective, when hunters would travel in groups."

"Okay. And ..."

"And ... if hunters wear these red cloaks, then they can see each other, but hide from lycans in plain sight."

"Huh?"

"Think of it as hunters' safety red. You go around wearing furs and leathers during an intense hunt and you're likely to get mistaken for an animal or a lycan, and end up with an arrow in ye. But lycans can't see red when we're transformed. Not very well, anyway. So when hunters wore red they could plainly see each other but, so long as they were downwind and standing still, they would blend into the trees and bushes and become invisible to my kind."

"Of course! Dogs are colorblind! Holy shit. *That's* why Red Riding Hood's hood is red?"

"Aye, it is."

After nothing was left but crumbs and crust, August and Faolán took Snow outside for a quick walk around the house. Faolan then called the sheriff while August took a shower in the master bedroom and then poked around Faolan's room a bit. There were no photos on the walls, only paintings, and everything was tidy except the stand next to the bed, which had a pile of small books and papers, with a pair of reading glasses sitting on top. She reached for the papers, but decided that was going too far. She then slowly made her way back out into the wide hall, which ended with a floor to ceiling window at one end. She walked over to it and looked out. The view was facing along the tree line. She could just make out one corner of the Rook and the barn in the distance. She patted her hair dry with a towel as she wandered down the stairs wrapped up in one of Faolan's plush robes.

He smiled when he saw her. "Well, don't you look cozy?"

"My hair is going to be a crazy, curly mess without all of the stuff I put in it to keep it under control."

"I've got some oils that Brigid gave me for my hair."

August grinned and gave him a suspicious look.

"Curly hair, men have it too," he pointed out.

"Okay. I'll bite," she flirted.

"I'm going to let that one slide." He went off to his bathroom and returned with the oil and a comb.

"Have a seat." He turned one of the kitchen chairs around and poured a thick golden liquid into his hands, rubbed them together, then ran it though her hair. It smelled of cloves and patchouli, cinnamon and orange rind, among other things.

"I'm going to smell like you."

"Oh no! A stinky old hound!" They both laughed again.

August closed her eyes as he ran a comb gently through her hair, lightly coating it with the spicy oil.

"I don't want to get dressed. I love this robe."

"Nobody is going to make you. You've got nowhere else to be right now."

They made small talk and played music and talked about things that had nothing to do with family feuds, damaged bodies and hopeless grief. After a while August called the hospital to check on everybody. Sorcha had stabilized, so they would be moving her to a regular room in the morning, and Brigid's procedure had gone well; she was already awake and fussing.

August left another message for her mother giving her the good news, and then they then retired to what Faolan called the game room. She'd still not seen his whole house and this room was new to her. It was off of the main hall and down a half flight of stairs. She noticed in particular its low ceiling; despite the length of it, it was a very cozy room, decorated with more historical pieces of art and furniture. At one end was an old and expensive-looking pool table, and curious cabinets mounted on the walls. Not far from the table was a bar with a large painted mirror behind it. There was also a pair of overstuffed velvet arm chairs near an ebony chess table with black and white stone pieces. At the other end of the room was the largest television August had ever seen—it was more like a movie screen in a tall wood cabinet. Facing the television was a huge sectional sofa, and this is where Faolan led her, letting her settle in while he adjusted the lights, rounded up pillows and a quilt, and fished through a drawer for a remote.

"Wow—this couch is cushy on my tushy. I like this cave, Wolf," August appraised with a nod. "I'd have to call it eclectic-masculine-chic. Very macho."

Faolan gave a short laugh. "Lie back and close your eyes, love. You are clearly exhausted."

She watched him arranging things and wondered how long it had been since he'd had a girlfriend. Then it occurred to her that he could have had a wife. Or even two wives. She wondered why she'd never thought much about his past relationships before now. She tried to form a question about the photo in his wooden box, but he was right, she was too tired to even think. When he joined her, the two of them scooted into the corner and put their legs up on a big ottoman. It was almost like being in bed together, and she wiggled in close to him. He threw the quilt across them both and Snow immediately bounded onto it and wiggled her way up to a spot between their legs and nested in for sleep.

"Maybe you should try to get some shut-eye," Faolan advised as he clicked on the big television. She put an arm across him and laid her head on his chest.

"No, I'm tired but I'm too worried to sleep. I'll just lay here and watch TV with you." She didn't even notice what he had put on—some sitcom with canned laughter, maybe. "My hair smells like you," was the last thing she said before she fell asleep with the gentle rising and falling of Faolan's chest.

August woke to Faolan gently petting her legs. She was only vaguely aware at first, slowly surfacing from a deep dark pool of sleep.

"Hey Red. August. Sweetheart, you want to get up now."

"No, I don't want to get up now."

He gently replied, "Yes, yes you do."

August's nose twitched to the aroma of coffee wafting in from the other room. It took a few moments before she could pull herself up to a seated position. She stretched with her eyes closed and smiled softly. "Mmmm, I smell coffee." She opened her eyes and confusion washed over her sleepy brain as she couldn't find anything familiar in the room. Then she remembered she was at Faolan's house, and everything from the night before crashed down on her. Her grandmother, Abel and Brigid were all in the hospital. Faolan's psychotic brother was on the loose. Her father was dead and her mother was all but living another life. And the man she loved was a werewolf. She gave an involuntary shudder.

"I'm sorry, I tried to wake you gently," his face clouded with concern.

She shuddered again. "It's not your fault. I appreciate it. I do want to get up, actually. I need to call the hospital."

August sipped her coffee, swallowed down a sugar-dusted doughnut, and at nine o'clock exactly she called the hospital. The report from the nurse was good: Brigid slept well and seemed to be recovering fully. Sorcha was still unconscious, but stable, and would be moved out of ICU. She was permitted to have visitors, and Abel had been with her since she returned to her room. August called her mother's hotel and still couldn't reach her, so she left an updated message with the front desk and promised to call back later in the evening.

August and Faolan drove to the hospital. They visited Brigid and Abel first, who were putting up a façade of good spirits, and they all discussed the necessity for them to figure out what to do about Ciardha. Brigid needed her client book and healing herbs from her shop—she had every intention of making their stay in the hospital as brief as possible—and gave August a list of what she needed. She also asked her to put up "Closed for Family Emergency" signs and make a couple of deliveries, then wrote out a shopping list for food that would help their immune systems. She half-joked that the hospital food was as bad for the patients as whatever had brought them to the hospital in the first place.

Faolan and August decided they'd go to the grocery while waiting for Sorcha to come out of intensive care, and promised they'd be back within the hour. But as soon as they reached the parking lot Faolan stopped in his tracks. August's hair stood up on the back of her neck.

"August, turn around and go back into the hospital."

"What's the mat—"

"Now, August."

She took a couple of hesitant steps backwards and then hurried back into the hospital. Faolan had not followed. She turned back around to watch him from the glass door.

Faolan seemed to root himself in place. He squared his shoulders as a man approached him. He had shoulder-length jet black hair with a few thin white streaks. He was about the same height and build as Faolan, if a bit heavier, and though his face bore some resemblance, he looked much more ragged and leathery and appeared to have one blue eye and one brown. They barely moved, like dogs eyeing each other, jockeying for alpha positioning. Faolan stood taller and locked his position, as the other man barely flinched and held his ground. He made some kind of parting remark at Faolan that made Faolan lunge slightly—an animal gesture she'd never seen him do. She knew then this must be Ciardha, and her blood turned to ice. She wanted to go out there and pound him with her fists, gouge out his eyes. There was a clatter at the info desk behind her and she looked away for a second, then looked back up and Faolan was standing inches from her on the other side of the glass. He looked grim.

"We need to get out of here," he said as he opened the door, with a tone that denied any argument.

"What about Brigid and my grandmother and—"

"We're taking them with us. Go and tell Abel to meet me at the back door on their hall. We're going to have to run to the house and get Snow and my other vehicle. You stay here! Abel and I will go by the herb shop and get the stuff Brigid wanted before we come back. We can get the supplies after we're on our way. Tell them Ciardha's close. And don't leave this building until I get back. He won't come in here while there are so many people, so just stay and don't leave this building for anything!" Then he was out the door.

August stood frozen, her mind refusing to process what was happening. The sound of Faolan's engine revving snapped her to attention and she took off down the hall to Brigid and Abel.

Three hours passed before Abel and Faolan returned, and for much of that time August had been trying not to imagine them shredded and bleeding by the side of the road. Only her faith in Faolan's abilities, and the knowledge that Brigid and Gran needed her, kept her from dissolving into a puddle of anxiety.

"We cannot move Sorcha," Brigid told them immediately.

"We have to," Faolan gritted.

"If we move her, she could die, Faolan. They've only just taken her out of ICU. It's too risky."

"Brigid, if we don't move her she will certainly die. My brother will come here after hours and kill her in her sleep. He knows she can't be moved, and that's why he's waiting for me to leave. Brigid, please—show me where she is."

They waited in Sorcha's room for the shift change. Once the nurses momentarily retreated from the station and the floor was quiet, they slipped out of her room to survey their escape route. Brigid stopped short when she realized they were walking past a cabinet full of drugs. "D'you still have those keys, Mr. Sly Wolf?" she whispered, and Faolan produced a slim case, looked at the lock, and pulled out a notched brass flat. He slipped it gently into the lock and wiggled it until the handle moved, and stepped out of the way. Brigid examined the bottles and plucked a few from the shelves, slid the others to cover the gaps, and silently closed the door again.

"You'll have to teach me how to do that," August whispered to Faolan, and Abel politely shushed her.

Once they decided the route was clear they returned to Sorcha's room. All she was connected to was an IV and a catheter. Brigid peeked beneath the blankets and inspected Sorcha's wounds. "Her coloring is good. Her wounds are very clean. Abel, you'll need to take the IV bag from the stand and hold it up as we go, but first, in that drawer behind you, there are probably a couple more of those, yes, and some of those bags and tubing for the urine." They filled a pillowcase up with bags and tubes and gauze.

"You two, you're going to have to do this bit yourself. August, carry the supplies. Faolan, it's up to you to carry Sorcha. It's lucky the rear exit off of this floor is just down the hall."

Brigid took a peek down the hall. "Okay, now is good."

Faolan scooped up Sorcha as August led the way, checking around corners and propping open doors. Then Brigid took them to the end of the hall and down a half-flight of stairs. They saw no one outside, and walked as quickly as they could to a black Cherokee Chief. August saw Snow's head pop up as they approached. It took some gentle maneuvering, but they managed to arrange Sorcha on the pallet of blankets and pillows piled up in the back of the cavernous Jeep. Faolan attached her IV onto a garment hook and Snow hopped into the back, licked Sorcha's hand, and curled up next to her, wedged in tight against some suitcases. Faolan and August helped Brigid and Abel into the back seat and August climbed into the front bench with Faolan. He stood up on the rocker panel, scanning and smelling all around the lot for any sign of Ciardha.

Then he gently closed the door, started up the vehicle and drove them quietly away, as though any sound would bring disaster down upon them.

"A'm guttin," Brigid said, breaking the silence.

"What?" August looked over her shoulder at her.

"I'm starvin', girl. We need to stop and get something to eat!"

"Me, too," Abel said in agreement, though he seemed less urgent than Brigid.

"We'll stop at the grocery store," Faolan said. "I want to put some miles behind us before we take a chance."

August found an apple and a Three Musketeers bar in her purse. Brigid handed the apple to Abel and sniffed at the candy. She gave August a funny look, but she ate it anyway. For the next hour they rode on, Brigid keeping a close eye on Sorcha, Abel napping, and August trying to find the place they were going on a map that had been printed in 1962. They stopped at a Giant grocery just outside of Baltimore. Almost as soon as they parked, a Baltimore County police car pulled in next to them. They hadn't done anything wrong, but August wondered what happened at the hospital after they left, or who might have seen them. Brigid and Abel feigned lighthearted conversation. Faolan stepped out and exchanged casual greetings with the officers. August came out to join him on the walk in front of the store.

One of the officers looked at them a bit longer than seemed warranted, then shot a glance at the back of the vehicle. The smoky windows in the back of the Chief obstructed any view of Sorcha, but this cop's sixth sense was keen. He followed them into the store and watched the pair as they shopped. Faolan and August tried to act naturally, talking and laughing but not touching. Their age difference would inspire suspicious glances even on a good day. Eventually the officer was caught up in a conversation with his partner and a pretty cashier. The last time August saw them they were headed back out to their cruiser. "Bleah! Finally!" she proclaimed with relief.

They loaded up two carts quickly, including everything on Brigid's list—gallon jugs of distilled water, honey, dried turmeric and other spices, plenty of fresh produce, garlic cloves, ginger roots, ginger beer, ginger tea, dark chocolate, and red wine. They also collected a lot of other things like coffee, matches, fire starters, dog food, paper plates, soaps, dry milk, and plenty of canned goods. It reminded August of the couple of times she'd been camping with her family, and for the first time since they'd escaped she thought of her mother. "We're going to have to figure out about Mom," she advised Faolan.

"Aye, we will."

Finally they stopped at the deli counter and got sliced ham and provolone. Once back at the vehicle August made ham and cheese sandwiches on her lap—just cheese and lettuce for Abel—and finished each one with a squirt of mustard. She passed back the sandwiches along with fruit and small bags of chips to Abel and Brigid, who devoured them. She pulled the tabs off of a couple of cans of ginger ale and handed those back as well. Faolan loaded the shell on the top of the Jeep with their supplies while August chewed on her sandwich, sharing bites with Snow. Brigid checked Sorcha's IV, then offered Abel a root to chew on, and shook a small packet of powder on the back of her tongue. She made a face and swallowed down the last of her ginger ale, then gave Faolan the OK to start the journey. They drove through the city and followed the bay north for another hour before stopping in an old town at the mouth of the Susquehanna for a fill-up and a stretch-and-pee. The sky was fading but the waning full moon was already growing bright in the east. Then they followed the river, turned off onto a dirt road, and drove through forested parkland for another twenty minutes in the dark to a small clearing on a ridge with a large log cabin.

"Oh, Faolan, I haven't been here in a long time," Brigid said.

"That makes two of us," Abel said. "I don't remember this place lookin' so nice, either."

"Is this yours?" August asked Faolan.

"It is. And there's only two people who aren't in this car that know where it is. There's no way my brother can find us here. Now let's get a bed ready for Sorcha in there, and after we unload we can talk about anything you want to, alright love?"

August nodded. She and Faolan took flashlights to find the kitchen, followed closely by Snow. Faolan opened an electric panel and switched on two breakers. Lights came on, though dimly. "It's off the electrical grid," he explained. "We have solar panels and batteries, but it's not exactly high-powered around here in the winter. And I'd rather not kick on the generator, if we can avoid it. So no TV, young lady," he winked. He led her into a bedroom and they dragged a single large bedstead into the center of the room, piling pillows at the headboard. Then they went outside and opened the tailgate. Sorcha was still unconscious, and Brigid was trying not to seem worried. "Her IV is almost done, but at least her catheter's working. I'm glad we didn't get here any later."

August and Faolan lifted Sorcha gently out of the truck and carried her to the bed without much issue. Brigid changed out Sorcha's bags and checked her wounds, then began sorting through the packages that Faolan had brought from the herb shop and the boxes they'd gotten at the grocery store.

Even in the low light August could see the cabin was impressive. Honey-colored log walls, a big fireplace, and heavy, comfortable furniture made it cozy, while it also boasted a long dining table, a full-sized kitchen with gas and wood stoves, two bathrooms, and three bedrooms, each outfitted with big beds, fire grates, dressers, and closets stacked with bedding, most of it new.

Abel lit candles and fired up a railroad lantern to give Brigid more working light.

"We should get a fire or two going tonight, but we'll want to bank them down by morning to keep the smoke to a minimum," Faolan noted, building up a stack on the grate and slipping fire starters underneath.

"This is a fine hideout," marveled Abel. "It's like you thought of everything. And how do you keep it so clean? I don't think there's a mouse in here."

"Well I was just here before I went to Scotland," Faolan confessed. "It took a bit of cleaning and stocking, to be sure. But, I had an inkling I might need it."

"I'm feeling beat. I'm glad to be settling in for the night," Abel said. "My arm's achin', I think I need to take something for it and lay down."

Once they were unpacked and settled in, Brigid changed the dressing on Abel's arm and gave him some stronger pain medication and a special tea blend. Brigid retired to the room Sorcha was in, where Faolan had set up a surprisingly lush roll-away bed for her to lay alongside Sorcha's bed. She said she wanted to be there in case Sorcha woke up, though August had the clear impression Brigid intended to be a human heart monitor for Gran. Abel took the room next to theirs and Faolan invited August to sleep in the room at the end, which had its own bath.

"What about you?" she replied immediately. "Aren't you going to sleep with me?"

"August, do you really think that's a good idea? You know how we are. Good intentions and all."

She was hurt by his assumption; she wanted nothing more than closeness at the moment. "I didn't mean it like that," she scowled, and padded stiffly towards the room he offered.

"I'm sorry ... I just meant, it's a lot of temptation and we're all tired."

She couldn't resist a bit more pouting, even though she knew she had earned her reputation. "It's okay," she sighed. "Sleeping on the couch, I guess?"

"You guessed."

"Oh, shit! What about Mom? What am I going to tell her? How can I even call her? What if she called and couldn't reach any of us?"

"It's okay. You left her an update earlier today. We'll just drive to Deerville in the morning. There's a payphone outside the pharmacy." He was so calm, his voice so reassuring, that August never doubted him.

"I don't even know what day it is anymore," she said leaning her face into Faolan.

"It's Monday. Though not for much longer." He cupped the back of her small warm head with his hand and nuzzled the top, letting August's tired, frizzled curls tickle his nose.

"Oh Wolf, what a big nose you have!" She gave the best laugh she could muster under the circumstances and he laughed softly back in appreciation. She untied her hair and began digging through her suitcase, flinging various clothing items onto the bed and chair behind her.

"I need to wash up, Wolfy. I feel gross."

"Good hot showers only happen in the afternoon, I'm afraid. But I can heat you up some water on the stove and you can take an old-fashioned bath, if you like."

"I do like, thank you very much."

The huge claw-foot tub seemed to take forever to just fill half-way with tepid hot water, but Faolan had poured two big pots of near-boiling water in. August peeled off her jeans and underwear and stepped into the steamy hot tub and sighed. It felt so good to wash off the stress and sweat of the day. She had improvised bubble bath with her lavender shampoo and now frothed the bubbles up into mountains. She held her breath and slid beneath the water, leaving her hair floating like a mermaid's. When she emerged from the bubbles she scooped up a handful and blew them across the room, old-movie style, and then arranged them into a sort of bikini for her upper torso. Ah, simple pleasures of life, she hummed to herself. She was surrounded by bottles of soaps and conditioners, wash cloths and scrub brushes, and the glow of a half-dozen candles. There was only one thing missing.

"Faolan," she called out sweetly, though not too loudly. "Could you come here, please?"

Faolan cracked the door, but didn't look into the bathroom. "What can I do for you, Red?"

"Would you please wash my back? Don't worry, I'm covered in bubbles and I promise not to compromise your virtue."

He opened the door a bit wider and she could see his smile. "Well then, I wouldn't want it said that I failed to serve m' lady when she needed me."

August flashed him an impish grin. If there was one thing she learned as she recovered from the death of her father, it was to take humor and joy where you could find it, even if it was in the middle of a great big mess. And now she was finally learning not to feel guilty about it. A small bit of wisdom, hard won and well learned, she figured.

She yearned to be touched, to be calmed and soothed by physical contact with someone she loved and trusted. For the first time in a long while, she just wanted closeness and to be taken care of, and nothing more.

Faolan stepped in and closed the door after him. Then he knelt down beside the tub with a washcloth in his hand and plunged it into the soapy water behind her. She was pink, and glowing. She thrilled to see that he looked happy, for the first time since their readings by the stream.

"You stay in that tub and keep your bubbles on or I'll turn right around," he cautioned her, and began sweeping the washcloth across her back in slow, gentle circles. August's toes curled.

She sighed and made "mmm" sounds.

Faolan dipped the cloth again and rubbed her shoulders, then swept up her hair and washed her neck as she bowed her head. He rinsed the washcloth out again and reached for the lavender shampoo.

"Just sit up straight, love," he instructed, then poured a generous dollop in his hand and began massaging her head. August closed her eyes and melted into him, as his fingers dissolved away all the day's anxieties, allowing them to slide right off into the suds. The ecstasy of Faolan's hands in her hair, gently but purposefully rubbing every inch of her scalp, made her feel loved.

"I love this ... so much."

"Rinse, little mermaid," he told her, and she submerged. He saw her body moving under the water, and he felt his heart cry for her. He still had that look on his face when she came up blinking and rubbing her eyes. He gave her a corner of towel.

"What is it?" She put her hand on his.

"I can't help but feel like I should have done more to protect your family. To protect you from all of this pain."

"Faolan, if it weren't for you I'm pretty sure I'd be dead right now." She kissed his hand and reached to pull his face closer, so she could kiss his lips. "I love you, beautiful man, and whatever we have to go through we'll go through together, and that's the only way I want it."

He nodded, and smiled, and held her wet chin in his hand. "Aye, love. Together we shall be." He kissed her one more time.

August gripped the tub and rose up out of the water and turned to him, letting the bubbles cascade down her body, and Faolan stood back, pausing to admire her beauty as he'd never seen it, as he always wanted to remember it, glistening and golden in the candlelight, before spreading the towel open and gently wrapping it around her.

"You are magnificent," he said low in her ear. "I don't know what I did to win your heart, but I am the luckiest man alive."

"I love you. God, I love you so much," August said, feeling overwhelmed with both joy and uncertainty.

"I love you, too." He held her face in his hands, she gazed up at him and he kissed her forehead.

Not long after, they were curled up by the fire in her room. She was wearing a short flannel nightdress and wrapped in a quilt, with her arms wrapped around Faolan.

"This is a quilt I found in the window seat at the Rook."

"It's lovely. Very artistic."

"I think my gran made it. It looks like the Little Red Riding Hood story." She ran her hands over the quilt, tracing the stitches and outlining some of the shapes with her fingers. "Here, trees. The path in the woods." She ran her hand to another square that hugged her hip. "Here, a girl in a red hooded cape. That's me. And look ... here you are, the wolf."

"Would you like me to read you a book?"

"I would love that."

The last thing she remembered was listening to the rumble of his rich Scottish baritone, her ear pressed to his chest, as he read to her from a book of E.E. Cummings poems.

August awoke in her bed, and saw Faolan already dressed and sitting in her room by the fire with a notebook on his knee, gently separating the still-burning logs to keep the smoke down. She rubbed her eyes and propped herself up on her elbow to watch him.

"Good morning," he said, and she could actually hear the smile in his voice. He set the notebook and poker aside and kneeled next to the bed to put his nose to hers. She inhaled his breath and leaned into his mouth with hers for a tender and brief kiss.

"Good morning," she responded with a lazy smile, putting a hand to his cheek and holding it for a moment while they gazed at each other. She inhaled and said, "Well, I suppose I need to get dressed, so you can drive me into town and I can call my mother."

"I suppose so," he said. "I'll pour you a cup of coffee."

He left and she pulled on fresh jeans and a sweater. The room was nice and toasty from the fire and she so looked forward to a cup of coffee—cream, five sugars.

Once in the kitchen she wrapped her hands around the giant mug, sipping gently as they checked on their friends. Abel was up already, trying to cut an orange with one hand. He became a bit agitated when Faolan tried to help him, but he was smiling again when he devised a technique of quartering them using the back of a muffin pan and the long bread knife. Brigid was giving everyone morning medications, while Sorcha's coloring was good and her blood pressure and pulse seemed to be normal, even if she still hadn't opened her eyes.

After a quick breakfast of oranges, doughnuts and bacon, August and Faolan stepped onto the porch into bright sunshine, as naked trees cast hard morning shadows across half of the clearing. They stood next to each other looking out at the view. It had been difficult to see last night, but they were up on a bit of a hill that looked out over trees and a portion of the river. Their breath was visible in the air and the crispness was exhilarating. August couldn't help but feel like it was going to be a good day. They stood close, almost touching, and August leaned in a little against him, then rocked away and back in again, like a moored boat.

"It's beautiful here."

"Aye," was all he said and then he pressed the car keys into her hand.

She screwed up her face. "What do you want me to do with these?"

"You're going to drive," he said, as if there would be no further discussion on the matter, even though she'd only driven a handful of times, and never in a vehicle as big as the Chief. Nor had she dealt with anything other than nice, smooth roads.

"Well, if you're sure about this."

"I am. You'll do just fine." He opened her car door and she hopped in.

She felt like a child sitting in a grownup's seat for about a hundred different reasons—some of them emotional and intellectual, as well as physical. At least her feet reached the pedals, if barely.

Together they went over a list of driving points, in order to make sure she remembered everything correctly. She did. She started the vehicle and pointed it downhill, and she felt quite accomplished when they made it to the drug store in once piece. She threw the door open and bounced out of the truck to the payphone.

Faolan was sitting in the truck jotting in his notebook when he sensed panic outside, and looked up to see August bounding towards the car. She yanked his door open, "You have to drive. I'm too upset. The nurses said my mother called the hospital yesterday, I guess after I talked to her, and she told them she would be coming back as soon as she could. What if she gets to the house before we get there? What if your brother is waiting for us?"

"Let's not get ahead of ourselves. We'll just call the house and if she doesn't answer, we'll leave a message that we're on our way. We could also call the police and tell them that the house isn't secure and your mother doesn't know it and is on her way home. They'll go and check on things. You and I can be back in Mahigan Falls in a bit over two hours."

August took a deep breath and nodded. They both walked over to the payphone and Faolan dialed the house number. After three rings it was answered with, "Detective Baker, who is calling please?"

Faolan shot a look at August, who looked concerned. He tried to keep his demeanor relaxed, for her sake. "Hello, is Sylvia there, please?"

August knitted her brow and tilted her head. "Who's at my house?" she whispered urgently, and Faolan gently put a "just a minute" finger in the air.

"Who is calling?" the detective asked again.

"This is Faolan Conall. I'm Sylvia's neighbor. Sylvia's daughter is with me and she is trying to get hold of her mother."

"I see," the detective said, grimly. "I think you'd better bring her down to the station. We need to talk to her."

"Can you tell me what this is all about?"

"It's best described in person."

"I understand. We're a bit of a drive from town. We could be there in a couple of hours."

"Where are you? Can you give me an address?"

"No need, we're on our way."

"Fine. I'll see you at the station," the detective replied, giving no hint of the situation.

"Of course. Detective?" August's eyes widened at the sound of the word.

"Yes?"

"Could you please leave a uniformed officer at the house? Sylvia is due back soon and I am a bit concerned about her safety. After what happened the other day."

"There will be officers here. Goodbye."

"What's wrong? Why do we have to go back? Who was at the house?" Faolan's silence was killing her. "Tell me what's going on!" She shouted, and a mother with her toddler in tow turned to look over her shoulder and then scurried away with him.

"I don't know, honestly. But they want us to come to the police station. He wouldn't say why on the phone. It's entirely possible they are looking for your grandmother, since she and her friends are gone, and you and I couldn't be found. We did rather abscond with her. They may want to make sure we didn't hurt her. Police are suspicious by nature, it's their job." He didn't mention that he wondered why they had a detective he'd never heard of at the house, rather than Sheriff Two Feathers.

"That's ridiculous. Why would we hurt my grandmother?"

"Well, some people would think the house and life insurance would be worth it."

"What a terrible, awful thing to say!"

"I just mean, they have their usual routes of suspicion. Even if the sheriff has known for some time that weird things happen in his town, he doesn't know all of what that is. All three of them disappeared from the hospital at once. It's going to make you and me, and even Sylvia, look suspicious. Plus, well ... we did steal some medication. We're not going to mention that, okay? We'll go over our story in the car on the way there. You're going to drive. You need to learn to do things for yourself when you're under stress. It will make you sharper."

August nodded.

They stopped by the cabin to tell Brigid that they would be back by dark.

On the ride to the station they went over their story.

"The main obstacle to our story sounding realistic is the fact that Sorcha is still in a coma. That seems reckless. Stop sign—apply your breaks sooner next time. So we'll tell them she woke up and made quite a fuss to get out of there right away. The detective is new, I've never heard of him before, but the sheriff knows Sorcha and he will have no doubts that Sorcha's demands were persuasive."

"What if they ask us why we didn't just take them back to the house?"

Faolan let out a grunt. "Good point. We'll tell them that they didn't feel safe at the house, so we took them somewhere they would feel safe."

"That makes sense," August said, her eyes glued to the road and her hands clenched onto the wheel.

"Try not to grip the wheel so tightly. And relax your posture a bit. Just watch the horizon, keep an eye out for deer and check your mirrors every few minutes. You're doing great."

August exhaled and relaxed a bit and allowed her hands to loosen a little. The drive was peaceful and she tried to just enjoy the bright scenery and Faolan's close proximity, but after an hour she was exhausted, and she was getting a headache from the flashing shadows of trees along the wooded roadways. Finally she gave up and pleaded with Faolan to take the wheel. Once they got going again her mind vacillated between the beauty of the drive and her concern over what awaited them in Mahigan Falls.

There were no parking spaces left in the lot at the sheriff's office. "Looks like a popular place today," observed Faolan. Official cars with different county names and a few animal control vans from other towns were sitting in the lot. There was a news van pulling in as they arrived.

Inside the station, the phones were ringing non-stop, while officers from various jurisdictions stood around drinking coffee, munching on doughnuts and writing in notebooks. August and Faolan approached the desk and asked for Detective Baker, who appeared almost instantly—a slight, elegant man, who looked to be at least partially of Asian descent. After brief introductions he whisked them away to an interrogation room.

"I didn't know we had a detective in tiny little Mahigan Falls," Faolan said as he pulled off his scarf and folded it onto the table in front of him. August removed her hat and scarf and did the same, stifling the urge to put her hand in Faolan's. She knew it might not be the best time to give any indicators that the two of them were romantically involved.

"Actually I'm from the county. Can I get you a cup of coffee?" They both shook their heads. He positioned himself across from them and sat down.

"I'm going to turn this tape recorder on, unless you have an objection." They shook their heads. "I don't want to alarm you," he said more to August than to Faolan, "but your grandmother has gone missing from the hospital. Her two friends who were attacked by a wild animal are missing as well." He emphasized "wild animal" and eyed Faolan at the same time. "Do you happen to have any ideas where we might look for her?"

August cleared her throat. "Actually, yes, I do."

"Oh?" He opened his notebook and clicked his pen open and stared at her.

Faolan noticed that the detective seemed surprised, as though he expected her to disavow any knowledge. He probably had worked out a whole scenario about August and Faolan killing the grandmother for her money and house.

"They are in a safe place," August said with as much casual confidence as she could muster.

"Where is this safe place?"

"Well, we'd rather not say," Faolan interjected.

"We?" He looked back and forth between the two of them.

"Yes, we, detective," August affirmed. "I phoned my mother last night to tell her about what happened. She talked to Faolan and me, and insisted I stay with him, for safety." August hoped she didn't sound too defensive, and plunged on. "Listen, my grandmother doesn't like hospitals. They scare her. She didn't want to be in that hospital and neither did Abel or Brigid. They were still traumatized from the attack and they wanted to feel safe somewhere far away from Mahigan Falls. So Faolan, who happens to be our long-time neighbor, said we could stay at his vacation property. Abel and Brigid have both been there before. They thought it would be a good place to rest and heal." The detective stared at August through her pause, so she continued. "Brigid's a pharmacist and a natural medicine expert, Abel has a pharmacology degree—they know a lot about these kinds of things. Faolan helped me pack their stuff and off we went. He's a good neighbor. He's also been helping out my gran and me since my mom has been gone."

Faolan looked casually on, trying his best to emanate a non-threatening energy, while also trying not to show how proud he was of August's performance.

Baker tilted his head and crossed his arms. "Why all of the high drama of pulling them out of the hospital without properly having them discharged? That is pretty reckless."

"It's true. It's true," Faolan said. "But the shift change had just happened and we had a long way to travel with injured folks and we just really wanted to get out of the door in a reasonable amount of time. It has been a traumatic couple of days, as you can imagine."

"Which brings me to something else I'm worried about," August went on. "We didn't have a chance to tell my mother much about the animal attack, and now she's coming back here and there could still be that dog, or bear, or whatever, out on our property. We want to get back to the house and warn her. So we would really appreciate it if you would let us do that."

Baker sat back in his chair and let out a breath. "There are two officers at your house right now," he assured her. "As for your version of events, it all makes sense to me but I'm afraid we can't just take your word for it. First of all, some controlled medications went missing from the hospital last night."

August never flinched. "Okay, but what's that got to do with us? I suppose if someone there wanted to steal some drugs, wouldn't they take advantage of a situation like this?" She was surprised at how quickly plausible ideas were coming to her. She felt a little guilty too, for creating suspicion for some innocent hospital staff and patients.

"We need to confirm your grandmother and her friends are safe."

"Well, I'd suggest calling them but we're too far out for a phone," Faolan noted. "And it's more than two hours' drive from here. I know the sheriff out there though; what if she were to check on the cabin to confirm they're all fine?"

Baker nodded and waved at the mirror behind him without turning around. A phone was brought into the room. He held up the receiver to his ear and looked at Faolan expectantly.

"Harford County, Deerville, Sheriff Géroux," Faolan supplied.

The detective had the switchboard operator find the number. For a few awkward moments no one had anything to say, so August tried to look politely impatient. The phone rang back and the detective identified himself before handing the phone to Faolan, who explained the situation to the sheriff. "Nothing to do but wait thirty minutes or so," Faolan said as he hung up.

"So, Miss Archer, what makes you think an animal attacked your grandmother and her friends?"

August's throat dried up. "Well ..."

"Because that's what Abel told us and that's what the responders felt the evidence bore out," Faolan offered. Detective Baker kept his eyes locked with August's.

"That's a pretty big house your grandmother has. An original to the town, and so well-maintained. Practically looks brand new. Must be worth quite a lot of money by now considering your grandparents paid it off in the early 1960s."

August wasn't sure what he wanted. "I have no idea," she said simply.

Baker sighed and stood up. "Alright, well, it's lunch time. You two hungry?"

August was, in fact, starving, but she didn't want to spend another moment in Baker's company. She shook her head. All she could think of was getting out of there and finding her mother.

"Suit yourself then. Officer, could you bring some water for these people?"

August had no doubt Detective Baker would be eating his lunch behind the glass and watching them. She did her best to make small talk, acting the impatient child, encouraging Faolan to play the part of the fatherly neighbor.

After what seemed an eternity he came back to the room. August couldn't put her finger on it, but he looked different.

"Miss Archer, we appreciate your patience. I'm sure we'll have you all cleared in just a little while."

"Okay, thanks," she replied, and almost immediately the phone rang.

Baker picked it up. "What? You're at the cabin. Everyone's fine? I can't hear you. Three ...? Sorcha Archer, Abel Jefferson, Brigid Herne. Yes ..." He covered the mouthpiece and told Faolan that Brigid wanted him to bring saline for Sorcha. "Alright. Yes. Thank ... thank you, sheriff."

After hanging up with the sheriff, the detective's face clouded and his eyes flashed something, then looked away.

"Well, it's all as you said. They're fine and resting." He handed the phone to the uniformed officer outside of the door, then closed it and turned back to them.

August and Faolan stood and reached for their scarves and hats.

"I'd like you to wait a moment. Please, sit back down."

"Actually, I'd really like to catch up with my—" Faolan interrupted August by placing his hand on her arm. She fell silent and looked confused.

"Maybe you could just tell us what you need to say and we can be on our way, back to our friends. They need us."

"Yes, of course," Baker seemed to be composing himself.

August's heart began to thud. Something bad was coming. She grasped Faolan's forearm while holding her breath, but still trying to act casual. Because if you act casual, nothing bad can happen.

"I'm very sorry to tell you this ..."

August's heart sank.

"I'm afraid your mother has been ... killed."

Everything went black.

***

What seemed like moments later to her, August blinked her eyes open. She tried to focus on Faolan, sitting in a chair pulled up to the side of the bed. He put his hand on hers and squeezed. "Hi, you," he said with a tender look.

She gave him a groggy smile. "What happened?"

But as she came out of her haze and saw the naked sadness on his face, saw her hospital bed and her gown, she remembered. A primal howl rose up from her gut and she grabbed at him, clutching fistfuls of his shirt and pounding her head into his chest as he leaned over her. He stroked her hair as she shook and sobbed, and he absorbed her muffled screams until her voice was hoarse.

"I'm sorry, love," he said again and again. "I'm so sorry."

August finally pushed away from Faolan's chest. Her head

throbbed and her eyes were swollen. But there were no tears left in her. Her father and her mother had both been ripped from her. Everyone she loved had been viciously attacked by this killing thing—hunted down by a mindless, murdering animal. When she looked up again, her jaw was set and her eyes were steel.

"Ciardha," she said, and it was an indictment.

He nodded, grim. "He is a disease, full of vengeance and Veritas ideology about his dedication to purity." The words were bitter in his mouth. "My father and my brother both were seduced by their anger and impotence to join in that stupidity, and it only ever fed their worst impulses—as though working things out with the other beings on this earth would somehow make them weak. They're addicted to the thrill of the hunt, and their target is what they call their natural enemy, the ones who would hunt and contain them. The Veritas hate all hunters, of course, and they despise lycans who have bred with humans. But they reserve a special venom for those they imagine have betrayed them—the lycans who have married into the hunter clans."

"My mother?" August croaked between clenched teeth.

"Aye, Sylvia. Her lycan family blood had long since mixed and diluted with the rest of humanity, but for her to marry a hunter, even with the trace of lycan in her, was a black mark. And after the Archers' personal battles with my family, I was afraid that one day it might come to this."

August looked into his eyes, filled with so much sadness and regret. She was trying not to blame him for failing to stop his brother—for not killing him right there in the hospital parking lot. Or years ago in Scotland, which would have saved her father from his death. Faolan could have prevented all of this.

She couldn't imagine how frightened her mother must have been when Ciardha took her. She thought of the red hooded cloak and the bow, the things her father had said before he died, and saw in them the hints of what he was going to teach her. She choked on the realization of all the things that would never be between them. And she understood that that untroubled girl who loved nothing more than to throw her arms around her daddy's neck was gone now too.

This was how hunters were made, wasn't it? They were taught by love how to hate. She flushed hot, and an ancient trace of lycan blood surged through her limbs and her heart, and she was over the bed rail and on her feet in the blink of an eye. But just as quickly she turned cold. Her muscles coiled, her eyes and ears seemed to reach every corner of the room, and she went still as though she could stand in that place for the rest of her life, if need be. She was a hunter. She was an Archer. She knew, without a flicker of doubt, that she would put one of her father's arrows into Ciardha's neck.

"Easy, love! You've had a concussion! Right now we need to take care of the living."

She silenced him with a piercing glare. Had he recognized a change in her? She saw in his eyes that even brave Faolan could feel fear, though for what she did not know. He seemed to be holding her to protect her from something. Herself, perhaps.

"I know you're angry, lass."

"Don't talk to me like that right now. Lass! Lass! Just stop it with your lass!" She was twisting her mouth, red-faced and mocking.

"You could have done something to prevent this! You could have stopped this evil before it took away my life, Faolan! How can I love somebody like you? How can I love you when you let your brother kill both of my parents? I'm sick of this! I'm sick of all of this hunter, werewolf, war, hatred, animal bullshit!" She grabbed fistfuls of his shirt and pushed into his chest with her head, wanting to drill into him, punch him, hit him, hurt him, and also wanting him to throw his arms around her and comfort her. She felt like her skin might split open and snakes and spiders would crawl out of her insides.

"August, I am so sorry it went this way."

She stood back from him and yanked out her I.V., spraying droplets of blood across the floor and Faolan's shirt.

"August is gone," she flashed. "All that's left is Red."

~~Red Vulticulus~~

Several nurses rushed to Red's room when they heard her yelling for her doctor to let her out of there, and they talked to her until she had quieted down. Dr. Schaffer finally appeared and gave her a brief exam. If Schaffer was unhappy about the way they'd taken Sorcha and the others away, she didn't say anything. She noted that Red's reflexes were "excellent," and since her concussion was a mild one she was released in the early evening. Until then she sat in cold silence, her eyes narrow and her mouth a hard line.

Red sat quietly in the Cherokee toying with her hospital bracelet while Faolan drove towards a diner. He told her that overnight Sorcha had awakened from her coma. And that Abel was feeling much better and Brigid swore she was better than new.

Red was listening, and was glad for the positive news, but she was ashamed about how divided she felt. She had been inundated and overwhelmed with too many conflicting feelings in the past month and it was taking its toll. She didn't want to be angry at Faolan; she knew she didn't have a right to be. How could she expect anyone to kill his own brother, let alone someone as decent and gentle as Faolan? But having decided she didn't want to be mad at him, she also had no idea how to make that happen.

"I'm sorry for all of the harsh stuff I said," she began. She spun the bracelet around on her elfin wrist.

"Don't fret," Faolan said as he pulled into the diner's parking lot.

Faolan understood her pain. While Red was in the hospital he had gone to the morgue to identify Sylvia, though he did not recount the whole ordeal to Red. As soon as the young female morgue attendant led him into the room he was nearly knocked over with the scent of Ciardha. He had urinated and sprayed all over her. And though the attendant seemed oblivious to the stench, Faolan's eyes fairly watered.

"I'm sorry for your loss," she said, imagining his watering eyes were a cue.

"Thank you."

She lifted the sheet for him. There hadn't been enough left of her face to get a positive identification, but it was a formality, really; the coloring, height and weight were Sylvia's, and the purse near the body contained her identification. The sheriff's department reluctantly concluded that Sylvia was the victim of another animal mauling at the house. They must have been wondering what would have made the animal repeatedly attack inside a house. With three injuries and one death on their hands—from what the medical examiner determined was some kind of large predator—the sheriff called in a game warden from the state, although Faolan suspected that it might have been for show. Sheriff Two Feathers knew a few things about Mahigan Falls, including Algonquin stories that stretched back long before a Freemason's cut stone was laid in the town. He had been wise, however, in putting out public warnings all over town. Deputies drove out to the more remote locations to warn citizens of the danger of a vicious roaming dog or wildcat, possibly even a bear. Faolan knew their efforts would be in vain, of course, and he imagined the sheriff did, too.

One other thing that Faolan hadn't fully elaborated with Red was about the person who was supposed to have been watching over Sylvia. Shan was a paid bodyguard, but Faolan had been unable to find her last night or this morning. This set him on edge. Ciardha couldn't have paid her off—Shan had proven herself before, and she had no love for the Veritas. More likely, Ciardha dragged her off into the woods and ate her. When Red was still unconscious, Faolan had tried to pick up scent trails out at the Rook, but they had aged and become confused, and the smell of his brother simply ended at the creek. He hoped Red wouldn't ask about Sylvia's bodyguard just yet; her pain had taken a disturbing direction and he didn't want to aggravate it any further.

Once inside the diner they both ordered burgers, fries and milkshakes. Red was a sorry sight as she hunched over the table. Her hair was tangled in all directions, unbrushed after two wild days. Her hospital bracelet was still on her wrist, and she hadn't even bothered to change out of her gown—she'd simply pulled her jeans on under it. Worse, she had a nasty bruise on her left cheek where she'd struck the table after she passed out at the police station, and as the waitress took their order she eyed the couple and squinted hard at Faolan.

"You okay, sugar?" she asked Red, pausing her gum-chewing long enough to lean forward and get a little closer to her.

Red just nodded. The woman took a deep breath and looked again at Faolan suspiciously, but decided not to make any more of a fuss.

Once it came, Red's burger disappeared quickly, with little conversation. But when she was down to the last few fries she said, "So, who was supposed to be watching my mother?"

Faolan set down his burger, picked his napkin up off of his lap and dabbed his mouth. He sighed heavily and met her gaze. She thought to herself how fatherly he was in that moment. "Her name is Shan and I haven't been able to get ahold of her."

"So, did you pay this woman money to watch my mother? Or is she a close friend or something? And why the hell didn't she do her job?"

"Red, she was a paid bodyguard, but I trusted her as much as you can trust a friend and a hired hand. I'm sorry."

"It's not your fault. The woman obviously is a shitty bodyguard and she'd better not cross my path or she'll be explaining why the fuck she's alive and my mother is dead while ... fuck ... never mind."

Faolan said nothing while she finished her fries and then waved the waitress down and ordered fried chicken.

"You were hungry."

"You saw what they tried to feed me for lunch. Limp iceberg lettuce and red gelatin. Gross."

"Hospitals aren't notorious for their fine dining experiences."

"When we're done here Faolan, I want to stop by the hunting shop."

His eyebrows went up. "Want to tell me what you're hoping to find?"

"Arrow shafts. You told me to practice." She didn't want to look Faolan in the eyes, so she looked off for the waitress. "Where's my chicken?"

"You only just ordered it. They need time to tell the cook what you ordered."

"Very funny," she said, and crossed her arms.

Faolan contemplated pushing her for details about what was going through her mind, but instead he clanked his ice around in his glass, watching her as she turned from her waitress lookout to focusing her full attention on the last crusty fry-end on her plate.

"Okay. We'll do that ... head over to the shop," he said, and put his hand on hers. She didn't resist.

"Thanks." There was a long pause. "I'm trying not to blame you. I know you already feel bad enough. But, it's hard. I feel like I should still be pounding you in the chest and asking you why you didn't kill your shithead brother years ago, knowing what he was capable of."

Faolan, full of shame, just nodded as tears began to roll down her face and drip onto the table.

"Faolan ..."

"Yes?"

"I like it when you call me lass."

"I know you do." He gently stroked her hand.

After the chicken arrived she realized she didn't actually want to eat it, so they wrapped it up and headed off to the hunting supply store where they found the shafts and fletching. A long afternoon of stewing in anger was wearing on Red, and once she'd thrown her supplies into the back and climbed into the truck she started to sob. Faolan slid across the seat and took her in his arms.

"I'm going to have to bury my mom," she managed, between sobs. "I don't know how to do that. I wish my dad was here. I wish we were by the creek reading books, instead of here ... me, mad at you ... buying stuff to hurt people. Or whatever they are. I don't want to bury her. Please don't make me do this." Her lament was deep and Faolan petted her and held her tight, waiting for the wave of sorrow to pass.

"I will handle the arrangements, sweet girl. Don't worry about it a bit."

She nodded into his chest and sniffed, wiping her nose on her sleeve. "I want to go see my gran right now."

He drew in a deep breath, held it for a moment and tried to release the tension he'd been accumulating all day. "I think we should swing by my place and grab a few more things first. Seems like we might be in the cabin for the long haul."

"Isn't that dangerous?"

"Ciardha will not cross the markings of my den. He respects the old ways above all things. The house is, without question, my territory."

"Why didn't you mark the Rook? Oh. Well, I guess there was no way Gran was going to let that happen."

"It's not really my territory, it's your mother's."

"I don't know if I will ever understand this."

"Sometimes I don't, either."

"If he won't cross your markings, then why didn't we just stay at your place?"

"There are many advantages to holing up in the cabin. It's safer, for now."

Red sniffed one last sniff. "Right. Well they better hope they never find me." She buckled in and they made their way back to Faolan's place.

Once on the front step however, Faolan caught the scent of something and whipped his head around. "Take out your knife," he whispered.

"What is it?"

"I'm not sure, the scent is muddled. Stay behind me."

"I smell it too. It smells ... familiar. Well, some of it does."

They crept around the side of the house to the back door, peering into windows along the way. The sliding door was locked and a stick was jammed into the track. He cast a concerned and confused look to Red, who shrugged. They went around to a side door that opened into a mud-room on the other side of the kitchen. Once inside, Faolan sniffed again. "Female," he whispered. "But don't let your guard down."

After another few steps his body language relaxed and he stood up straight. He shouted into the dark house, "I can smell you! Come out! We aren't going to hurt you!" Silence.

"You say it," he told Red.

"Why should I say it?" she whispered back.

"Just do it," he insisted.

"Do I say the part about smelling them?"

He shot her a look.

"Okay. Sorry," she whispered, and called out, "Come out! We aren't going to hurt you!"

The library door creaked open. "August? August, is that you?"

A woman emerged, covered in scratches, and limped towards them.

"Oh my god, Mom? Mom!"

"Oh, baby!"

Sylvia rushed towards her daughter and they embraced, both sobbing.

"They told me you were dead!" August was so overcome with relief and feelings she couldn't name that she crumpled to the floor and held onto her mother's waist and sobbed in a heap.

"I know sweetheart, I'm so, so sorry!" she said, kneeling onto the ground and kissing her daughter's face. "Oh, I'm so glad you're here, and safe! Let's sit down, sweetie. My leg hurts. You smell so different."

"So do you," August said, realizing she could pick out a number of individual scents on her mother—peat, grass, blood, beef, ale, lavender soap, and pheromones—hers and probably Ciardha's as well.

Faolan helped them stand and they all sat around the big table near the kitchen, where just a few days earlier August had first learned about the Conalls and the Archers. Faolan looked at Sylvia's leg.

"What happened, Sylvia?"

Sylvia looked at August, then back to Faolan.

"You can say. She knows. About me. And about your blood too."

Sylvia shook her head, and reached out to touch her daughter's face. "I am so sorry. I wish none of this had ever happened. I should have told you sooner. Your father and I both, we should have told you when you started your moon cycle."

"It's okay Mom. It's done. I'm just so glad you're okay." They embraced again.

She turned her attention to Faolan, without letting go of August's hand, "Well, I flew in from Arizona and went straight to the hospital. Of course there were cops all over the place, so I called from the payphone outside and spoke to the nurses who told me that Brigid, Abel and Sorcha had gone missing. I hoped it was because you'd taken them somewhere safe and that August was with you."

"Ciardha approached me in the hospital parking lot. I knew I had to get them out of there, so I took them to the cabin."

Sylvia nodded.

August looked to her mother and said, almost under her breath, "You know about the cabin, too? I hope I know everything now." She removed her hand from her mother's and crossed her arms like an angry child.

Sylvia ignored it the way a mother ignores a child throwing a tantrum. She turned to Faolan.

"You had a vulticulus watching me, right?"

Faolan nodded. "Shan, was her name."

"I owe her my life. So, I parked here and walked through the Rook to the woods to see if I could see or smell anything. That's when I saw the vulticulus. I must have lost her at some point and she went to the Rook to find me, I guess. She was creeping around. You know, you could have told me you were having me watched."

"Honestly, it was Evan's idea that I not tell you. He left instructions with me, in case anything were to happen to him. He suggested you might be … resistant to such a thing."

Some nice memory of Evan crossed Sylvia's face. "Yeah, well, what did he know?" She wiped away a tear. August reached out again to hold her mother's hand and squeezed it. Sylvia smiled.

"Anyway, I think she knew he was following her because she'd made her coloring and clothing similar to mine. I think she was trying to look as much like me as possible, and I guess it worked. She seemed to be luring him into the Rook. She circled around twice, then went in Sorcha's suite door. I thought maybe she was going to go up the back stairs and come down the front and get him, maybe she thought the smells in the house would confuse him, I don't know. But after she went in, he followed."

"I'm going to get something for that leg." Faolan rose and went to the hall for bandages.

Sylvia called after him as he rooted through a hall closet. "I hoped you were at the cabin, but there was no way to know until I could get out there. Maybe she would have managed to get him, but I don't think she expected two of them."

Faolan rushed back into the room. "Two of them?"

"Yes, there was a woman, too. I didn't even see the female until they were leaving. I still don't know how or when she went in. Do you know who it could have been?"

Faolan stammered for a moment and Sylvia and August studied him, waiting.

"I don't know who it was," he finally managed.

Sylvia narrowed her eyes and studied him a bit harder, "What do you know?"

"I don't. I haven't seen my brother in a very long time. Anything I guess would be purely that, a guess. I'd rather deal in facts."

Sylvia resigned with a sigh and nodded. "I understand."

August began washing her mother's leg while Faolan unspooled a bandage wrap. "I think you actually need a shower, Mom."

Sylvia agreed and they helped her to the bathroom, where she showered and Faolan provided her with a fresh tee-shirt, which clung to her hips and hung nearly down to her mid-thigh. Her jeans took a wash and tumble while she ate the diner chicken and August wrapped her ankle. It seemed to be only a sprain.

"I don't know how he found this town," Faolan wondered. "I always break my trails. Sometimes three or four times."

"He must have been following me somehow. I did go poking around his neck of the woods. He still has a few loyal pairs of eyes. I've put you all in danger." Sylvia's voice quivered.

"Mom, stop. This monster was bound to find one of us sooner or later. And Gran's lived here forever. Now go back and tell me about this vultico thing. She looked like you?"

"Vulticulus," corrected Faolan.

"Yes, sweetie. The vulticuli can change the pigment in their hair and skin and eyes. She's a similar size to me. Wearing similar clothes, she looked a lot like me. When I saw her, I dropped my purse and ran around the house screaming for you. I took off up the hill hoping you were here and forgot my purse. I suppose a body that looked like me and had my purse laying nearby was enough for the police.”

“Can’t you people come up with things that don’t sound so similar?” August piped. “Veritas and vulticulus? How the hell am I supposed to keep all of this straight? And how exactly did this Shan person change her pigment?” She paused. “You know, I ask these questions and I just can’t even believe the strings of words that have come out of my mouth the past few days.”

Sylvia blinked at her daughter. “You’re one of us ‘people’ dear. And the two v-words are just a coincidence, but I take your point. Anyway, they can control the melanin in their skin and hair—I have no idea how. But I’ve never met a vulticulus I didn’t like. They tend to be intelligent and selfless and most of them are kind.”

“Okay. Wow. So, there was never any traveling RN job? Never any work conferences?”

“No sweetie. I’ve been hopping all over the country and Europe trying to track down your father’s killer. Always just a few steps behind him.”

“I can’t believe this. I just can’t even believe it. I don’t even know what’s real anymore.”

“I’m sorry, baby. I hated lying to you. But why would I ever want you mixed up in this? I just wanted to find him myself and persuade him to leave my family alone. Whatever that took. I should have told you something though. I don’t know why I thought this wouldn’t happen. It’s not like any of his clan accept me, or even tolerate me. They’d all like to see my head on a spike.” She petted her daughter’s hair and her eyes were filled with tears. “How’s Sorcha doing?”

Faolan gave her a hopeful look. "She's awake. I had Sheriff Géroux check in on her at the cabin. I'm afraid Abel lost an arm, though."

"Oh, poor Abel! I saw the mess at the Rook and I knew it was bad. I was so worried they'd gotten you somehow, but there was no way for me to check."

Faolan stood up. "We're all heading back to the cabin. I need to pack some things. I think I have some crutches here. I'll put them in the truck." He went off into the depths of the house. August helped her mother back to the library and sat her on the couch. Then she went to the shelves.

"What are you doing, sweetie?" Sylvia asked as she winced and lifted her foot onto a pillow.

"Packing books to take to the cabin. So, you knew about the cabin, too? Hah—and here I thought I was protecting you from all this."

August grabbed books by Pratchett, Sagan, Rice, Lewis, Atwood, and Tolkien. She also pulled a couple of poetry collections, some of Faolan's ancient-looking tomes about creatures and hunting, and what seemed like an encyclopedia of fairy tales. She scooped a handful of pens and markers and paper from the desk and tossed them into a wooden box that previously had contained only dust bunnies.

"Your dad couldn't get enough of books. You're so like him in that way."

"I remember." Pretending to concentrate intensely on book spines, "Do you miss Dad?"

"What? Yes. Yes, of course I do. Why would you ask me that?"

"I don't know. I thought you did, but now I'm realizing nothing was as it seemed."

"August—look at me sweetheart. I loved your father more than life itself. But I guess, somewhere in the back of my mind I knew I might lose him some day. We've had this hanging over our heads for a long time. I'm sorry if it seems like I don't miss him. I miss him terribly."

A slight sniffle was followed by the "fwpp" of a tissue being pulled from the box. Sylvia dabbed her nose.

"How did you hurt your foot?" She asked Sylvia.

A sniffle and a blow. "Running up the hill to this house. I twisted it on a rock. Should have been watching where I was going." Dab, dab.

August sat on the couch and peered at her mother. She wasn't even sure she was the same woman who raised her. "Are you telling me *everything*?"

"*Everything*? What do you mean *everything*?"

"I don't know, Mom. I just feel like you're hiding something from me."

"All I was ever trying to do is protect you." She sniffed and dabbed again.

"So you knew about all of this, right? Gran and her scars and Faolan and what he is and that Dad was killed by, you know ..."

"A werewolf?"

"Yes. That."

"Yes, I knew, honey. Of course I knew. Because of what I am.

And what your father was. We all suffered because your father and I were in love. We weren't supposed to be in love. Life is hard enough for cumanta ..." August's eyes searched her mother. "It means 'ordinary people.' It's hard for cumanta, but there are many more of them than us. Really, it's their world. Our clans grow a little thinner every year. And we're different. Our bodies and minds are different. Our social structures and ways of life. We did okay when we could stick to our lands and keep our numbers under control. It's been a difficult assimilation for most of us and some of us cannot even begin to live anything but a mystical existence. Can you imagine what it's like for the mermaids in the lochs? And all of this hate among the various clans, it's been devastating. You saw what it's done to your grandmother."

"So, is that everything?"

"I'm sorry you're upset that you didn't know these things. But I'm not sorry we hid it from you. Sweetheart, you're alive and healthy because we brought you here. I'll never apologize for that. But I *am* sorry we didn't prepare you better. The truth was bound to come out eventually. Listen, sweetie, in all of the things Faolan told you about, did he talk about Iseabail with you?"

"No. Why?"

"I just wondered if you understood how ... well ... if he explained it all."

"What are you trying to say?"

Faolan burst into the room. "All packed! Let's go!"

August sighed. "I have some books and a box of stationary supplies. Would you mind?"

Faolan examined the ladies and flexed his jaw. "Everything okay in here?"

"Yes! Please, would you give us another moment?" August asked, exasperated.

Faolan's face tensed slightly, but he let it go. "Aye," He bent over and kissed the top of her head, then piled the books onto the crate and hauled the lot away.

"It's impossible to tell you everything, August. It takes years of questioning and exploring. You seem to know what you need to know right now. Isn't that enough? Let the rest come in its own time."

August felt like the child at the grownups' table. What was enough? What was too much? Did she even want to know what she already had learned? She felt her throat get tight. Whatever else there was, she decided, she did know enough. For now.

"I'm with Faolan. We're, you know, together."

"I know. That's why I was asking if he's told you about Iseabail."

"Oh. Aren't you going to give me some speech about how he's too old for me?"

Sylvia let out a breathy burst of laughter. "He's too old for me, too."

August smiled, but looked confused.

"We aren't really like the cumanta. We age differently. We mature differently. Many of us also have some genetic memory. He's not too old for you in our culture. If anything, you're a few years behind other females of your kind, socially. Some would already be married by fifteen, though I wouldn't recommend that. Actually, because you are mix of hunter and lycan, it's possible you're a decade or more ahead of most girls your age, developmentally. That's really our fault. Mine and your father's. Trying to raise you like them. We knew what was happening, but to the rest of the world, you just seemed very advanced. Which you are—physically and mentally. Don't mistake that for wisdom, though."

"Except for the pointed remark about not being wise, I think that's the most comforting thing I've been told. It explains a lot. I've always felt so ... different. Not better than other kids my age, just on a different wavelength or something. Does that make sense?"

"Oh, yes. And, I'm sorry."

"Why the big deal about telling me stuff when I turned eighteen?"

"Well, in the cumanta society that's when you'd be emancipated. You were going to be moving out and heading off into the world eventually. We were trying to operate within the constructs of this society. We needed to let you know there was danger, if there still was. You also were going to live a lot longer than your human counterparts, which can actually be agonizing when you're in love with one. We didn't know what would come of things. Eighteen seemed the right bridge between our world and the human one."

August didn't know if she should be grateful or angry. She felt outraged that she'd been lied to, even if the reasons were loving. But she also had to accept the fact that her mother clearly was not the person she had been pretending to be all these years. It was going to take August some time to get to an understanding place in her heart.

Or a trusting one.

She frowned and nodded. "Okay. I think I understand."

"I know you're angry. You will come to understand, in time."

"So I've been told ... and told," she grumbled.

After a long pause, August softened and just tried to be grateful she had her mother and that she was okay. "When I found out you were dead ... or when they thought you were, I felt like I wasn't myself anymore."

"What do you mean?"

"I felt like I wasn't August Archer anymore. I was so overcome with rage, and bitterness. I wanted to hunt down and kill Ciardha for what he did to you and Dad. My heart was filled with vengeance, I felt like there was nothing left but that hunter part. And maybe my wolf part? But it wasn't just me in here. Does that make sense?"

"Yes ... it does." Sylvia held out her arms and August embraced her mother again.

"Gran woke up, and you're here, and now I can feel myself, the August parts of myself, again."

Faolan returned, leaned over the couch and scooped up Sylvia to carry her to the Chief. August secured the house and they all piled into the truck.

"You know there's a body in the morgue everybody thinks is you," August pointed out. "What are you going to tell the sheriff?"

Sylvia looked away out the window. Her expression was unreadable.

"Don't worry sweetie. I'll find a way to make this sound perfectly reasonable."

"Maybe we should just go now and get it over with," August said.

"I need some rest. It won't make much difference to poor Shan if I tell them tomorrow."

She wasn't too crazy about this new side of her mother, but at least she was sure that Mom knew what she was doing. August took the wheel as her mother watched from the backseat with a proud but faraway stare. They stopped by the Rook to pack up the things on their list and some items Sylvia needed, and then they were off to the cabin.

When they returned to the cabin Brigid prescribed a healing regimen for Sylvia's ankle. She suspected Sylvia had a hairline fracture, and treated it accordingly with a brace and bandages and a few plants—one of which grew in abundance there, according to Abel—that would promote bone growth and strength. Sylvia couldn't get over how leggy Snow had become, and the pup danced around the cabin for an hour before she collapsed in front of the fire Faolan had built up.

They found Sorcha was still in bed and rather groggy, and Abel was reading to her from *LIFE* magazine, adroitly flipping pages one-handed. But she perked up to see Sylvia hobble into the room, and they held each other for several minutes. When her granddaughter came in, Sorcha was overjoyed, and August held her hand until she fell asleep again. Almost from the moment Sorcha first woke up, Brigid and Abel had both been regaling her with accounts of Faolan's bravery and his protection of the family, but Sorcha wasn't quite convinced yet. It was going to take a while for that stubborn lady to change so much of her mind.

The fire crackling on the grate filled the main room with a warm and smoky atmosphere that satisfied some primal instinct for shelter. August stacked the books they'd brought onto the corner table by the armchair, and grabbed one to take to bed. She hugged everybody and said goodnight and padded back to her room. She opened the copy of

Wolf: The Ecology and Behavior of an Endangered Species by David Mech, but was barely three pages in before it was tented on her chest as she slept. When Faolan came in to check on her, he removed the book, marked her page with her red hair ribbon that had been abandoned on the dresser, then placed it on the nightstand. He climbed into the bed, clothes and all, and petted her hair until he fell asleep, too.

The next morning August woke up to find Faolan cooking a large breakfast for everybody. Waffles with strawberry compote, fat sausages and strong coffee were each making their way onto the long table in the dining area.

"You were in my bed last night, weren't you, Mr. Wolf?" she teased.

"Aye, well … your mother did say I should stay close, didn't she?"

The smells brought Brigid and Sylvia to the table, and Abel came out to collect a tray for Sorcha and took it back to her, balancing it expertly on one hand.

After small talk and too many cups of coffee August went out to the bright porch with Faolan on her heels.

"What is that thing your mother wanted so much?" he asked her. A hefty little trunk sat on the porch looking back at them, its hasp mouth closed, its metal nub eyes staring blankly.

August looked up, though she could only see Faolan in silhouette. "This is the chest that had some of my dad's hunting stuff in it. And I think," she posited, pulling the silver chain with keys dangling on it from her pocket, "that this is the key for it." She held up the larger, fancier of her two keys to show him. "This is the one my dad had locked in his box, my box—and wouldn't tell me what it went to 'til I was eighteen."

Faolan moved over a bit so she wouldn't have to squint up at him and it made her happy that she could now observe his curls and eye crinkles.

"Thank you for breakfast," she said.

"You already thanked me, darlin'," he fairly beamed.

He's so sweet, it almost seems fake sometimes. How could any one man be this wonderful? she pondered. *There's got to be something wrong with him. What's more, how is it that Mr. Conall doesn't already have wife? Why should I be the lucky girl he spends his time with?* She knew the answers to these questions weren't romantic, lighthearted serendipity, but the hard realities that had brought them together. Did it even matter? They knew each other now. She sighed. Was it her limited life experience that made her so susceptible to his charms, she wondered? Or was he just that damn charming? Her basis for comparison was a string of awkward teen romances and uninformed sexual relations. Either way, she counted herself lucky to have his attention. Sometimes she felt like a cat, pressing and nudging and sitting on his paper so he wouldn't lose sight of her. It was probably not the best habit to nurture, but if he didn't like it, he hadn't indicated his displeasure in even a subtle way.

She held her breath and slipped the key into the trunk lock and to her delight, it clicked and then turned. She reached into the oaken chest and lifted out a stack of slim journals, about eight of them. The oldest looked handmade; the newer ones she recognized as the same kind of Moleskine journals her father had preferred in his study to write and doodle in. There was also a collection of smaller, pocket-sized journals, several plain and fancy knives, some tools, and a pint-sized wooden box that sounded like it had marbles rolling around in it. In the bottom was a small metal pot with a handle and spout, as well as a linen pouch with little amber-colored pellets.

"What's that you've got?"

"The book is about the making and care of weapons. And I bet these are arrow tips. Points." She slid open the fitted lid on the box and dumped a heavy little pile of points out into her hand and set them down on the table, and some rolled free.

"Those must be old. They look to be pure silver. They don't make them like that anymore. Too expensive." Faolan reached forward to inspect one, and though August tried to snatch them back it was too late. He immediately dropped it like it had shocked him, and rubbed his burning fingers. "Mistletoe!"

"Yes. I'm sorry, love. I think they've been dipped in oil." She found a vial marked "Mistle. Oil" and held it up. "I should have said something before I showed it to you. Are you okay?" She reached out to examine him and he let her. Small red welts had developed on his hand, but were fading quickly.

He made a grim face while kneading his hand. "I'd forgotten about that little trick. It's been a very long time since I was chased by an Archer."

A chill ran through her body. The personal connection, the intimate way it affected Faolan, wasn't something she'd considered.

She knew, of course, that some of her family had chased and killed some of his, but until now it had been so abstract. She hadn't yet internalized the reality of that being an extension of herself. A personal history that she and Faolan shared before she ever knew him.

"Why is it that I can touch these and you can't? I mean, I am part lycan."

"It's actually not that mysterious. The lack of genetic diversity makes us sensitive. "Somewhere along the line, generations ago, somebody was severely allergic and it just got worse with each generation."

"Inbreeding."

He nodded. "You and Sylvia are not going to have the problems the rest of us do. Though, you seem to have some of the benefits."

She extracted the new shafts from a bag and dropped them onto the table, where they rolled into a neat row. She then lay the fletching alongside and got out her knife. "First I have to heat this dried sap in this little pot. Would you make me a fire?"

He wiggled his brows at her and she giggled.

"Oh, now you flirt. This is serious stuff, mister!"

"Of course, m' lady. As you wish." He soon had a small fire going in the grill and they poured the amber pellets into the metal pot and set it over the flames, letting it melt while she began sliding fletching into the arrow shafts. Faolan donned a pair of gloves and dipped the end of each prepared shaft into the sap then inserted it into the hollow end of a point. After a couple of hours they had about thirty new arrows to put into her quiver.

Early that afternoon Faolan took Sylvia back to Mahigan Falls to talk to Sheriff Two Feathers about the body in the morgue. They were back by dinner and everybody tried to just relax and recuperate from a crazy week. They all played Sorry and drank ale and talked about Scotland.

All at once everything that had happened in the past few days caught up to August, and she felt unexpectedly tired again and a headache was plaguing her—presumably remainders from the concussion. Sylvia gave her a quick exam and Brigid fixed her a medicinal tea and suggested she turn in early, which she didn't think sounded like a bad idea. She went to Faolan and told him she was tired.

"I think I'm ready for a long nap. Will you please read me a story so I don't have to think too much about all this ... stuff?"

"I'd be glad to."

She looked like she might tip over and he stood to catch her, and pressed his face to the top of her head. The pair of them lumbered through cabin living room together like a swaying sloth.

Once in her room, which she now would be sharing with her mother, August snuggled down under the covers and Faolan lay beside her on top of them.

She tried for just that moment to feel okay with everything. To just relax and enjoy the security of that moment. But her rage was still too hot. "I'm going to have to kill your brother," she said, and buried her head in the crook of his arm.

"I know."

"You have to let me do it. It's part of who I am. I know that now."

"I know." He squeezed her a little tighter.

"Read *White Fang* to me."

She had already placed the book on the nightstand. He scooted into more of a sitting position as she cuddled to him, and after a few minutes of Faolan's gentle reading cadence, she was asleep.

The cabin was roomy and cozy, but with that many people in one house, and limited hot water, there were bound to be some flared tempers from time to time, though nothing too serious ever came of it. Most of the time was spent cooking and playing cards, practicing defense skills and reading books.

Thanksgiving was an interesting one at the cabin, with Abel, August, and Brigid all in the kitchen making do with the local produce, and Sorcha eyeballing Faolan over the table. She hadn't relinquished all of her suspicions about Mr. Conall, as she called him, nor was she ready to completely forgive him for the death of her daughter Blair. She knew it had been self-defense, even if she wanted to lay it all at Faolan's feet. She was beginning to see how the terror of those days could cause people to make mistakes—even her darlings—and Faolan's unceasing charm was beginning to win her over. By Christmas she even had knitted him a red cap, as a symbol of honorary acceptance into the Archer clan, and for all the following week he wouldn't be seen without it.

Yule was spent burning a big log in the main room's hearth, singing songs and exchanging handmade gifts. The most stunning of the gifts were the Fair Isle scarfs made of Blackface wool that Sorcha knitted for everybody. Abel and Sylvia baked their most popular holiday cookies and Brigid made tea blends customized for each person. For August, it was strawberry and mint. For Sorcha it was a relaxation blend. August gave everybody a wooden carving of a star with their first initial on it and the edges burned for effect, with a twine hanging loop threaded through a hole. Faolan gave each of them small origami boxes made of thick, beautiful handmade paper he must have had tucked away somewhere. Inside each box was a tiny scroll with a saying on it, sort of like Japanese and Celtic fortune cookies. August's had two inside, one read, *Whit's fur ye 'll no go by ye!* Which Faolan said meant, *What is meant to happen will happen.* The second, and most precious to August, read *Mo Ghaol*, which she recognized immediately because it was on the insides of her parent's wedding bands. It meant "My Love."

As the days grew longer by inches they celebrated Hogmanay into the earliest parts of January. Sorcha kept threatening that she would have made haggis if only she had what she needed. Then in February, when the winter weather began loosening its grip, it became clear the trail on Ciardha and his companion had gone cold. Sylvia and Faolan had taken turns calling in favors and looking for answers, none of which amounted to much. It was as though Ciardha had fallen off the face of the earth. Nevertheless, the cabin land had become an effective training ground. Even Sorcha practiced her skills, having recovered enough to take up throwing knives. She also went on long hikes with Abel, who for his part, took up the sling. He had decided not to get a prosthetic yet, insisting it would only slow him down. His thought was that if he couldn't have two arms, he would take advantage of the benefits of having one—although

Sylvia nearly had him convinced that she could design a prosthesis that would be more useful than the arm he lost.

Faolan and August were slowly getting to know each other on more intimate levels, no longer needing books to make communication comfortable. They were learning about each other, letting the layers and colors of each moment of bonding unfold, and beholding it like a beautiful sunset. With these discoveries and connections came a sense of joy and wonder and of something bigger than themselves.

March 17, 1984

It's the end of a long, but happy day. Brigid prepared an unfussy St. Patrick's Day dinner, with the help of Abel, both of them chatting and smiling and teasing each other. I didn't realize that Brigid was Scottish and Irish. For some reason I kept thinking she was just Irish. I don't know why I bother to make any assumptions about where people come from, or even what they are for that matter. I've noticed there's also a lot of rules that people—or wolves or creatures, or whatever—make up about who is allowed to love who. It's exhausting.

We've spent the better part of the winter training. All of us, even Gran. Mom isn't much with wielding weapons, but she's fantastic at making things. As it turns out, she's got a mind for cobbling things together and making them work. She's reminding me of the Professor on Gilligan's Island. She says years of nursing has helped her think about how things work, since there is no machine more complicated than the human body.

Brigid has fine-tuned her special bag of herbs and potions—a sort of hunter's cure-all kit. She's given us all little satchels that we can carry emergency supplies in. I don't know that we're going to need them because we've completely lost Ciardha and whoever his companion was. Telegrams to Scotland haven't yielded much about the remaining Veritas. It's as though they've all vanished into thin air. I don't know whether to be more relieved or worried about that.

I'm amazed by Abel the more I get to know him. The man doesn't have a negative bone in his body. He just takes everything in stride and with grace, like a good king would. I think there couldn't be anybody better for my gran. I hope she'll let him in. I see glimmers of her walls coming down with me and with Abel. She's afraid of losing again. I don't blame her. Months ago, before all of this stuff happened, he hinted about wanting to marry her. I'd be very glad to call him my grandfather.

My archery skills are badass. I'm amazed at my own abilities, honestly. The only thing I worry about is choking at a crucial moment. My anger towards Ciardha has not softened at all. It makes me wonder how much like Sorcha I am and what that means for the future of my heart. I don't want to shut myself off from my own feelings someday, but sometimes they do feel overwhelming. It would be nice to have a shut-off valve, or a barrier just to pause the influx of feeling or help it slow down to a trickle for a bit.

The days are getting longer and warmer, and so my affection for Faolan grows, too. That's me, practicing writing old-fashioned love letter style. Though I was positively giddy when we first started together, and I didn't think I could feel more deeply about him than I did then, I've since changed my mind about that. That infatuation has settled into something deeper and more comfortable. I always thought that comfortable began where passion ended. Or maybe one caused the other. This isn't true, and I wish a single magazine, movie or TV show had explained to me that comfortable can be beautiful and the beginning of something, not the decline.

I suppose I haven't written much the last couple of months because I've been so absorbed in training and getting to know my family much better. My history, too. Faolan finally told me his age. I couldn't believe it. He will turn 109 two days from now. He said he doesn't celebrate it anymore, but I'm going to make a big feast. Everybody else has already agreed. I was a bit shaken at first, but I had my suspicions. I was already insecure about our age difference, and this did make me feel more vulnerable, but I also realize I can't do anything about it. I thought my inexperience would come as a disadvantage in our relationship. As it turns out, I am thinking it's more of an advantage. Faolan seems a bit hung up on past relationships. We've only touched on them briefly, but I don't have that kind of serious baggage when it comes to men. Maybe I'm just making excuses. Maybe it just feels so good to be with him, I will justify it any way I can. Maybe I want reasons at the ready for anybody who would challenge our relationship. I'm not ruined the way so many people are, who have been injured by love. Injured by love. That's a sad thought. Seems counterintuitive. Injured by love. In any case, I think it makes me a bit braver in love. Love. Love. Love. I let him see all the most vulnerable parts of myself. Okay, maybe not all of them, but enough of them that I feel like he knows me. Like he sees me. And that's really important. Sometimes I don't feel like I could possibly be all that interesting, and then we have an intense discussion or I hear myself say something witty and charming and I realize, hey I am worth something.

The rooms have gone through some re-arranging. Abel and Sorcha sleep in the same room. Brigid and Mom sleep where Abel was, which has two twin size beds, I realized. That's because Mom insisted on moving out of the master bedroom so that Faolan and I could share it.

She told me that there wasn't any use in pretending that Faolan and I didn't want to sleep in the same room—everyone knew it—so we should just put all of them out of their misery and share the same room already. She also said that she'd feel better knowing Faolan was right next to me, if anything were to happen. I'm not sure if Mom meant we should have sex or not, but we don't. I want to, but I've stopped pushing the subject. At least, I try not to. I don't want him to think I don't want him, but I also don't want to come off as disrespectful of his wishes. It's tricky. I confirm my desire through other kinds of touch. I put my palm into the curve of his low back and hold it there. I twist a finger into his curly hair. Or I rest my cheek in the cradle where his neck meets his shoulder. There are times he reaches out to pet my back or stroke my bare leg and I am quiet. And he is quiet. And I don't want to tell him to keep doing it. I feel all turned inside of myself. Awkward even. Is he thinking my leg is nice? Do I have any bumps on my back? Is he enjoying petting me or simply ignoring the flaws? Where does that negative voice come from, anyway? I don't want to say, "Keep stroking me." But I don't want him to stop either. And here is the wicked part: sometimes I can't help but wonder if he's sizing me up for a bite or if some small part of him thinks of what a mouthful of my meat would taste like. It seems like a dark thought, but I always giggle at it and, well ... if I'm being honest ... I get a bit turned on.

What would it feel like for his teeth to sink into my thigh, flesh and muscle, hitting bone causing an electric current of warning to shoot through my skeleton? Would I scream and fight? Would I greet death with a knowing nod, believing I deserved what I got because I knew who I was climbing into bed with? There is the tiniest part of me that doesn't trust him. I am overthinking things. Just enjoy the leg stroking, August. Just melt into his touch.

It was warm for mid-March, so August and Sylvia decorated the yard, opening up two long folding tables and draping them with yards of sheets and tablecloths. They bought some lanterns and lights at the dinky department store in Deerville, and hung them on the tree closest to the table. They put Faolan at the head of the tables, which were piled high with breads and meats and cheeses and fruit. Everybody gathered 'round to pat his back and wish him a long life. Even Sorcha gave him a nod and a wink.

The table was full of hearty chewing and munching sounds, glasses of ale sloshing and clinking together. There was so much joy and laughter it filled August up. She studied and memorized as much of the moment as she could, holding all of them close to her heart.

August ducked into the cabin and got the cake she'd made—a round, two-layer brandy and peach cake with vanilla frosting. He grinned wide at seeing it, or maybe at seeing August bring it to him.

Sylvia clinked her glass with a fork and said, "Speech! Speech!" Everybody else started clinking their glasses with flatware.

Faolan just shook his head and put up his hands and said, "Alright, alright!"

"I want to first thank this beauty, August, for ignoring me when I said not to make a fuss. This, lass, is a lovely fuss. A delicious fuss. Thank you!"

The group shouted "Hear, hear!"

He turned somber for a moment, "I know that our families have had a terrible past, but I think if you look around this table you can see what we can be. What we are all capable of."

"I'll drink to that!" Brigid took a giant swig of her ale.

"Let's all drink to that," Faolan said and held his cup high, then leaned in and clinked it with all of the other cups, saving August for last. They kissed each other, lightly, and tipped back their glasses.

After everybody was good and sauced Brigid started telling the tale of "Little Red Riding Hood"—the real version, she called it.

"Once upon a time there was a young girl who was a very smart healer, but was lacking in the hunting skills of her people. She often was sent off to make food, or pick herbs, and sometimes to visit her grandmother when she was sick, rather than hunt and guard, like the other girls her age. Some say her name was Rose, some say it was Kait, but all say she couldn't use a knife or bow to save her life. Kait-Rose's mother wrapped her in her red riding hood and gave her a basket, which she filled with herbs and teas to heal her ailing grandmother. She warned little Kait-Rose not to take off her cape and not to talk to wolves, for they were bad and liked to eat little girls."

August squeezed Faolan's hand and gave him a sly look. He squeezed her hand back and winked at her, and then they both pretended like nothing had just happened.

Brigid continued, "Once in the woods, however, the little girl found herself distracted by all the herbs she recognized, and would pick the useful plants and tuck them into her basket. When rounding a sharp bend in the path she ran right into a man. He was tall and lean and he startled Kait-Rose, so much so that she dropped her basket. He bent over and gathered her things and handed them to her and apologized. Then he tipped his dusty hat and gave her a wink.

"Kait-Rose was eased by his apologetic nature and fooled by his friendly grin. Her senses as a hunter were not serving her and she didn't even realize that she was in the company of a wolf.

"'Where are you taking the food and herbs, Little Red Riding Hood?' he asked.

"'I am taking them to my sick grandmother who lives in a cottage near Broom Loch,' she told him.

"The man nodded and told the girl that he wished her grandmother well. And though it pained the wolf to let such a tender morsel slip through his hands, he was also a patient and sly wolf, so he ran ahead of the young girl to make an easy meal of both of them.

"He found the cottage but could not find an ailing grandmother, though he did find her nightgown and night cap. He thought he would have himself a bit of fun and play with the girl before he ate her. He transformed into a wolf and put on the clothing and crawled into the bed, for Little Red Riding Hood was nearing the cottage. When the girl came in he moaned and cried out as though he were a little old lady that was feeling ill.

"'Come closer granddaughter,' he moaned. 'Bring me some healing teas.'

"Kait-Rose got closer to the wolf, who she thought was her grandmother, and sat on the edge of the bed.

"'Grandmother, you do look strange today. Perhaps you need stronger teas than I have with me.'

"'Oh no dearie,' the wolf said. 'I will be just fine once I eat.'

"'But grandmother, what big eyes you have.'

"'All the better to see you with, my little dove.'

"'Grandmother, what big hands you have, and they have grown hairy as a dog's.'

"'All the better to embrace you warmly with, my darling girl.'

"'Grandmother, your nose is so big, bigger than any nose I've seen.'

"'All the better to inhale the herbs and get well, my dear.'

"'Grandmother, what big teeth you have!' And at this, Kait-Rose realized she was in danger and went to stand up. The wolf ripped off his disguise and revealed himself to her, furry and drooling and frightening.

"'All the better to eat you with, Little Red!'

"And as the wolf lunged towards the little girl an arrow sang past her, cutting the air. Kait-Rose turned to see her grandmother outside of the window and turned back to see the wolf laying on the floor of the cottage, a large red pool growing around his head.

"The end."

Brigid and Sorcha clapped and hooted. Sylvia clapped politely and wore a strained smile. Abel raised his brows and tipped back his ale.

August wasn't sure what to make of it all. Faolan's face was stoic. She couldn't tell if he was offended or just observing. He stood and poured some more ale and took a swig and said, "Tha mo bhàta-foluaimein loma-làn easgannan."

August heard the string of foreign words escape expertly from his mouth and realized it must be Gàidhlig— Scottish Gaelic.

"Your *what*, is full of eels, Faolan?" Brigid laughed hard, a little ale escaping in a spray.

"His hovercraft, I think he said," Sorcha said. "Don't be a spoilt-sport, Faolan!"

"The tale—it's not the way I heard it, ladies. Though hunters have been known to polish a bit. To put a bit of a shine on a story, y' see?" He was bemused and waved an accusatory finger at them.

Snow stood up at the commotion. She made a tight circle, examined the people, then barked. She repeated it several times, as though she were telling everybody to settle down.

August watched the matter unfold and decided it was a bit of fun they were having with each other and nothing serious. Brigid and Sorcha were laughing so hard that Brigid could barely squeak out, "I'm ... a'gon' ... a'gon ... ta pee myself!" Then she took off for the cabin with an awkward knock-kneed walk-run.

After the party, after everything was cleaned up, everybody else retired to their rooms while August and Faolan stayed outside and gazed at the night sky. An evening chill was setting in and they wrapped themselves in a giant quilt, and slow-danced under the string of lights to nothing but the music of their hearts.

~~Home Again, Home Again, Jiggity Jog~~

April 6, 1984

We returned home last week. Faolan marked a tight perimeter around the Blue Rook and we've installed some security measures that will at least notify us if there are trespassers. It's nice to be home, but the cabin had a certain magic that I'll miss. It's not like I can never go back, but the time we were all there, you really can't go back to something like that. It's too special. Know what else is special? Bright lightbulbs and hot showers any time you damned well please.

I think we should get a dog for the Blue Rook. Snow and I stay with Faolan so much of the time, I'd feel better knowing there was a dog here. Faolan is going to contact the sanctuary where he got Snow to see if they have any pups available.

Things are quiet, despite the fact that we know Ciardha is out there somewhere. Faolan thinks we're safe for a while but once he realizes his mistake, killing a bodyguard instead of my mother, he's going to be very angry. I understand that kind of intense hatred now. I'm also painfully aware of how it eats itself, it's a sick cycle of hatred. I don't want to be part of that, but I'm too angry to be otherwise. I know I should want to be rid of this overwhelming sense of wanting vengeance, but for now, it's an important part of me. Good or bad, it stays.

Brigid has decided to shut down her shop in town and sell off most of her non-apothecary inventory to a young man who has opened up a crystals and incense boutique at the other end of Main Street. She came home to find some rather distraught customers. She gave all of them discounts on larger supplies of their herbs, so if they ever had a gap in their supply again, they'd have some extra. Brigid says the new shop owner will be especially glad to get supplies before the summer visitors come for the antique shops, B&Bs and art fairs.

I should keep up with this journal more. Writing these things down helps me solidify the reality of them in my mind. It also helps me work out weird thoughts and figure out problems. It's not like I can just go to a therapist and tell her that I'm living with my werewolf boyfriend and his brother is trying to kill us. This process of writing, it helps engrave these things on my life in a way that makes them easier to absorb. It's amazing the power that pen and paper has.

~~Smoke and Mirrors~~

April 8, 1984

We have a new puppy! The wolf and wolfdog sanctuary had a few puppies that were just old enough to adopt and they drove one down from northern PA. The mother was abandoned by the owners because she was too hard to handle. Faolan made a big donation and they agreed to bring one right away, since they were relieved to find a home they considered suitable. They have a big chunk of acreage near the Allegheny Forest and evidently the operators are distant relations to Faolan.

Unfortunately, people keep trying to breed wolfdogs and don't realize that they don't make the best human companions, especially if they have too much wolf in them. Brigid just clucked her tongue and said, "Cumanta," when Faolan told us that the sanctuary was feeling the burden. Gran is thinking about adopting one of the older abandoned ones as well, which might actually be good for her. The puppy is black with gold eyes and Gran named him Smoke. They think he's a Black Wolf hybrid with a high wolf content. Very bad for humans to raise because of how unpredictable their development can be. Faolan says some of the lower wolf content hybrids make better pets. He also said that some humans do make good pack leaders, but from his perspective, they should stick to domestic breeds.

Smoke is as much a puffball as Snow ever was. I can barely keep from picking him up. It's hard to even let him sleep! And Snow's so big now, every bit as big as a large German Shepherd. She picks him up and carries him around and licks him. It's so cute I want to squeeze them until I can't breathe!

On another note, being back at the Rook seems to have brought back some of my anxiety about Tanner. I've been having nightmares about him. And sometimes at night, before bed, when I'm out on the balcony looking down the slope towards the Rook, I think I see him standing in the woods. I don't want him to inhabit any part of my mental space. I'm going to keep evicting him until he doesn't return.

I did mention these uncomfortable feelings and memories to Faolan last night and he said something that made me realize that the wild animal that attacked Tanner was him. I don't know what the right words are to convey this idea, but it was like he told me, without telling me, and also knew that I didn't want to hear it outright. He wanted to tell me. I wanted to know. But neither of us wanted to talk about it. We have a type of communication on a level I've never had with anybody else. He just reads me so well, and I think I read him pretty well, too. Every day we spend together, we discover something new about each other. There seems to be reams of information we could share, as though it will never run out. That's probably naïve, but I don't care.

It also occurred to me that this means "guy rescues girl and girl falls for guy." Am I a cliché? How lame is that!? Or does it not count since I fell in love with him before I knew he ultimately saved me from some terrible fate? Maybe I'll rescue him from something. Then we'll be even. Does it even matter who rescues who if we're all just good to each other? Can't a love story just be a love story *without so much scrutiny? Maybe I'm over-thinking all of this.*

Speaking of relationships ... there's been an interesting development with my mom. Apparently when she and Faolan trekked out to the police station in Mahigan Falls to tell them about the mis-identification of Shan, the sheriff was extremely relieved. At some point in their past he'd had a bit of a crush on my mom. When we got back from the cabin Mom stopped by the post office to collect all of our mail that had been gathering there for months, and there were about six letters from Sheriff Two Feathers. Mom was actually blushing. It was pretty adorable. It's entirely possible that she had a crush on him, too. But I don't want to put much thought into that. I'd rather think my parents were madly in love and never noticed anybody else, ever. Anyway, I think she might consider responding to him. I really don't know how I feel about that right now, but I know being happy for her is the right thing, so that's what I'm going to work on.

Also, I miss Lainy more than ever now that I'm back home. I'm going to try and call her tomorrow, though I don't know how I'm going to explain where we've been. It's really hard to not tell Lainy about all of what's happened, so maybe it's better to stay out of touch. I guess I need to consult the family and figure out what's best. I don't want to drag Lainy into our lives and put her at risk. Why does it feel like I'm always losing somebody?

The Rook and Faolan's place were both dusty, moldy, spider-webby messes by the time they got back from being at the cabin for months. Now that the weather was turning towards spring, they threw open all of the windows and dusted and scrubbed every inch of both houses, and restocked the refrigerators and cabinets. In the process they located a number of family photos and scrapbooks that they all planned on digging through some night soon. August stopped to touch a few of the photos of her father. She removed some of them from the storage containers and tucked them in her special box in the window seat. As she did she examined the photo of Iseabail again. Issy. She thought she might be ready to hear about Iseabail, soon. She'd pieced together that the Faolan in the letters was her own Faolan. Obviously they were deeply in love. She wondered whatever happened to Iseabail, but decided it was of no consequence to them. Or at least she needed to convince herself of that. After all, Iseabail was no longer part of his life. August felt close enough to Faolan now, secure enough, that the memory of another woman wouldn't make her jealous. She was certain of it. He couldn't help his past any more than she could help hers. August knew she could look in the mirror and be proud of these things.

~~Domestic Red~~

Faolan's room; the enormous bed is the centerpiece, piled high with opulent quilts of satin and silk. August lies naked on her stomach across it, nearly swallowed in the landscape of downy textiles and pillows. A sunbeam highlights her low back as she languishes, tracing the designs of the multi-colored quilt with a long finger. Faolan watches as she sighs and nestles a cheek into the bedding. Her locks slide off of the silk, falling in long black curls, almost to the floor. She gives him a soft smile and a slow blink, like a sleepy cat. He feels a tug below the waist as his erection begins pressing hard inside his trousers. Faolan smiles and inhales deeply as he rounds the bed, and August tracks him. He pulls his loose linen shirt over his head and throws it onto the bed beside her. She grabs fistfuls of the fine fabric and buries her nose, inhaling. His musk is intoxicating. She inhales deeply again, smiles, then drops the garment onto the floor. A satisfied sigh.

Faolan considers the tender, vulnerable bottoms of her feet and resists a momentary urge to tickle them. His heart is full and wants to open to her and tell her all of the things she longs to hear. A calm surface hides a tempest of excitement. He wants to give her every loving protestation of every lover who has ever lived. He traces her contours with his gaze and thrills at the sight of her naked bottom. He can't decide whether to take off his pants or cup her bottom with his hands and pepper it with kisses—he must do both, immediately.

He opens his trousers and steps out of them, pushes down the front band of his underwear revealing the tip of his cock. A sharp intake of breath from August at the sight of it. He removes his encumbrances, his cock almost pointing upwards, bouncing in air with each movement. She lets out an audible groan then gives her bottom a little wiggle. An invitation.

He bows over her body, arms stretched out caressing her shoulders, touching as much of his flesh to hers as possible. His face on her bare back, his chest pressing to her perfect, creamy bottom and his cock resting against the bedding, between her legs.

He kisses the entire valley of her spine, working his way downwards towards her low back to the lovely divot where her bottom cleavage begins. He cups and kisses her bottom and gently bites until August raises it higher with building urgency. He helps her onto her knees, her most vulnerable parts now directly in front of him. Dark downy curls of short hairs fringe the sweet pink wound splitting the engorged, peachy flesh. Were he not a well-grown man and experienced lover he would have come at the sight of it. He can feel his nipples tighten, his flesh bump up and his cock almost jump as he inhales her scent, and then gives her one long lick, up from the excited bump nestled in the flesh of her mound to a deep dip into her opening. The smell and taste of her, like the ocean and salted cream, is on his lips, his nose, his cheeks, his chin. He wants to rub every part of him against her pink slickness until she is panting and spent.

She leans into him more firmly, wiggling and pressing urgently against his face, against his chin. He clasps her at bent hips and nuzzles her harder, licking and sucking, rubbing his chin against her, gently humming. She began moaning, then crying out in short bursts of yes, yes, yes.

She says, "I want to turn over. I want to look into your face. I want you inside of me!"

He doesn't want to stop kissing and nuzzling, diving into her with his face, but she is so urgent—and he undeniably wants to put his cock inside of her. They move together in helping her onto her back.

He takes in the sight of her, first all at once, then starting again at her crown of raven locks, savoring each plane and curve of her face. Her eyes, green gems like the grasses of Perth. Her breasts, perfect handfuls of glowing peachy flesh topped with puffed rosebuds. Her belly and thighs, achingly beautiful, a master's sculpted marble, and he can feel his appetite rising in a ferocious animal wave inside of him. Now her lovely mound. But something is different. Out of place. Her downy thatch is no longer black, but orange-blonde. Confused and startled, he looks up at August's face and instead of long ringlets of dark hair, there is pale. And as he meets her eyes, grassy-green has turned to sky-blue. And what had been his new bright love, August, is now a face from his haunted past, Iseabail. His lost love lies naked before him as she did ninety years ago in a heather-strewn field in Scotland.

Faolan goes cold, and takes a stunned step backwards.

"What's the matter? Don't you want me?" She pleads, her hands and arms stretched out towards him. "I've missed you so."

She is as beautiful as ever, and just as he remembers her. There is something haunting, almost alien about her manner.

"My darling," she continues, sitting on the edge of the bed. She grabs his hips with both hands, guiding him closer, "Haven't you missed me? Feel me."

She stands and takes one of his hands and places it on her naked breast. He can feel the firm nipple kissing the center of his palm. He wants her, despite his conscience—his love for Iseabail now fully awake, his desire, overwhelming, for both his new love and his old. He is pulled hard across a chasm of disloyalty—both to Iseabail for wanting to abide by August, and to August for wanting to bed Iseabail. What kind of hell is this?

"It feels like you have been missing me, my lover." She places her hand around his firm cock and begins stroking it lovingly. He doesn't have the strength to demur her advances, even as a sense of shame blushes his neck and ears.

Knowing, she reaches up and gently pinches his ears, "Your ears still pink. Do not worry, my lover. Do not feel ashamed. Come, lie down." They turn a slow spin and with his back to the bed, he lies against the great pile of pillows and she straddles his thigh. "Do you remember how we used to do this?" Her smile is bewitching and the words full of sensual memories.

"Aye, I do, lass." His words are thick with his native brogue and it feels so good. It feels so good to not hold back his accent, his love for Iseabail, or to hide his cock from desire and his conscience from his old love. She understands his shame and absolves him of it. The floodgates of emotion, now open, could not be closed against the force flowing out of them now.

"I used to wear nothin' beneath my gown. You'd come to me in

your kilt and sit on the stump in the middle of the apple orchard and I'd have a merry ride. This before ya put a babe in me, remember?"

"Aye ... lass, I ... I ... could never ... forget it." His words falter with passion and tension as Iseabail slides her nakedness back and forth against his thigh, her full round breasts swaying an inch from his face. Her body is softer and rounder than August's and he lets his fingers sink into her. He alternately suckles her nipples and buries his face into her lush cleavage as she rubs. She is leaning, one hand holding the bedpost and the other stroking his cock while she whispers into his ear, and just as he is about to climax she begins to say, "Why don't you want me? Why don't you want me?" He feels a sting of embarrassment and a hot pinprick in his brain lets something ancient seep in. His aspect comes upon him, and his body starts to change, his teeth sharpening, his fingernails growing into fierce claws.

Iseabail grins too widely and laughs, "Yes! Yes! That's it my lover!" Then she straddles his cock, sitting down on him, taking him into her, screaming his name. He could feel her warmth and wetness wrap around his cock, slick, clenching, even as he transforms and it grows larger and longer inside of her. At his peak he feels the contracting release, spurts and quakes, hips jerking and pressing of their own volition—euphoria and release wash over him silencing all guilt as Iseabail keeps repeating his name, "Faolan. Faolan. Faolan!"

He woke with a start, sweaty and disoriented in a tangle of sheets and blankets. August was standing beside the bed, nudging his arm rather firmly, "Faolan!"

He blinked and rubbed his eyes and noticed that his hand was
partially transformed and he shook it as though it had fallen asleep
and then tried to tuck it under the sheet. His body was tingling and
he remembered he'd been dreaming. Or having a nightmare. He
couldn't decide which. Then came a flush of shame and
embarrassment as though he'd betrayed August. The sheets were
damp in spots and stuck to him. He needed a way to discreetly usher
August out of the room so he could clean up.

"Are you okay? You were yelling and howling. You even looked
like you were starting to transform a bit."

"Aye. I mean, yes. I'm fine. I just had a hunting dream. That
happens sometimes. I hope I didn't scare you."

August grinned and tilted her head. "You didn't. But you seem
... weird. Are you sure you're okay?" She reached for his hands,
"Why don't you come here and—"

"No!" He said it a little too sharply and it wiped the grin right
off of August's face. He realized he needed to be calmer, or she
might start asking questions and he'd have to lie some more, which
he didn't want to do, even about a dream. "No. I'm sorry. I was just
really rattled by that dream. I'd like to forget about it."

"I understand." She waited for some kind of response, but he
still seemed dazed. "Are you hungry? You've been sleeping for
hours."

"Aye—yes. Yes, I'm hungry. Famished." His accent wanted to
come out thick as if he'd never left the highlands. For some reason
he was making a concerted effort to minimize it. "Would you please
make me something to eat while I put on some clothes?"

"I'd kind of like to watch you put on your clothes," she said, and teased his shinbone through the sheet with her finger. His face changed. She did her best to play it off like it didn't sting. She opted to try a cheerful tone. "I'll make you a big sandwich."

"Thank you." Weak smile.

"You're welcome, love." She skipped out of the door. Actually skipped. That may have been overplaying her hand a bit, she thought, but it was too late now. She headed down to the kitchen and tried not to feel dumb.

August stacked a plate high with fresh baked slices of sourdough and meat and thought about *that look*. That *you know we can't*, look. It always made her feel a little undesirable. Along with trying to let him know that she wanted him, so he didn't ever have to wonder, she wanted him to be affirming towards her, too. She knew he wanted her. If he were her shitty teenage ex-boyfriend, the one that made her walk to his apartment and didn't even come downstairs to open the door, they could be fucking all over the place and it would be fine. And he'd be trying to force her to drink watery beer and have sex on the stairs like in some movie he saw and saying stupid things like, "Touch it, help me, it hurts," or "Bareback is better, baby."

She knows Faolan is putting her off because he thinks he's protecting her from the Big Bad Wolf. Isn't he? It isn't because things don't work, even at over a hundred years old, because she's seen him, worked up, and sometimes working out the tensions they built together. She'd peek, through the bathroom door. She guessed that maybe he knew she was peeking—why else leave the door cracked? August was growing tired of these mixed-up laws and rules, so many of which didn't even apply to her. On top of it all, she had to wait until a big talk he wanted to have.

So many questions. She should just ask him! Maybe he was dangerous during sex, she suddenly thought. Like, he could hurt her or lose control. No, he would have told her that already. Besides, if there was the slightest chance of that, he never would have let her get this close. It has to be something more ... more ... emotional. She kept waffling between being frustrated with him and trying to just relax about it. The urgency, it's a big indicator that bad decisions might follow. He was right about that.

Maybe she was not considering things from his perspective. She trusted Faolan. He's always had her best interests at heart, it seemed. Sometimes she wished her hormonal fog would clear so she could focus a bit better. Her desires were always screaming at her, turning even some of the most mundane duties and conversations towards thoughts of sex. Frustration added fuel to the fire because it seemed ridiculous to frame their relationship in the terms of human relationships. It was obvious her hormones and genetics were in conflict with the social constructs of the little town they lived in. Maybe things would be different if they were with their own kind. This was the first time she truly longed for Scotland.

Snow stood at the back door and barked. August wandered over and let her back in. She fed her some roast beef scraps, which she finished in one swallow and went to the couch, climbed up and curled into a ball.

August could feel her frustration rising. She was slamming

things as she made the food. Snow put her head up and tilted it. August stopped, took a deep breath and tried to accept that, at the moment at least, Faolan's wisdom outranked her screaming lust. She congratulated herself for being mature and resigned herself to a long night of wiggling around in the bathtub by herself. With the door cracked.

She found a large tray made of several types of wood creating a beautiful pattern. She loaded the tray up with plates filled with food—the sandwich, chips, pickles, cookies and a glass of red wine and took it upstairs. Faolan had already showered and dressed and was in the middle of making the bed with fresh linens.

"It was time to change them. I think I need to turn the AC up a bit. I mean down. Wait, which is it when it's AC? Up or down?"

She laughed. "Up, I think."

He smiled then averted his eyes, unable to shake the guilt that clung to him. August noticed, but pretended not to.

"Here's your sandwich. Lots of meat on Sorcha's homemade sourdough bread." She held the tray out proudly.

"Cookies and red wine. A lovely pairing." He laughed. "Thank you. Looks great. Red, I'm sorry if I scared you." He walked over to her and kissed her on the forehead.

His energy still seemed off to August but she tried not to let it worry her. She put the tray on the round table in the sitting area and sat in the armchair to watch him make the bed. She was surprised to feel touched by it. Something having to do with the domesticity of him making the bed, and her bringing him a sandwich. It was another way of deepening the groove of affection she felt for him.

And because she had accepted that there would be no sex between them for the short-term, she was able to recognize the ways they were already intimate. Ways that didn't have anything to do with sex, and that soothed her.

"I like watching you make the bed."

"You just like a man who can tuck a proper sheet corner." He paused his work long enough to grin and squeeze her knee.

She let out with a hearty giggle. "Yeah, I think that's it. I mean it, though. I like watching you do domestic things."

"I understand," he said, while finishing up.

Snow bound into the room and right onto the bed, sliding the fresh linens into a bunched up mess. They both laughed and Snow barked.

Faolan wished he could fast-forward past all of the awkward conversations about Iseabail. He wished that August could suddenly be older and more experienced. But this was the uncomfortable space they lived in at the moment. At the edge of something wonderful or something sad, depending on how she felt after *the talk*.

They sat in silence while he ate his sandwich, tearing off large bites and swallowing them in two chews, occasionally tossing one to Snow, who expertly caught them without moving from her spot. August stole potato chips and nibbled their edges. She scooped up his abandoned dill pickle and ate it.

When he turned back around he said, "Hey, that was *my* pickle!"

August shrunk a little. "I'm sorry! I thought you didn't want it. You left it there, all abandoned and lonely."

"No I didn't."

"Then why didn't you eat it?"

"It wasn't pickle time yet!"

August burst out in a fit of laughter at this and tried to mimic him, "It wasn't pickle time yet!" But mostly halted words and hoots came out and she slid off of the chair onto the floor, rolling around in silent spasms while Faolan stood there staring on with wonder.

"You are a silly girl," he said, his r's rolling hard.

When she started to settle down, she sat up on the floor and leaned against the seat of the chair and wiped away tears. "Oh my god ... oh ... my god ... my sides ... hurt." Some more chuckles and tears. "Pickle time ... oh goodness!" When she could finally breathe again she sat back up in the chair and let the final bits of laughter sputter softly out and she said, "I want you to teach me all about pickle time." They both laughed as Snow did circles and barked in quick succession to get them to cut it out.

He chucked August's chin, and put his arm around her waist. They went downstairs and fed Snow three cans of food.

"She is really turning into the most gorgeous beast I ever saw," August said.

"She's a fine wolf, aren't ya girl?" He rubbed her between the ears and knelt down and buried his face in her neck and gave her a big hug. He looked up at August, who was watching them. "I hate this dog," he said with a wink, then resumed giving her vigorous rubs and scratches and ear squeezes.

"Uh-huh." She smiled wide, arms crossed, enjoying the closeness of their little family they were forging.

"Let's play some chess, Little Red. Shall we?"

"Okay, but I kind of suck at it. My dad was trying to teach me ... before ..."

"Well, let's play chess and you can tell me all about your favorite things you used to play with your Da."

"I'd like that." And August realized how some of the emptiness of remembering her father had been filled by the idea of invoking happy memories. Instead of pushing away thoughts of him because they hurt, she wanted to tell Faolan all of the stories she could think of, engraving them on her heart.

After chess they took Snow for a walk in the late April breezes and headed down to the Rook to see Abel's garden in bloom. It seemed as though he arranged the plants so something was blooming throughout most of the year but April through July promised to be stunning. Abel was now living at the Rook, staying with Gran in the suite downstairs. This meant the garden was more lush than ever, as though it was trying to show off for him. Brigid moved into one of the Rook's upstairs rooms now that she didn't need to live over the shop any longer. They made an interesting little crew, Sorcha, Sylvia, Brigid and Abel, and now Smoke.

They all had talked about moving again, going into hiding again, but they all agreed the best thing was to face this head on, or they'd never have peace. For the time being, there was guarded peace.

~~May Aye~~

It was well into May and August still couldn't bring herself to approach the subject of Iseabail with Faolan. She'd tried to make small talk with her mother about it, to get an idea what might be in store for her, but her mother just said, "You really need to talk about this with Faolan." So she dropped it. But every time she tried to broach the subject with Faolan she felt queasy, so she took it as a sign it wasn't time. Not yet. For his part, Faolan seemed hesitant to talk about it as well. This played on August's concerns and she would journal about them, to tamp them down and try to focus on the present, which was pretty wonderful. Sure, a murderous werewolf who hates her family could show up and try to slaughter them at any time. Sure, there is some big secret or hurt about this Iseabail. But there's also love, and books, and family, and walks along the creek. A lot to be thankful for, she reminded herself.

She looked ahead to her coming eighteenth birthday and knew that there was a good chance she and Faolan would finally have the opportunity to consummate their relationship. She tried not to fantasize about that particular moment anymore. She wanted it to be its own thing, not tainted with a bunch of unrealistic ideals. Then she would go back on that vow, and fantasize about it after all. *It's exhausting trying to constantly talk yourself out of something you want so badly*, she wrote once in her journal. *And every now and then I'll have a moment where I look at him and think, "What the hell am I doing? I don't know this guy!" It's funny how the mind plays tricks on you. Sometimes you have to remind yourself not only why you're on the path, but that you're actually on a path at all.*

On this fine morning in May, August baked blueberry muffins and apricot scones from scratch for Abel and Sorcha's engagement party. They were like a couple of kids and it was fantastic. She cooled the muffins on the window and tied her hair up in a red ribbon and slipped on the red sundress that was once her mother's, one of the treasures found during the big spring cleaning in April. She put on her pearl necklace—the Conall pearl—and checked herself in the mirror, straightening a few stray hairs. She smoothed a sheer red lip gloss that smelled of strawberries over her lips, rubbing them together and making a kissy face. She smiled at her reflection, content.

"Faolan, do you have a basket?"

"Aye, here ya go, Red."

She put the muffins and scones in the basket, along with framed photos of their little family she had wrapped up as gifts for the walls of the Rook. Then she and Faolan and Snow walked down the path, through the fat full trees of the forest to her grandmother's house.

www.ingramcontent.com/pod-product-compliance
Lightning Source LLC
Chambersburg PA
CBHW031139120726
47905CB00006B/1740